Heat crept up Josh's neck.

"What kind of person do you think I am?"

Tara shrugged. The gesture was elegant, and he couldn't help thinking that she'd look more at home at a French château than in Montana. "All I know is what I've seen between you and Walt, and the way you acted at the clinic," she said. "Oh, and the way you've done your level best to get rid of me. It hasn't been impressive."

She had a point. He'd never expected things to turn out this way. Sometimes he didn't recognize himself when he was arguing with Walt or pulling his hair out over a cowhand quitting.

As for Tara?

On one matter they totally agreed—they didn't care for each other. That was okay, although he was fighting an undeniable attraction to her, a response that was purely chemical.

Dear Reader,

I have always been interested in geology, but lately the variety and beauty of this planet's stones have been a particular passion. It may sound funny, but in many ways, rocks are like people. Some are harder, some softer, and each have their own particular beauty. Of course, as with people, it may also take a little work to discover the beauty inside. One of my favorite rocks is moldavite, a glass-like stone that was created when a meteor hit the earth. Love can be like that. It lands with unexpected force and creates something new.

My hero and heroine in *The Rancher's Prospect* are both strong, stubborn, independent people who've set a course for their lives that isn't necessarily the best for them. A world traveler, Tara has developed a cool outer shell to protect herself, but she isn't nearly as tough as she appears, while Josh is working single-mindedly to achieve his dream of raising organic beef cattle on his own ranch.

It was interesting to pit these two very different people against each other, with the beautiful state of Montana as the backdrop to their story. Montana, by the way, has some very interesting geologic history, some of which naturally found its way into Tara and Josh's story.

I enjoy hearing from readers and can be contacted c/o Harlequin Books, 225 Duncan Mill Road, Don Mills, ON M3B 3K9, Canada.

Callie Endicott

CALLIE ENDICOTT

The Rancher's Prospect

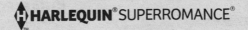

Recycling programs
for this product may
not exist in your area.

ISBN-13: 978-0-373-61005-1

The Rancher's Prospect

Copyright © 2016 by Callie Endicott

Printed in U.S.A.

Callie Endicott's life refuses to slow down, but lately she's taken a small amount of time to indulge her interest in rock hunting...in various rock shops. She still doesn't have enough hours to do everything she wants, but Callie figures life is a juggling act and practice makes perfect. She's interested in everything, but her particular passions include history and nature, which fits perfectly with her love for writing, reading, hiking and walking on a beach. Between her cats, her guy and everything else, boredom is never a problem.

Books by Callie Endicott

HARLEQUIN SUPERROMANCE

Montana Skies

Kayla's Cowboy
At Wild Rose Cottage

That Summer at the Shore
Until She Met Daniel

Other titles by this author available in ebook format.

To Carol, and in loving memory of Joe

PROLOGUE

JOSH MCGREGOR REINED in his horse when his satellite phone rang. He pulled it from his saddlebag and saw his parents' phone number on the display.

"Hey, what's up?" he answered.

"Josh, can you get to Montana right away?" asked his mother in a trembling voice.

Alarm went through him. Mom would never sound so shaky unless something terrible had happened.

"What's wrong?"

"It's…your…" She stopped and he could hear her crying and saying something about how she'd thought she could handle it.

His stomach twisted.

A moment later his father came on the line. "Josh, there's been a car accident. Grandpa Walt and Grandma Evelyn. A drunk driver…"

Gripping the phone so hard his fingers hurt, Josh tried to sound calm. "How bad?" He couldn't bring himself to ask if they were still alive.

"Bad. They were airlifted to the hospital in Helena and are both in surgery. You should get here as soon as possible…just in case." The last words were very soft, as if that would keep them from reminding his wife that her parents could be dying.

"I'll be there, whatever it takes," Josh promised, his throat tightening unbearably. He loved both his grandparents, but he had a special bond with Grandma Evelyn.

"Just get here safely," said his father. "Hear me?"

"I hear. Don't let Mom worry."

"All right. We love you, son."

Josh urged his stallion into a gallop and they quickly covered the three miles back to the large barns of the Texas ranch where he worked. He tossed the reins to a ranch hand. "Take care of Lightfoot for me, will you? I've got a family emergency."

"Sure, boss."

He stopped at the ranch house to let the Gordons know he was leaving, and also to phone Mark Eisley, his second in command. A call to the airline got him on the next flight leaving for Montana.

A FEW HOURS LATER Josh charged into the reception area of the hospital.

"Josh," a soft voice exclaimed. Emily, his new sister-in-law, jumped up from one of the seats and gave him a fierce hug. "Come on," she said. "They're in intensive care. It's this way."

Grateful, he followed her through the hallways.

"How are they?" he asked.

She shook her head. "No change in their conditions in the last couple of hours. They're still critical. I get updates now and then, but I told Trent to stay with your mother while I waited for you. She needs all the support she can get right now."

Until Trent had gotten together with Emily, Josh wasn't sure his brother's presence would have been much comfort. She'd softened his edges in ways no one else had been able to do.

The rest of the family was in the intensive care waiting room. Mom was leaning against Dad, and Trent was on the other side, holding her hand. His sister, Madison, who lived in Seattle now, was already there, as well. There was a pained stillness around the room. Even DeeDee, his brother Jackson's lively stepdaughter, was unnaturally solemn.

His dad got up and gave him a fierce, silent hug; Parker's embrace alone would have told Josh, if he hadn't already known, how serious the situation was.

Sarah McGregor also stood and put her arms around him. "I'm so glad you're here, son," she murmured. "You can see them next."

Josh understood the drill at ICUs. Only two visitors, at limited intervals.

Ten minutes later an aide came into the room. His father nodded, and Josh went with her through a wide door. His grandmother lay in the first cubicle.

Agony shot through him as he saw the bandages on Evelyn Nelson's head and left shoulder.

He leaned over the bed, took her right hand and whispered, "It's Josh, Grandma."

Her fingers tightened for a moment.

"She squeezed my hand," he whispered to the nurse who was adjusting an IV.

The woman gave him a kind, sad look. "It's likely just a reflex," she said gently, but Josh didn't believe it.

He turned back to his grandmother. "I'm going to see Grandpa now," he whispered and felt her thumb press against his palm. "I love you."

If possible, the nightmare got worse when Josh saw his grandfather. Walt's face was bruised and swollen, and a machine was breathing for him. His leg was swathed with bandages, blood staining through, and Josh wondered how extensive the damage might be. Lord, Grandpa would hate to be disabled; running his ranch was everything to Walt Nelson.

"Hey, Grandpa, it's Josh," he said, slipping his hand around the slack fingers. But this time there wasn't any response, not even something his imagination could build upon. "I…I just saw Grandma. She sent her love." It was possible to say that much, given the pressure of her thumb when he'd spoken about seeing her husband.

A moment later the aide nodded toward the door and Josh reluctantly left the ICU.

Back in the waiting room, Trent silently stood and gave Josh his place beside their mother. No one was talking. His sister-in-law Kayla lay on the floor with her feet elevated, probably related to her being seven months pregnant. But she seemed all right otherwise. Jackson sat next to her, holding her hand.

Sitting and waiting was hard for Josh; he was used to long days of vigorous activity, the same as the rest of the family. But it was good to be together at a time like this, even though all they could do was wait and pray.

CHAPTER ONE

TARA LIVINGSTON LOOKED through the taxi's window at Notre Dame and other familiar Parisian landmarks as they headed for the airport. She would miss France, and it seemed especially hard to leave as spring approached, though Paris was wonderful in every season, despite its ever-growing traffic problems.

In a rare email exchange a few months before, an old college roommate had claimed Tara was living the dream life. Maybe she was—her Facebook album contained photos of everything from Stonehenge, the Bavarian countryside and her climb up Mount Fuji to scuba diving off the Australian coast. She'd lived in five countries over the past ten years, with visits to others, and had thoroughly enjoyed each of them.

But now she was headed back to the United States…to Montana, of all places. Her few belongings had already been shipped to the temporary apartment she'd asked Lauren to find for her, though there was no telling when they would arrive.

The butterflies in Tara's stomach had nothing to

do with returning to the States, and she kept telling herself there was nothing overly significant about seeing Lauren again. Their initial meeting had been awkward, but that was to be expected when twin sisters were reunited for the first time since they were babies.

If they couldn't find a way to connect…?

Well, Tara had always managed by herself, and the world wouldn't fall to pieces if she continued that way. Things would be simpler, at any rate. It had often seemed that family complicated the lives of her coworkers and tied them down. She wanted to be free to live different places and do all the traveling she wanted to do.

At the airport she checked her suitcases and settled in to the first-class seat paid for by her employer—a reminder that they wanted her to sign another contract as soon as possible. They'd even given her a choice of countries. She tucked her purse under the seat while wondering if she should pick somewhere new or go back to one of the places she'd loved so much.

A decision could wait until she began negotiating with her company about a new contract. She planned to be in Montana for three months. Lauren had invited her to stay in her spare bedroom, but Tara had wanted her own place. Lauren Spencer might be her twin, but she was still a stranger, and Tara wasn't ready to live with another stranger. Her entire childhood had been spent living with strangers, being shuttled from one foster home to another.

The trip went well, albeit with a few layovers and transfers, but Tara was used to travel and made the connections to Helena without a problem.

"Tara," called a voice as she arrived at the baggage claim area after landing. It was her sister, smiling tentatively, and their alikeness surprised Tara all over again. They had the same long blond hair, the same blue eyes with tiny flecks of gold, and the same height and build.

"I thought you weren't coming," she said. "I have to get a rental car, anyway."

"I caught a ride with someone so we could travel back together—I couldn't let you fly in without being met."

"That's nice." Tara was far more accustomed to disembarking alone than she was to having someone greet her. Still, it was a nice gesture from her sister, and the effort was appreciated.

"Is this all you brought?" Lauren asked, looking at Tara's two bags when they arrived on the carousel.

"I mailed a few boxes, but I travel light. I'll buy anything the apartment lacks and leave it behind when I go."

"Hopefully the apartment will be all right. It's just a block from where I live and fully furnished the way you wanted, but the landlord said he'd understand if you decide to find somewhere else.

He was surprised you didn't want to choose your own place."

"I'm used to it," Tara explained. "The company I work for makes my living arrangements, which saves time. Besides, I'm not fussy. It's just a place to sleep."

After picking up the vehicle she'd reserved, Tara set the GPS and headed for Schuyler, a small town a couple of hours away.

"How was the flight?" Lauren asked after they'd passed the Helena city limits.

"I slept part of the way, which made it shorter."

"Even so, you must be exhausted. The jet lag got me pretty bad when I flew back to California after visiting you in Paris."

"Right. I'll probably go to bed almost as soon as we get to the apartment."

It was a good excuse to cut the day short. They ate supper on the way, and there was a second hug after they arrived at the furnished apartment, which was much nicer than Tara had expected in a small town in the wilds of Montana.

"I'll come to the clinic tomorrow and take you out to lunch," Tara promised. She didn't want things to be uncomfortable with Lauren, but she didn't know how else to act. Her twin was obviously better with people than she'd ever learned to be.

Lauren brightened. "That would be great."

So Tara had the evening to regroup and unpack

her bags, and she could sleep late the next morning. She reminded herself that nobody could expect to build a sisterly relationship overnight. After all, anybody who believed twins automatically connected had never spent more than thirty years apart from their sibling.

"WHAT DO YOU MEAN the order was canceled?" Josh barked into the phone. "I was expecting it to arrive this week. I've got heifers ready to breed."

"I'm sorry, Mr. McGregor, but that's what our records say," explained the woman on the other end of the line. "We received a call that you didn't need it."

"*Who* called?" Josh demanded, though he was certain who was responsible.

"Walt Nelson is the name on my form. He had the purchase order number as confirmation."

"Thank you," Josh said crisply. "In the future, please note that I'm the only one who can cancel orders."

"Very well."

He slammed down the receiver and strode out to the yard where his grandfather was sitting.

"Why did you cancel my order from the Double J Ranch?" he asked.

Walt set his jaw. "Because we don't need any frozen bull semen. Especially from *Texas*."

"There's nothing wrong with Texas," Josh returned, trying not to lose his temper. Grandpa was an old-school rancher and had never forgotten the remark from a visiting Texan about Montana's "little ole cows." He'd never forgiven it, either. Josh supposed it hadn't helped when he'd taken a job in the Lone Star state. Fifteen years ago, he'd tried working on the Boxing N during first his summer break in college but had been treated like a peon with no horse sense. Things weren't much better now.

"Huh." Walt crossed his arms over his chest. "They might have done mail-order breeding at that fancy-dancy ranch where you worked down there, but my cattle are already first-rate. If we want to vary it up, we make arrangements with our neighbors."

Why couldn't he understand? Josh wanted to produce top-grade organic beef. He had started the process of getting the Boxing N's grazing land certified as pesticide-free, but even in the parts of the ranch that couldn't be certified, he wanted to improve the stock. And borrowing a bull from a neighbor's ranch *wasn't* the improvement he had in mind. The Double J Ranch had prize-winning bull semen for sale, and it was exactly the upgrade he wanted.

Of course...he *could* go to his brother. Jackson's breeding program was well-known, but Josh didn't want to slide in on his family's coattails. It already felt as if he was behind the curve since Grandpa had delayed his retirement so long.

The thought sent a mix of sorrow and guilt through Josh.

Twenty-five years ago, Grandpa Walt and his brother had made plans for the futures of their respective ranches. Since Mitch was older and didn't have children and Walt had two grandsons, Jackson and Josh, they agreed that Mitch would retire and give his ranch to his great-nephew once Jackson got out of college. Walt, in turn, would give the Boxing N spread to his younger grandson, Josh. Except Walt Nelson *hadn't* retired when Josh graduated college, he'd kept working…until the accident.

"I have a plan for the Boxing N, and bull semen from the Double J is part of it," Josh said as calmly as possible. In the four months since Grandpa had given him the ranch, he'd danced around, trying to be considerate and respectful, but the situation was wearing on him.

"Fancy-dancy nonsense," Walt proclaimed. "That isn't the way we do things here." He stood. "I'm going to see how Grasshopper is doing. It's her first foal."

As Walt Nelson limped toward the foaling barn, Josh held back a howl of frustration. Grandpa couldn't let go of being boss, but you couldn't have *two* bosses on a ranch, especially two with such dissimilar ideas.

Perhaps it harked back to the old rivalry between the Nelsons, Josh's mother's family, and the Mc-

Gregors, his father's. It hadn't been a blood feud, but it was fierce nonetheless, and it must have been a terrible blow to Walt when his only child fell in love with someone from the enemy camp. Walt still didn't really approve of the McGregors.

Needing space, Josh went to the barn, saddled Lightfoot and rode toward the north section of the ranch.

His frustration doubled when he saw slack wire on a fence. One of the ranch hands should have found the problem and taken care of it, but they were confused about whose orders to follow, who was doing what and when to do it. And they were also shorthanded since several men had quit, telling Josh that they'd return once Walt was out of the picture. Between the two problems, things were getting missed.

Taking the tools from his saddlebag, Josh began repairing the fence. Grappling with wire was preferable to the tug-of-war he was having with his grandfather. He would have used his trust fund to buy a different ranch years ago if he'd known everything would turn out this way. Now he was stuck—Walt couldn't handle the Boxing N alone, and Josh couldn't abandon the old guy, no matter how crazy the situation made him.

Distracted, Josh felt his hand slip. The wire cutters slashed across his palm and blood immediately welled from the ragged slice.

Damn. Damn. *Damn.*

TARA WALKED DOWN the street, following the directions to the clinic that Lauren had given her. It was almost surreal to see so many people dressed in jeans, boots and cowboy hats, as if she'd walked onto the set of a Hollywood Western.

Just three days before she'd been at the Chartres cathedral, brushing shoulders with visitors from around the world. It had been a farewell trip to one of her favorite French landmarks since she didn't know how soon she'd be back. Now she was living in the land of cowboys and hitching posts. She only knew they were hitching posts because she saw a horse tied to one.

Stopping in front of the Schuyler Medical Clinic— a modest title since apparently it covered a vast array of services—Tara straightened her shoulders. The drive from Helena with her sister had been filled with awkward silences and even more awkward bursts of conversation. Still, it was too early to draw any conclusions about how well they would get along.

It didn't help that she wasn't good at relationships in the first place. Her most serious boyfriend, Pierre Montrose, had made her failures in that area abundantly clear.

Pushing the memory away, she entered the clinic.

The receptionist's eyes widened. "You must be Tara. The two of you really *do* look alike."

Tara tried to smile. She would probably hear that often while she was in town.

The other woman looked at the clock. "Lauren should be ready soon."

"Thanks."

Lauren was a physician's assistant and had moved to Schuyler the previous year. She'd come for a friend's wedding and had immediately decided the small town suited her much better than Los Angeles. It wouldn't have been Tara's choice, but to each their own, she supposed.

As she perused a rack of magazines, the outer door opened. A man stomped inside, his left arm wrapped in a bloodstained towel. He was attractive, with dark brown hair and intense blue eyes, but his face was flushed and scowling.

"Good, you're here," he said, thrusting his injured limb at her. "I need this stitched up, and please skip the lectures."

Tara raised her eyebrows. "I'm afraid you—"

"Give me a break, Lauren. Just do it without one of your speeches."

His manner was startlingly abrupt…surely *all* Montanans weren't this rude.

"I was trying to explain that you've mistaken me for my twin sister, Lauren," Tara said, keeping her tone as even as possible. It wasn't easy. She'd never had a cat, but she knew it annoyed them if you rubbed their fur backward, and that's how she felt…as if she'd literally been rubbed the wrong way.

"What the hell?" His eyes narrowed suspiciously.

"I'd like to point something out, however," she added smoothly. "Declaring you don't want a lecture suggests you may need one."

"You've got one hell of a nerve saying that," he snapped.

"Didn't I get it right?" she asked. "Tell me what happened and I'll try to tailor my lecture."

"Hell."

"You seem to have a limited vocabulary. That was your third 'hell' in less than a minute."

He glared and turned to the receptionist. "Is Lauren available?"

"I've already paged her, Josh. She'll be out in a minute. Has the bleeding stopped?"

"Mostly."

A minute later Lauren hurried into the waiting room and checked Josh's wound. She looked at Tara apologetically. "I need to take care of this," she said. "I'll understand if you don't want to stay."

"Don't be silly. I'm happy to wait while you deal with the results of someone's stupidity."

Lauren's eyes widened, but she simply gestured to her bad-tempered patient, who followed her into the rear of the clinic with a last fierce look at Tara.

The receptionist chuckled once the door had closed behind them. "Oh, my gosh, Lauren said you had opposite personalities, and now I see what she meant."

"Oh?"

"Yeah. She's a terrific PA and very sweet, but

she would never stick it to Josh the way you did. Good job."

"Thanks. Is he always like Napoleon with a headache?" Tara asked, using one of her French coworker's similes.

"Lately, at least. He's getting on everyone's nerves and keeps—"

The woman stopped abruptly and looked down at the papers on her desk; perhaps she'd been about to say something prohibited under privacy regulations. She seemed relieved when someone else came through the door and stepped up to the window. A protracted discussion about insurance ensued, so Tara settled into a seat and leafed through a news magazine. She read with interest an article on international relations with France. The thought of returning to Paris for her next contract was compelling, but there were so many other places to see. Rome and Berlin called to her as well, along with Madrid.

In the background, she heard a comment about something Josh needed and pictured his face again. Maybe she shouldn't have sounded off since the clinic was Lauren's place of employment. But who did he think he was? Lauren was a professional, not a flunky who was supposed to jump when he snapped his fingers.

As for lectures… Weren't medical personnel *supposed* to advise their patients on healthy living?

She was on her third magazine when the interior door swung open.

It was Josh…What's His Name. While his hand was neatly bandaged and elevated in a sling, getting it treated obviously hadn't sweetened his mood. The thunderclouds on his face did nothing to diminish his good looks, but Tara wasn't impressed—she'd known too many handsome jerks over the years. He glanced at her, and she gave him a wickedly sweet smile, which made him glower all the more fiercely before marching from the clinic.

Lauren joined her several minutes later.

"I'm free now," she said. "But I'm afraid that took part of my lunch hour."

"That's okay. Where shall we go?"

"How about the restaurant down the street? It isn't gourmet, nothing like the places where we ate in Paris. Schuyler doesn't have any fancy restaurants, but the Roundup Café is fast and clean."

"Not a problem. I enjoy indigenous foods."

Lauren just blinked at the tongue-in-cheek remark, so Tara wasn't sure whether her sister shared her sense of humor. Or maybe they simply needed to know each other better before that sort of thing could be understood between them.

JOSH STALKED AWAY from the clinic. The throb in his palm had subsided thanks to the anesthetic Lauren had used before sewing it up, but it would undoubtedly begin hurting again as that wore off. She'd also written a prescription for pain pills. He had insisted they weren't necessary, but she'd reasonably pointed out that he might change his mind after the clinic had closed.

It didn't help to know he'd acted worse than a hungry bear right out of hibernation. The series of accidents he'd had in recent months had made him feel like a ten-thumbed greenhorn. What's more, once he got back to the Boxing N, Grandpa was sure to make a remark that would send his blood pressure sky-high.

On Josh's last two visits to the clinic, Lauren had suggested he needed to pay more attention to what he was doing, especially when tense or angry. It was irritating to be told something he already knew, and he hadn't wanted to hear it again. Still, Lauren Spencer was a nice sort, and he shouldn't have barked at her…or at the woman he'd *thought* was Lauren. The story of her long-lost twin sister had gone through Schuyler with the speed of a grassfire, but he hadn't realized they were identical.

Well, not *really* identical, at least in personality. Lauren was quiet, almost shy at times, with a down-to-earth practicality, while Tara had a cool, sensual polish. If he'd known she was in town he never would have mixed them up, but he'd heard she lived in France. She *did* seem foreign in Montana, while her sister had fit in from the beginning.

It was a good thing. Getting medical professionals in Schuyler was an ongoing challenge; the town had even resorted to offering a bonus for anyone agreeing to stay three years or longer.

Josh snorted grimly. People in Schuyler wouldn't be pleased if he said anything to make Lauren unhappy. It wasn't just that they needed a good PA, they liked her...a whole lot better than they liked *him* recently.

Grimacing, he fished his cell phone out, awkward from being temporarily one-handed. Finally he untied the sling and stuffed it in his pocket. His phone had rung several times in the clinic, but he hadn't been able to answer while Lauren was stitching up his palm.

The missed calls were from his parents' home number, so he dialed back, trying to ignore the small clutch in his chest. It had only been six months since they'd lost Grandma Evelyn, and the whole family remained jumpy about the possibility of more bad news.

"Darling, are you all right?" asked his mother in an anxious tone. "Dora Payton phoned. She said you went into the clinic covered in blood."

"Dora overreacted, as usual. It's just a cut and Lauren put in a few stitches."

"Thank God. Not that I'm happy you were hurt, I'm just glad it wasn't worse. Why don't you come over and lie down for a while? I'll make you lunch."

Sarah McGregor couldn't resist playing mommy, even for her grown children.

"Thanks, but I'm fine. As long as I'm in town, I'm going to run an errand."

"Oh. All right. Call if you need anything."

"Will do." Josh disconnected before she could suggest pulling out his old teddy bear for comfort.

He returned the phone to his pocket and headed for the bank. After taking care of his business, he'd stop and grab lunch before going back to the ranch. Maybe along the way he'd get a little inspiration on dealing with his grandfather.

As she and Lauren stepped into the Roundup Café, Tara was instantly aware that they'd become the center of attention. Heads swiveled their direction, the rhythm of the conversations changed and several people left their seats to crowd around them.

"My word, Lauren," an older woman exclaimed, "you mentioned having a twin, but it didn't sink in that you'd look so much alike. Your hair and eyes… I can hardly tell you apart."

"Did you really meet for the first time in the last year?" someone else asked. "That's amazing."

Their curiosity was understandable. Separated

and reunited twins weren't common, and Tara knew she might be equally curious in their shoes.

"Tara," Lauren said, "this is Vanta Cooper, she's an attorney, and that's Mark Corson, and this is Rob Mueller..."

The introductions continued and Tara lost track of the names; it seemed as if her sister knew everyone in town.

Vanta Cooper leaned toward Tara. "Don't worry, nobody expects you to remember who we are. Lauren gets to know us at the clinic and other places."

Nevertheless, Tara was getting distinctly edgy. How had her sister become friends with so many people? She'd only lived in Schuyler since last October. Maybe it was a Montana thing, the open ranges and isolation drawing everyone together. Or it could simply be that Lauren made friends easily.

Tara's smile got harder to maintain as the introductions continued. She hoped nobody expected her to be like her twin, because she wasn't. Life as a foster kid had taught her there were risks to getting close to people. As an adult she'd spent two years in each country where she'd worked but couldn't claim to have friends in any of them; knowing she was leaving made it seem best to keep her distance. Naturally she had acquaintances, though she rarely kept contact with them once she moved on to a new position.

After what seemed like ages, folks returned to their seats while she and Lauren found a table along the wall.

"You've obviously gotten to know a lot of people here," Tara commented after they gave their order to a server.

"Medical personnel are popular in Schuyler," Lauren explained. "And my best friend married into one of the oldest families in town, so that helps. Everybody knows the McGregors."

Tara frowned thoughtfully. "I thought Emily married someone named Hawkins." Her sister had sent Emily's name as an emergency contact after moving to Schuyler.

"She did, but Trent's mother was a McGregor. When his parents died, he and his sister, Alaina, were adopted by their maternal uncle and aunt. The family is terrific and everybody here is so nice. I was really impressed when I came for the wedding, and since Emily loves the place so much, I decided Schuyler would be a good place to live."

"I see."

Just then the café door opened and in walked the wounded jackass from the clinic. He looked around, probably searching for an empty spot in the crowded restaurant, and Tara hoped he didn't expect to join them, because while sparring with him might be interesting, she was sure it would make her sister uncomfortable.

"Hey, Lauren," he said, stopping nearby.

"Hey, Josh." Lauren looked at his bandage before focusing on his face. "What happened to the sling?"

"It's in my pocket. I want to thank you for taking care of me. Sorry I was so abrupt."

"No worries. I, um, should properly introduce you to my twin sister." She gestured. "Josh McGregor, Tara Livingston."

McGregor?

Oh, great.

For a moment Tara wondered whether Lauren might be sweet on the guy; that might also explain the "lecture." If so, her move to Montana made sense. But if they were involved romantically, Tara knew she might cut her stay short—watching someone careening toward an emotional train wreck wasn't her idea of fun. Her sister was far too quiet and shy to deal with Josh McGregor's volatile personality. Work was the only part of Lauren's life where she seemed confident.

"Hello," Tara muttered, and he gave her a short, almost imperceptible nod.

"Please keep your arm elevated as much as possible," Lauren urged him. "That spot on the hand is especially vulnerable to infection. And take it easy. You need to let it heal."

"You bet. Thanks."

When they were alone again, Lauren leaned forward. "I realize Josh was in a rotten mood when you met him earlier, but he isn't always that way. Emily says he's a good guy," she said softly.

"Deep, *deep* down, right?" Tara guessed, deciding that Lauren wasn't interested in Josh, after all, except as a patient.

"He can be difficult, but from everything I've heard, he's going through a rough time right now." Lauren nervously adjusted her water glass. "Anyhow, I was thrilled when you said you were coming for an extended visit, but can you afford to be off work that long?"

"It isn't a problem."

Tara wasn't accustomed to sharing personal details with anyone, and didn't elaborate on her financial situation. For ten years she'd enjoyed generous salaries, a full living expense allowance and hefty bonuses. She'd bought company stock and was well fixed. Employment wasn't about earning a paycheck any longer; it was about seeing and living in new places and getting better at her work in accounting and records management. She'd specialized in both.

Their food came, and as Tara ate, she saw Josh McGregor inhale an enormous hamburger so fast he probably didn't even taste it on the way down. The corner of her mouth twitched as she saw a splash of sauce from the burger hit the neat bandage on his hand. He wiped it quickly and got up, tossing money on the table.

On his way to the door he gave her another polite nod, but Tara wasn't fooled. Whatever had been burning under his facade was still smoldering.

CHAPTER TWO

THE THIRD NIGHT after he'd cut his hand, Josh wished he'd filled the prescription for painkillers from Lauren; instead it was still in his wallet. He'd decided to tough things out.

He lay in bed for another few minutes, listening to the sounds that drifted in through the open window—cattle lowing, the neighs from the horses...a night breeze through the trees. Finally, he rolled out of bed and took two aspirins before dropping into the living room recliner.

The house Josh lived in was a couple hundred feet from the main house. His choice to stay in the foreman's residence, instead of with Walt, was another source of tension between them. Walt thought his grandson should be at his immediate beck and call, though not because of uncertainty over his health. He just wanted to yell that the barns needed to be checked or to do some other task...usually something Josh had already handled or assigned to someone.

Josh's mouth tightened.

Unreasonable expectations were why the foreman's house had been empty. Grandpa was an old-school rancher who believed in running things with an iron fist, and no foreman worth his salt was willing to be treated as a glorified flunky. Walt had never kept anyone for more than a few months.

Belatedly recalling the recommendation Lauren Spencer had made, Josh raised his injured arm and draped it above his head.

Maybe if he hadn't repaired the corral his hand wouldn't be throbbing so much, but he *couldn't* take any time off to let the gash heal—there was too much to do.

Now another cowhand had quit, leaving with the wry remark that he *hoped* to get his final pay. Josh presumed it was a reference to the deplorable state of the ranch office. Walt's name remained on the ranch accounts and he insisted that he could continue writing the checks, but payments were erratic. When Josh had brought it up earlier, the old man had furiously claimed he had a plan and would get it done.

Right, a plan.

His grandfather kept an old-style ledger book to carefully track the number of foals born each year, but all the other ranch accounts were in shambles. Walt practically considered a computer to be blasphemy and the internet a passing fad not worth thinking about. Apparently it had escaped his notice that his wife had owned a computer *and* used the internet.

When Josh had moved in, he'd had the internet service transferred to the foreman's house. His next step would have to be getting a computer online at the ranch office, though he could imagine his grandfather's explosion when he did so.

Josh released a heavy breath.

God, he missed Grandma Evelyn. She was the one who'd kept peace between her husband and the rest of the family. But it was more than that. She'd been a wise, beautiful, laughter-filled presence in his life. Losing her had left a hole that refused to heal.

His family kept urging him to have patience with Walt, but they didn't know how bad things had gotten. Legally Josh now owned the Boxing N and could do what he wanted, but how could he oust his grandfather? Hang the legalities; it was still Walt's ranch. But like it or not, Josh knew he'd have to take control of the office at some point. Bills and the payroll needed to be properly managed, along with any stock sales or purchases. He didn't want to get a reputation for being unreliable.

The throbbing slowly eased in his hand, and Josh had fallen asleep, when the phone rang. He grabbed the receiver, adrenaline racing through him.

"Yes?"

"We need to get to the hospital," said his grandfather.

Josh shot to his feet. Walt had been frail since the accident, and his continuing health issues had put stress on his heart. Was it possible their heated discussion about the ranch office had brought on a heart attack or stroke?

"What symptoms are you having?"

"It isn't me," Grandpa returned irritably. "It's Alaina. Your sister has gone into labor."

Josh's pulse slowed. It was good news, not an emergency.

"If it's just started, we don't have to rush," he said. "Mom says first babies take time. Get some more sleep and we'll go in a couple of hours."

"No, *now*."

Josh released an exasperated breath. He might have known Walt wouldn't budge. His grandfather was crazy about Alaina, despite her being related to the McGregor clan rather than the Nelsons. It *had* taken Walt a while to accept both Trent and Alaina after they were adopted by his daughter and son-in-law, but Alaina had totally won him over.

A few minutes later Josh stepped outside. Grandpa was waiting on the porch of the main house and without a word climbed into the cab of the truck, maneuvering his bad leg into place.

Josh headed for town, his hand pulsing again. He could take the pain med prescription to the pharmacy in a couple of hours, but he hated the way that stuff made him feel. That was one of the few things he shared with Walt; his grandfather didn't like taking anything for pain, either.

Tara exited her apartment complex and saw Lauren coming down the block toward her. They'd discovered a mutual fondness for early-morning walks and had agreed to meet each day at 6:00 a.m. so they could go together. It was a relief to finally discover something in common.

Tara fell in step with her sister, who had started toward the edge of town. "Do you always take the same route?" she asked.

"Usually. I guess that makes me boring, but I enjoy the fitness trail. It's great to get away from houses and power lines. I could never do it easily in Los Angeles, but would you rather go another way?"

"This works for me."

Beginning at the hospital, the path continued out to the county park, where it branched into different directions. Tara had first seen the park on one of her drives; it was a pretty place and she looked forward to exploring it thoroughly. But as they walked through the hospital's small parking lot, Lauren's pace slowed.

"That's Trent's truck," she said, gesturing to a vehicle with Big Sky Construction painted on the door. "Emily is only five months along—it's too early. Do you mind if we… Well, you don't need to go in. You should continue on without me."

"No, I'll come with you," Tara told her. It didn't seem right to ignore Lauren's concern for her friend. Besides, with nothing else to do in Schuyler, she could walk whenever she wanted.

"We'll need to go in through the emergency room because it's so early," Lauren explained, leading her to a side door.

The hospital wasn't large, but from what Tara saw as she followed her sister, it was clean and modern.

Lauren turned into a hallway marked Maternity and stopped when she saw the waiting room full of people.

"Em, are you all right?" she exclaimed, rushing over to a woman in a navy blue maternity dress. "We were going for a walk when I saw Trent's truck outside."

"Nothing is wrong," Emily assured, patting her rounded tummy. "Alaina went into labor. The whole family gathers for stuff like this. Isn't that wonderful?"

Lauren nodded fervently.

Tara wasn't sure what she'd expected of her sister's oldest friend, but while Emily Hawkins wasn't a raving beauty, she was pretty and positively glowed as she hugged the arm of a tall, handsome man who had to be her husband. A strange envy went through Tara when she saw the tender way he looked down at his wife.

Recalling that Josh McGregor was a member of the family, Tara scanned the room and saw him in a corner, his hand elevated, with what appeared to be fresh blood on the bandage. Curious, she went over and saw the wrapping was no longer pristine white, but dingy from a lot more than the hamburger sauce she'd seen him spill on it. Undeniably, there was fresh blood, as well.

Josh's mouth tightened at her obvious interest, but he stood nevertheless. Certain age-old male courtesies were alive and well in Schuyler, Montana—cowboys tipped their hats and men stood in a woman's presence.

"It looks as though you need another lecture," she said softly.

Beyond a set jaw, Josh didn't react.

A youngster sitting nearby was staring at Tara in fascination. "Golly, you *do* look like Lauren," she declared, then cocked her head. "But in a way you don't, only I'm not sure why."

"DeeDee, at least introduce yourself before spouting off," scolded a woman with auburn hair. She stood and smiled at Tara. "I'm Kayla McGregor, and this is my daughter, DeeDee."

"It's nice to meet you. I'm Tara Livingston."

"Why isn't your name Spencer, like Lauren?" DeeDee asked.

"Because Lauren was adopted by the Spencer family and they changed her name," Tara explained, hoping the youngster wouldn't ask more questions. She didn't enjoy thinking about her childhood or telling people that *she'd* never been adopted. Instead, she'd grown up in foster homes until she'd aged out of the system at eighteen. The situation wasn't unusual, but when you were a kid, hoping for a family of your own, it was hard not to wonder if something was wrong with you rather than understand that some people were reluctant to adopt older children.

Across the waiting room Lauren was talking to a man dressed in surgical scrubs; a moment later she hurried toward Tara. "Everything is going well with Alaina," she said.

A perverse mood nudged Tara. "Mr. McGregor's hand might be the exception."

"I'm fine," Josh snapped.

"Really? I could swear that's fresh blood. But since you're at a hospital, I'm sure you can get help if you need it," she added, mindful that her sister was off duty.

Lauren immediately turned to Josh. "Let me check it for you. I can probably get supplies from the emergency room."

His head shook once in a definitive rejection. "You said there would be drainage, and that's all this is." Yet he flinched in obvious discomfort as he shifted his arm.

Lauren hesitated as she looked at the grubby bandage. "Uh, Josh, you need a clean dressing at the very least, and if you're in excessive pain, you could have an infection."

"I'm just, uh, late with a pain pill, that's all. I'll put a fresh wrapping on it later."

His tone made Tara wonder if there was more to the story, but maybe she'd prodded him enough. She wasn't even sure why she had done it the first time, unless it was the universal impulse of poking a sleeping snake to see if it was alive…and seeing how quickly you could jump out of striking range.

"Okay," Lauren said, though she didn't sound convinced and shot another worried glance at the filthy bandage.

It was curious that she wasn't being more forthright, but on the other hand, Josh McGregor did the tough he-man thing so well, it would take someone far more self-assured to challenge him. Besides, he hadn't come for follow-up medical care; he was just waiting for his sister to give birth.

Lauren crossed the room to speak with someone else, so Tara decided to prod Josh a little further, after all.

"Personally," she said, "even if the inside is okay, which I doubt, the outside of that bandage looks like something from a horror film."

That was when he turned and stalked out of the room.

Tara stood back and waited as her sister made the rounds of the waiting room, then became aware of an older man a few feet away. His head was cocked as he stared at her.

She smiled. "Hi, I'm Tara Livingston."

"Nice to meet you. I'm Walt Nelson. You, uh, remind me of my wife when we first met—beautiful and sassy."

"I…have a feeling you just gave me a lovely compliment," she answered. No one else was paying any attention to the two of them and there was a strange air of intimacy, even in the midst of the group.

"Yeah, but don't let it go to your head."

An instinctive liking for the elderly man washed over Tara. "I'll do my best," she promised. "I do records management, so I'll just file it under Compliments to Be Ignored."

Walt leaned back in his chair and she realized he seemed tired and frail.

"Records management," he murmured. "That's interesting." That was all, and after a few moments, he appeared to be growing drowsy, so she shifted the other direction so he wouldn't feel he had to continue talking.

Aside from that brief, odd interchange, Tara felt more out of place than the first time she'd landed in a foreign country. Still, there was something pleasant about the atmosphere in the waiting room, everyone showing up to welcome a new baby.

Family, an inner voice whispered.

A familiar ache went through Tara, but she refused to poke *that* spot; her own life was just fine being traveled solo.

JOSH TRIED NOT TO glare at Tara Livingston as he returned to his chair with a cup of coffee from the vending machine; someone might notice and he didn't want his foul mood to become the subject of a family discussion. However, it didn't stop him from deciding that Tara was an annoying termagant—an old-fashioned word he'd picked up from Grandma Evelyn. But the term fit Tara, who was so unlike her sister. Lauren, with her friendly nature, had quickly found a home in Schuyler. Perhaps that was the pot calling the kettle black, considering his own short fuse the past few months, but there was no denying that Tara had a sharp tongue.

Now that he wasn't being taken by surprise, he saw fewer and fewer similarities between the two women. There was a superficial likeness, but their personalities were completely different. Even their clothes were distinctive—Lauren wore a loose dark blue sweat suit, while Tara had chosen form-fitting jeans that showcased every delicious curve. As for her snug designer T-shirt...? It reminded him that she was remarkably well built.

"Hello. You're obviously Lauren's sister." His mother's voice intruded into his thoughts. Always gracious, she'd come over to introduce herself. "I'm Sarah McGregor, and you must be Tara. How nice of you to come with Lauren to check on Emily."

"Not at all. I'm glad your daughter-in-law is all right," Tara said politely. "I take it Alaina, the one having the baby, is your daughter?"

"Yes, I'm so blessed. Five children and three of them married now."

Josh leaned forward, interested by Tara's discomfort in talking to his mom. It seemed strange since she hadn't quailed under his bad temper, but you never knew.

His mother glanced at him and back at Tara. "I gather you met my son before this morning…?"

"That's right," Josh interjected, hoping to head off any revelations Tara might make. "We ran into each other when I went to the clinic for my hand."

"Yes," Tara agreed smoothly. "He thought I was Lauren, but I don't have a medical background. I do accounting and records management for an international company based out of London."

His mother seemed oddly disappointed. "Then you won't be staying in Schuyler?"

"Not permanently. I'm a freelance contractor and my latest contract just ended. An extended visit seemed the best way to get better acquainted with my sister."

"Isn't it wonderful?" Lauren said in a soft, enthusiastic voice. "Tara says she can take a few months off before she goes back to work. Of course, then she'll be heading off to Berlin or Singapore or some other faraway spot."

"But you'll be here until then?" Sarah pressed Tara.

"As far as I know."

Josh restrained a groan, suddenly realizing why

his mother was so curious. Now that he was back in Montana, she'd decided it was time he got married. She'd had mixed feelings about him falling in love when he worked in Texas…since a wife from the Lone Star state might expect him to remain there instead of come home.

But Josh had no interest in marriage, not until he got things in order at the Boxing N. Then…*maybe*. Great-Uncle Mitch had never married and seemed quite happy. Meanwhile, Josh enjoyed dating, but it had nothing to do with looking for a life partner.

"Do you enjoy horseback riding?" Sarah asked Tara.

"Very much, though I haven't gone for a couple of years. Mostly I was able to ride while living in England. I also got a couple of chances when visiting the Australian outback."

England? Australia? And most recently she'd lived in France? Boy, was his mother barking up the wrong tree. When and *if* he ever wanted a long-term relationship, it wouldn't be with someone whose lifestyle took her all over the world. Someone like that would never stay long in Montana.

A rancher needed a wife who loved ranching alongside him. Josh had already seen how hard a marriage could be without a shared passion. Grandma Evelyn had come from San Francisco and never completely adjusted to ranch life. Actually, Josh wasn't sure what had held Walt and Evelyn together. It must have been a case of knowing they could have married more wisely but were making the best of things. His grandfather's priority had been the Boxing N above everything else, and Grandma Evelyn had loved art, music and flower gardens.

He glanced at his grandfather, who'd briefly fallen asleep earlier but was awake and blinking groggily. If only Walt would try to make the best of things *now*, but he wanted things his way and only his way. Ironically, Grandpa never would have put up with that behavior when he was a young man; stories of the battles between Walt and *his* father were epic. Of course, those battles might have started his stubborn refusal to see anyone else's point of view.

"You're welcome to go riding at our ranch whenever you want," his mother told Tara. "Lauren, too, of course."

"You'll have to excuse me," Josh said, hoping to head off his mother from suggesting that he give Tara and her sister a personal tour of the McGregor spread. "I'm going to the cafeteria for some better coffee than this sludge. Who wants some?"

There were several raised hands, along with a rueful shake of the head from Kayla, who was holding her four-month-old daughter. Kayla was forgoing coffee until she was no longer nursing— she'd discovered that even decaf gave the baby colic. Josh knew how hard that must be for her;

she'd once lived in Seattle, which was a mecca for coffee lovers, and deeply missed the brew.

When he returned with a tray of steaming cups, Lauren and her sister had left. His mother was still talking about them, though, and he was convinced she had matchmaking in mind.

He would have to be careful. The past few months had been hard on the family, especially for his mom. She'd lost her mother and watched her father go from being an active, vital rancher to a querulous old man with disabilities. The arrival of Kayla's baby had helped, along with having his sister, Alaina, pregnant along with Emily. Still, he didn't want to raise her hopes that he'd get married anytime soon.

Right now he was solely interested in the ranch he'd dreamed of building. Grandpa was providing enough roadblocks; he didn't need any more.

LAUREN PRESSED HER fingers to her stomach as she walked with Tara toward the emergency room exit. She wished negative emotions didn't bother her so much. Heck, half the time she was wrong, misinterpreting a frown or shrug and losing sleep over what it might mean or questioning what she should do about it...even as she knew she was being ridiculous.

Josh McGregor was a prime example. The way he'd stomped out of the waiting room had seemed ominous, but it could be her imagination. And even if it wasn't, it didn't necessarily mean anything except that he was having a bad day.

If only that sort of thing didn't make her feel as if she was shriveling up inside.

It would be wonderful to be more like Tara. Karen—the receptionist at the clinic—had gleefully recounted how Tara had "stuck it to Josh" when he'd roared into the waiting room earlier in the week. Obviously Karen felt their patient had deserved a dose of comeuppance.

Maybe so, but Lauren was glad someone *else* had dispensed the prescription.

She hadn't talked enough with Tara to know if her twin was interested in settling down and getting married, but it would be wonderful if she stayed in Montana. There were plenty of nice guys in town. Almost as if summoned by the thought, Lauren saw two men in uniform coming through the double doors to the emergency room. The taller man grinned when he saw her.

"Hey, Lauren," Carl said. "I heard about Alaina, so we stopped to say hello to the family and wish them well."

Lauren nodded as other kinds of flutters started. "That's nice of you."

Carl was the local sheriff and the man with him was a new deputy. After living in Los Angeles with its frantic pace, she loved the small-town atmosphere in Schuyler. She couldn't imagine a big-city policeman dropping in like this at the UCLA Medical Center.

Carl had attended the Trent Hawkins–Emily George wedding, and he and Lauren had sat next to each other at the reception. Lauren had enjoyed talking to him, and after she'd moved to Schuyler last October, they'd gone out several times.

"Holy cow," Carl said, staring at Tara. "You said you had a twin, but it didn't hit me until just now what that meant."

"Sometimes I feel the same way. Tara, this is Carl Stanfield. And the deputy next to him is Noah Mercer."

"It's nice to meet you," Tara said.

"Same here." Carl cocked his head. "You almost have an accent, but I can't place it."

"I've lived in five different countries over the past ten years. There's no telling how much has rubbed off."

"That explains it. Noah is the same—he spent most of his childhood in New Zealand and Germany."

Tara turned to the deputy, asking about a place in Auckland that she'd visited, while Carl urged Lauren down the hall a few feet.

"I've stopped by the clinic to see you," he said, "but you're usually with a patient."

"They keep me pretty busy."

"I'm sure they do. But now that you've had a

chance to get more settled, I wonder if we could get together for dinner again?"

Renewed flutters went through Lauren's abdomen. She liked Carl…liked him enough that she'd excused any further dates by saying she needed to get more settled. Carl was attractive and her pulse jumped whenever she saw him, but they were incompatible, so it didn't make sense to continue.

"I'm sorry to put you off another time," she said slowly, "but with my sister here, I shouldn't take time from her visit." Darn it, why couldn't she just say no?

"Don't be silly," Tara exclaimed, apparently overhearing them. "You can't put the rest of your life on hold while I'm in Montana. Go ahead."

"Oh… I…in that case, it would be nice, Carl."

He flashed his wide smile at her. "Great. How about Saturday night?"

"I don't know, I'm on call for the next week," she said, still hoping he'd get the message that she didn't actually *want* to go out with him again. "I try to keep things quiet so I'll be at my best if I'm needed."

That was the truth. Medical personnel were limited in the area, and they took turns being available for after-hours emergencies.

"I understand. Would the following Saturday work?"

Obviously he wasn't giving up, and Lauren wondered if she was unconsciously sending the wrong signals.

"Uh, sure," she answered, unable to think of another excuse. A shred of irritation went through her. Most guys would have gotten the message with the first excuse she'd used, or at least the second. Even Billy Halloran, a notorious Schuyler flirt, had backed off when she'd told him that she wasn't free because she was painting her apartment and who knew how long it would take?

Of course, it was doubtful that sensitivity had anything to do with Billy's reaction. He'd disappeared at the speed of light, possibly worried she'd ask him to help.

Carl would have rolled up his sleeves and taken over the project, ignoring her protests. In the time they'd already spent together, his take-charge personality had been obvious, which was partly why she couldn't envision a relationship with him. Someone like her would get swept under, like a swimmer in a riptide.

"I'll drop by the clinic and we can discuss the details," Carl said, drawing Lauren's attention back to the present. He smiled again and walked with his deputy toward the maternity wing.

Outside Tara studied her curiously. "Is something wrong? You're flushed."

"No. Everything is fine."

To avoid further questions, Lauren headed for the fitness trail, setting a rapid pace that Tara easily matched, though in her case she made it look like a sexy, long-legged stroll.

It was too bad they still hadn't developed the close relationship that sisters should share. That way Tara might have teased her about Carl and she could have explained that she liked him, but that she wasn't his kind of woman...the main factors being his career and her unfortunate streak of timidity.

In the beginning, her old boyfriend in Los Angeles had found those qualities attractive—it had made him feel protective and manly. But after a while Kendall had suggested she take assertiveness training and get counseling for her self-image. She'd broken up with him not long afterward.

Carl was a sheriff who'd been a big-city cop. He'd dealt with everything from traffic violators to murderers. It would take him even less time than Kendall to realize he'd rather be with someone gutsier. But she couldn't explain that to her sister, who was strong and confident enough to live and travel alone in foreign countries. They barely knew each other—what if Tara thought less of her because of it?

"You're quiet," Tara commented after they'd circled the park twice.

"Just, um, getting my head together for work," Lauren said. It was true, more or less. She needed to think less about her abysmal love life and more about the good things she had going, such as connecting with her long-lost sister. That was great, even if being around Tara made her feel like the Cowardly Lion in *The Wizard of Oz*.

Taking a deep breath, Lauren decided she didn't have to make a big deal out of the situation. It was just one more date. Carl hadn't suggested getting serious; he'd just asked if they could have another dinner together. She didn't have to go out with him again once it was over.

She was both relieved and a little depressed at the thought.

CHAPTER THREE

A WEEK LATER Tara walked down an aisle at the grocery store, selecting spices. The restaurant food in Schuyler was tasty and certainly "indigenous," but she was ready to vary things up with her favorite dishes from the countries she'd traveled to. Not that there was a huge selection of exotic ingredients available, but she could make do. Cooking was often a question of style as much as content.

It would also be good to experiment with recipes off the internet. In fact, she was ready to try *anything* to occupy herself. She was accustomed to working regular hours and maximizing her free time to see everything possible in the places she lived. In Schuyler she didn't have a job, and her sister had long shifts at the medical clinic. Montana scenery was stunning, but nobody could spend all day, every day, just looking at the beautiful vistas.

Before long she'd realized she would go stark raving crazy without something more to do. Fortunately, that was changing since word had gone around Schuyler about the kind of work she did. More than once she'd heard, "I understand you do bookkeeping and organize stuff." It was a simplistic description of her professional skills, but that was okay. She needed to occupy some of her time and didn't mind trimming her fees to fit her new environment.

Today Tara was going to talk with a prospective client out in the country. His lawyer, Vanta Cooper, had contacted her, explaining that ill health had necessitated bringing in outside help. When she'd heard the name, Walt Nelson, she had immediately agreed, remembering him from the hospital.

Rather than use GPS, she studied a local map and memorized the route to the Boxing N. Shortly before two she pulled up next to a small building with a sign that identified it as the office.

"Good to see you again, Tara," Walt said as he limped forward to meet her. "When you mentioned records management at the hospital, it gave me the idea of having you work in my office here. My lawyer's office said they'd track you down."

"I'm glad they did, Mr. Nelson," she agreed with a smile.

"Call me Walt. You mind if I call you Tara?"

She smiled. "Not in the least."

"Come see the disaster zone."

He led the way into the building's main room and Tara knew what Vanta had meant when she'd said that "paperwork isn't Walt's favorite occupation." The chaos was obviously a long-standing condition. Papers were everywhere, and it was unlikely the ancient desk to the left had ever seen a computer.

But the room was pleasant, with windows that provided gorgeous views of rolling ranch land as well as the gardens around the house. On the right were comfortable chairs, a small sink, refrigerator, stove and coffeemaker. Plainly it was more than an office; it was also a gathering place, though she didn't know whether it was for employees or friends.

"I don't suppose what we need done here is like your work in Paris," Walt continued. "It may seem ridiculous to you."

"I don't think anyone's business is ridiculous," she told him honestly. "Your needs will be different from the records management systems used by an international corporation, but I wouldn't expect that on a ranch."

He peered at her, his faded eyes looking sad. "How did you like working in Paris and all those other places you've lived?"

Realizing he wanted more than a pat answer, Tara thought for a moment before responding. "There is nothing quite like living among people who grew up in a different culture. What's automatic for me may not be for them, and vice versa. It's an adventure."

Heaving a sigh, Walt settled into one of the easy chairs. "So you're a Magellan of the modern age."

"I don't have much to keep me anchored in the United States, that's all."

"The ranch was *my* anchor…perhaps my prison, as well."

The last words were mumbled, and Tara wasn't sure she'd understood him correctly. She sat quietly while his eyelids drooped; she wasn't in a hurry and he looked tired. After a few minutes, he shook himself and sat forward.

"My apologies. It's those blasted pain pills the doctor gave me. But I won't need them much longer. I'm set on that." His voice was grimly determined.

While she knew she might be romanticizing the moment, Tara suspected she was seeing the grit made legendary in movie Westerns, except this wasn't two stylized hours on celluloid. It was the real thing.

"I've got to check on a new foal," Walt said, lurching to his feet. "Go ahead and poke around. Vanta explained you work as a contractor, setting your own hours and such, which is fine with me. If you don't want to tackle such a mess, there won't be any hard feelings."

"Don't worry, Walt. I think it's going to work out fine. Just so you know, some of the time I'll work only mornings or afternoons, depending on my other commitments and whether my sister has the time off."

He nodded. "That's fine. Shake on it?"

Tara took his hand and was surprised by the firmness of his grip. She also realized that the odd sense of connection she'd experienced was even stronger than when she had met him at the hospital. He was different from the suave, cosmopolitan executives she normally worked with; there was something rough and genuine about Walt Nelson.

"By the way," he added, "just to be clear, *I'm* the one hiring you, not the Boxing N."

Not sure what the difference meant, she nodded. There could be a trust involved or something that made it important to clarify. She'd probably learn the reasons as she went along.

Once Tara was alone in the office, she began looking through various stacks and drawers, cubbyholes and shelves. There were at least fifty years of ranch records, many of them mixed up with current paperwork.

Twenty minutes later she ran across a yellowed handwritten invoice dated 1872, wherein a Zebedee Nelson recorded the sale of fifty head of cattle. The expense of the cattle drive bringing them to market was annotated on the bottom. It was a whole lot more interesting than most corporate historical records she'd seen, and as she sat studying the paper, a soft breeze came through an open window.

In Paris she'd worked in a modern high-rise, surrounded by desks, bright uniform lights and the hum of hundreds of people going about their business. This would be a nice break, at least for the time being. She had a feeling Lauren hoped she would consider staying in Schuyler, but Tara had always felt the need to be constantly moving forward. She couldn't picture giving up her career and staying in one place.

JOSH TURNED OFF his satellite phone as he rode toward the Boxing N ranch center. He was discouraged. After two days of having a help wanted ad in the local newspaper, his only calls had been from a high school senior looking for an after-school job and a retired pharmacist who'd moved to Schuyler the previous autumn and had "always wanted to be a cowboy."

Surely it would get better. And after he got more help on the ranch, there'd be time for some of the other things that had to be done.

A silver Toyota was parked by the ranch office, and Josh frowned. In the past, his grandfather had met his cronies there because they could smoke their cigars without bothering his wife. But Walt had given up smoking years ago, and since Evelyn was gone, he no longer needed the office as a separate gathering spot. Still, old habits died hard.

After grooming Lightfoot, Josh tiredly made his way to the foreman's house and slumped into an Adirondack chair on the porch. But as two figures came out of the ranch office and stood together beside the car, Josh leaned forward. One of them was his grandfather; Walt's labored pace was impossible to mistake. But the other was a woman, and even from this distance, Josh could see she possessed very attractive curves.

Curiosity drove him to his feet, and he strode toward the office. But as he got closer, he couldn't believe his eyes. It was Tara Livingston. What the devil was *she* doing here?

"Hey, Grandpa," he said as he came close. "Is everything all right?"

"Of course," Walt said. He appeared thoroughly self-satisfied, which was instantly worrisome. "As I recall, you've already met Miss Livingston. I just hired her to get the office in order."

Josh managed to swallow the "hell, no," that instantly leaped into his mouth. "Really?" he choked out instead. If it wasn't one complication, it was another.

"Yep. I've been thinking about doing it, and she came along at the right moment."

Tara's eyes sparkled, and Josh was sure she'd guessed his reaction.

"I see," he said. "Perhaps you could have consulted me first."

"No point," Walt informed him stiffly. "I *told* you I'd take care of things. Tara, when will you be starting?"

"Monday."

"Fine, fine. I'll see you then." With that, he limped toward the main house.

Josh watched his grandfather's retreating figure in disbelief.

"I'm sorry," he said to Tara, "there's been a mistake. This is my ranch now, and I'm still evaluating what to do with the office. Your services won't be needed."

A smile played on her lips. "It isn't your decision. Mr. Nelson was very clear that *he* was hiring me, not the ranch."

"That doesn't make any difference," Josh returned quickly. "Please tell my grandfather that you can't work for him. Anyway, I understand you're here on an extended vacation. Why would you want a job?"

She shrugged, and he couldn't help noticing the way her silk blouse slid over her breasts. *Crap*. It didn't make sense—Lauren had never made him react this way.

"It really isn't a vacation, I'm here to get to know my sister," she said. "But Lauren has her own job and I'm not used to being idle. So when folks started asking if I was available to work, I thought it was a good way to keep occupied."

"Why the Boxing N?"

"It's as good a place as any. I'm taking contracts at more than one location, but I have a feeling this will be my favorite."

"If you've got employment elsewhere, you don't need to work here."

Tara's blue eyes narrowed. "It's not for you to tell me what to do."

"That isn't what I'm doing. I was just pointing out that you don't seem to need the job here."

"Are you *also* the arbiter of what I need?"

"I didn't say that, either," Josh insisted.

"Sure you did. What's your problem, anyhow? I'm only asking because I'll be working at the Boxing N and your attitude affects me."

His head was starting to spin. "Then quit."

She shrugged. "Technically I'm a freelance contractor, but regardless, I have no intention of quitting. And if you think you can fire me, reconsider the thought. Do I need to point out again that Mr. Nelson made it very clear that I'll be working for him, not the ranch? I'll be looking out for his interests, not yours."

Josh counted to ten, then to ten once more. She had him over a barrel. As much as he wanted to lay down the law to his grandfather, he couldn't disenfranchise the old guy. Besides, if Walt had hired Tara as his personal employee or contractor, nobody else *could* fire her. Well, since he owned the Boxing N now, he could restrict her access to the ranch, but he could imagine the explosion that would follow.

For a brief second, Josh considered trying to convince Tara to help him get Walt to be more reasonable, but she'd made it clear where her loyalties lay.

"Very well," Josh said in a stiff, formal tone. "At the very least, I'd appreciate reports about your progress in the office."

"I'm afraid you'll have to ask Walt for any updates he wants to share."

She marched to her car and got behind the wheel. Waving as though they'd simply had a cordial chat, she drove down the road toward the main entrance.

Damn, she was aggravating.

His thoughts spinning, Josh returned to his porch, even more discouraged than when he'd gotten off the phone with the retired pharmacist. Without treating Walt with a disrespect he didn't deserve, Josh couldn't fire Tara, and he couldn't direct her work since he wasn't the one paying her.

A grim humor shook him.

One thing he had to give to his grandfather— he was a wily old coot. Walt had planned ahead, hired Tara and made sure she knew he was the one writing her paychecks. Josh couldn't help wondering why. There were qualified secretaries and accountants in Schuyler that Walt could have employed. Of course it was doubtful that any of them *looked* like Tara—so what was the possibility that his grandfather had been bowled over by a young woman's beauty? Not in an inappropriate way, but the way an old man appreciates the reminders of youth and a young man's vigor.

Josh didn't know, and it didn't matter. Of one

thing he was sure—Walt was a stiff-necked pain in the ass and couldn't let go of controlling the ranch, but he was honorable. And on that, Josh trusted they had a small amount of common ground.

CARL STANFIELD PULLED to a stop at the light and waved at Emmett Foster as he crossed in front of the sheriff's cruiser. Emmett was around sixty and ornery as sin, but Carl liked him. It was hard not to like most of the people in Schuyler. That wasn't to say his job was heaven on earth. No job—and no town—was perfect. But on average, it was considerably calmer in Schuyler than in St. Louis, where he'd worked for a good deal of his career.

St. Louis was a great place, but it was still a city. And after being a homicide detective for a decade, few things surprised Carl anymore—he'd pretty much seen the worst.

But in Schuyler he saw a lot of the best. Of course, he also had to deal with the occasional cattle theft. Then there was the time he'd arrested a guy for a DUI because he was drunk while riding a horse. Not that a DUI while riding a horse would hold up in court—officially the charge was drunk and disorderly—but folks in Schuyler loved the story.

After parking at the medical center, Carl went inside.

"Hi, Karen," he greeted the receptionist. "It isn't an emergency, but does Lauren have a minute?"

"I'll check when she's finished with her patient."

"Great."

Unable to relax, Carl stood at the window watching the traffic pass in the street. He'd been in Schuyler for over two years and it was working out well.

Now he wanted to get his personal life on track. When he'd lived in St. Louis, the idea of settling down had held little appeal. The divorce rate among cops was disturbingly high, but things seemed different in Schuyler. A small town sheriff surely had a better shot at a successful marriage than a homicide detective working all hours of the day and night. Besides, the town felt like a good place to settle down and raise a family.

Not that Schuyler didn't have its pitfalls. The area had quite a history of ranch rivalries and family loyalties, which was why the county supervisors had decided to look for law enforcement from outside the area. For the same reason, Carl had realized it might be best to date women who were relatively new to town...such as Lauren. Well, Lauren was the only one he'd dated, but there was something special about her.

"Carl?" Karen said, breaking into his thoughts.

He swung around. "Yes?"

"Why don't you wait in Lauren's office?"

"Sure."

That was better. He'd rather not talk to Lauren in front of the waiting patients, and particularly not in front of Karen after their recent encounter at Ryan's Roadhouse. She and her boyfriend had just broken up and she'd had more than her share of booze, though to her credit she'd given her car keys to the bartender the minute she ordered her first Long Island iced tea. Somehow she'd consumed five of them and had still been sitting upright.

Poor kid. She'd cried on his shoulder and asked what was wrong with her...following the question with a passionate kiss. Carl had declined the overture and made sure she got home safely. He doubted she remembered much about the evening and would rather keep it that way.

Karen gestured to the door on her left. "Go ahead. Room ten."

Carl spotted Lauren at a computer station as he turned the corner. She was entering information, only looking up when a patient approached her with a question. As she talked to the man and his child, her face lit with the smile that had drawn Carl from the first time they'd met.

Smiling himself, he stepped into her office.

He'd liked Lauren from their initial meeting at the Hawkins wedding and had been pleased when she decided to move to Schuyler. As the story went, a few days after the wedding she'd called the clinic to see if a job was available. A month later she was living in Schuyler. It was easy to imagine how delighted the clinic had been to hire a PA who didn't have to be convinced that moving to a remote town, two hours from a commercial airport, wasn't a fate worse than death.

Of course, that didn't mean she hadn't changed her mind once she'd arrived and faced the prospect of a long Montana winter. Could that be part of the reason she'd started putting him off…uncertainty she wanted to stay, after all?

Carl was annoyed at himself for making excuses for her refusals; he didn't suffer from a lack of confidence, but Lauren's absence of enthusiasm had tweaked his ego, especially since his instincts said that she liked him.

Restless, he got to his feet again. The office suited Lauren—well organized with personal touches that made it inviting without being unprofessional. On the bookshelves were a few photos of an older man and woman—presumably her adoptive parents—along with one that appeared to be a selfie of her and Tara Livingston in Paris, the Eiffel Tower behind them.

Just then the door opened behind him, and he turned around. It was Lauren.

"Hi, Carl," she said as she came into the room. "Karen mentioned you needed to see me. Is there a problem?"

"Not at all. I was driving past and wanted to touch base with you about tomorrow evening. We've tried some places here, so how about going to Windy Bluffs for dinner? There's a steak house, an Italian place, Mexican and Chinese. The Chinese place isn't as good as it could be, but it's edible. Does one of them sound okay to you?"

"All of them, I guess."

"Do you have a favorite?"

"Uh…usually Chinese," she told him, looking nervous. "But if it isn't that good, maybe it would be best to go elsewhere. How about the…um, Mexican restaurant?"

"Fabulous," he answered, pleased. Deep inside he'd wondered if she would say she didn't want to go out with him again after all. "Maybe after dinner we could see a movie, or perhaps take a walk along the river."

"Either would be nice. The trail beside the water is pretty, though I'm uncomfortable going there alone."

"It isn't a good idea to go into isolated areas by yourself," Carl agreed. "Let's see what appeals once we finish dinner. Okay?"

"Sure."

"I won't keep you—I know how busy this place is. How about tomorrow at five?"

"Sure."

"Sounds like a plan."

Carl walked out, refraining from whistling. She hadn't canceled and seemed to be okay with his suggestions for the following evening.

Eating in Windy Bluffs had been his top choice,

since he preferred going someplace where fewer people knew them. He had yet to eat a meal out in Schuyler without townspeople stopping to chat. As a rule he welcomed it, since law enforcement in a small community was partly about building relationships. But it had made his first dates with Lauren awkward to have so many interruptions.

Carl let loose a whistle as he climbed into his cruiser. Life in Schuyler was good.

LAUREN'S HAND SHOOK as she picked up the chart for her last patient of the day. When Carl had asked what restaurant she preferred, she'd forced herself to say something definite as a preference. She'd read that men usually wanted women to be clear about their choices.

After dealing with Mrs. Whittier's "sore" ear—the elderly widow mostly came to the clinic for company—Lauren walked to the Roundup Café to meet Tara for supper.

"Hi," she greeted her twin. "How was your day?"

Tara smiled, an impish expression on her face. "I had a *very* interesting afternoon. Walt Nelson hired me to work in his ranch office, and Josh Mc-Gregor did his best to end the job before it began."

"He fired you?" Lauren asked, dismayed. She'd be sick if someone did that to her, but Tara didn't seem disturbed in the least.

"Nope," her sister answered cheerfully. "He

asked me to quit. I refused and we argued like seven-year-olds grabbing for the same ice cream cone."

Lauren was amazed her sister could be so nonchalant. She wished she could be equally at ease with confrontation, but she'd learned at a young age how destructive arguments could be. Her adoptive parents had loved her, but they'd also hoped having a second child would heal their marital woes.

She'd been six when they'd taken her in. Her new mother had dressed her in pretty clothing, and her new daddy had proudly introduced her as his daughter. But they hadn't stopped arguing, and her new family had always appeared to be crumbling. Then when she was in high school, it fell apart completely.

She had responded by avoiding any sort of conflict. Her brother had responded to their parents' disastrous marriage by becoming a philandering jerk. It was always painful to think about him.

"Do you…er, think Josh is *really* opposed to you working there?" she asked, trying to push away her memories and the nausea they inspired. Mostly she didn't like that aspect of the person she'd become, startled by her own shadow and wanting to jump in a rabbit hole whenever someone raised their voice.

"Oh, yes," Tara said, "he *definitely* doesn't want me there."

"Won't it be difficult to work for Mr. Nelson if Josh is upset about it?"

"Not for me. I'm going to talk with Walt again to establish guidelines. If he has any concerns, we'll iron them out then. As for any issues Josh might have, that's his problem."

Lauren tried to relax and adopt her sister's off-hand attitude. It hurt to think they could have grown up together, and she had an idea that she might feel stronger if she'd had an ally all those years ago. She'd certainly taken enough psychology classes to see how it could have made a difference.

Silly. That wasn't the way it had happened, and there wasn't any point to thinking about the might-have-beens. At least she'd had a family, however troubled, and her parents loved her, regardless of how their marriage had ended. Tara didn't have anyone and had never had a real home. Maybe that was why she didn't worry about where she lived and always seemed to be looking at what was over the horizon.

It was odd, the way things had turned out.

THE NEXT AFTERNOON Lauren's nerves were tighter than ever. She wanted to ask Tara to come over while she got ready for dinner, except it would have meant revealing her tension over going out with Carl Stanfield.

The phone rang, and she jumped. She grabbed the handset, disgusted with herself for hoping it was Carl, regretfully canceling their evening. "Hello."

"Hey, Lauren," Emily said. "What are you wearing for the big date?"

"It isn't a big date," Lauren corrected automatically. "We're just going out to dinner. That is, we've already gone out a number of times, so it isn't something to get carried away about."

"If you say so. What are you going to wear?"

"I thought my black blouse and the matching wraparound skirt."

"Not bad. Just accessorize with something that makes a statement." Emily's parents were clothing buyers and her sister a supermodel, so she knew what she was talking about.

"I'm not good at making statements."

The doorbell rang. "Sorry, Em, someone's here. I've gotta go," Lauren said, disconnecting and running to answer it. She found Emily there, grinning at her, cell phone still to her ear. It almost seemed like old times back in LA, except Emily hadn't been pregnant then.

Emily came inside and settled on the couch, putting her feet on a stool. "I love being pregnant, but my feet swell. Okay, fashion-show time. Go get dressed."

Lauren put on the black skirt and blouse she'd bought in Los Angeles while shopping with Emily.

Her friend helped her choose a silver scarf to wear at her waist and place a large silver pin on her shoulder.

"You look terrific," Emily said when she got up to leave.

"I can't compete with Tara's elegance," Lauren answered. In contrast to her twin's sophistication, she felt as if she was a country bumpkin. Before they'd met, Lauren had figured she and her sister would be alike. After all, they were identical twins and she'd read stories of separated twins discovering amazing similarities and parallels in their lives. So far it hadn't worked out that way.

"Why would you want to compete with Tara?" Emily countered. "Her clothes work for her, but you have to be yourself, and anyone worth knowing would agree with me."

Lauren choked out a laugh and said good-night to her friend—at least *she* was going home to a husband who adored her.

The doorbell rang a short time later. It was Carl, deliciously handsome in a tan sports jacket.

His gaze ran over her in what seemed to be appreciation.

"You look amazing," he told her.

"I had help. Emily came over."

He smiled. "I'm flattered. You called in a fashion consultant for our evening together."

His interpretation was nice and she decided not to explain that her friend's most important contribution had been to calm her shaky nerves. It couldn't take much longer before he figured out what she was really like, and a dull melancholy went through her at the thought.

CHAPTER FOUR

WHEN TARA ARRIVED at the Boxing N on Monday morning, Josh McGregor met her at the office and she wondered if he'd make another attempt to get her to quit.

"The building is quite old. It was converted to the ranch office after my grandparents were married," he explained as they stepped inside. "Before that it was used for guests and as a second bunkhouse during the busy season."

"Where was the office before?" she asked.

"The house. The ranch hands were in and out a lot, and they smoked cigars. The tobacco made my grandmother ill, so she probably asked if operations could be shifted to another location."

From the corner of her eye she noticed Walt had come through the open door and was listening.

"The other day I found some historical records, including an invoice from the 1800s," she murmured.

"Really?" Josh seemed interested. "I wouldn't want anything like that thrown away."

She deliberately turned to address his grandfather. "Walt, I don't dispose of anything unless I'm asked to discard items older than a particular date."

The elderly man appeared to be assessing the situation.

"Older than a certain date?" Josh repeated.

"There are legalities involved with record keeping, but it's an owner's decision what to do with paperwork that no longer has tax or other legal implications."

"Okay. Put that sort of thing in boxes and I'll check it over."

"You aren't my employer, Mr. McGregor. Walt, shall I organize any historic material I locate?" she asked. Walt grinned while a flash of anger crossed Josh's face.

Walt nodded. "Can it be stored in a way that makes sense?"

"That shouldn't be a problem, but I'd suggest using archival storage materials. A lot of paper today is acidic, so putting old documents into files without protecting them could be damaging."

"Get whatever you need," Josh put in hastily. "We have an office supply store in Schuyler, and if they don't have what you require, they can order it."

Walt jutted out his chin. "I'll phone and tell the store you'll be making purchases for the Boxing N. They can bill me."

The two men stared at each other in silent combat, and Tara didn't want to find out how long it would take for one of them to back down.

"That's fine," she interjected. "Walt, we didn't talk about whether office records should also be computerized."

"No," Walt replied immediately.

"Yes," Josh said at the same time.

"You're working for me," Walt reminded her.

"Then I'll hire you, too," Josh asked. "Everything needs to be computerized."

Tara's head was beginning to ache; the tension between the two men was palpable. Maybe it wasn't fair, but her sympathies were entirely with Walt.

"Perhaps this could be sorted out another time," she said finally.

With a stiff, angry nod, Josh stomped out of the office building.

Walt settled into one of the comfortable chairs at the opposite end of the room while she started to work.

"My grandson is wrong," he said after several minutes.

"About what?"

"Evelyn didn't ask me to move my office out of the house. But I could tell cigar smoke bothered her, so I moved into this place."

The wistful expression in the old man's eyes made Tara curious, but she didn't try to probe.

"That was thoughtful," she answered.

"I would have done anything for my wife…at least, that's what I always claimed. She was an amazing woman. I should have…"

His voice trailed off, and he looked at the window behind her, though she didn't think it was the garden he was seeing. She'd learned the Nelsons had been in a terrible car accident the previous autumn; Evelyn had lingered for a few days before she passed, and Walt had been left with a painful limp. It was dreadfully unfair that he would have to spend his senior years without his wife. Again she felt that odd, powerful liking for the older man. His obvious loneliness reminded Tara of how solitary her own life was.

Since he seemed lost in thought again, Tara returned her attention to the chaotic office. Organizing it would take some time. The system—such as it was—appeared to be limited to creating the piles of papers she'd seen the first day, along with battered boxes and paper bags. Instead of holding paperwork, the ancient filing cabinets were stuffed with a miscellany of items.

After a while Tara glanced up and saw Walt had left. That made things easier. She combined several partial boxes so she'd have containers to unload the cabinets. Opening one of the file drawers, she pulled out a large tangle of leather straps.

"What have you got there?" Josh McGregor asked.

Tara jerked at the unexpected voice, her heart

skipping. She made a mental note to keep the office door closed while she worked and to look for a bell that could alert her when anyone was entering. For such tall men, both Walt and his grandson moved quietly, and she didn't enjoy being surprised. One coworker had claimed she was worse than a cat, jumping whenever startled.

She examined the dried-up leather straps and metal pieces. "It appears to be old horse tackle."

"What a terrific place to keep something like that."

Though Tara silently agreed, she was annoyed by Josh's wry tone. Equally annoying tingles shot through her as he brushed her arm, lifting the jumble from her hands.

"I doubt this has been used for thirty or forty years. It isn't worth much now, but I'll see if there's anything that can be salvaged."

She hesitated. The relationship between grandfather and grandson was obviously complicated, and they were putting her in the middle; she was starting to feel like a bone being growled over by two dogs. "I'll discuss it with Walt," she told him firmly.

Josh's jaw tensed in a way that was rapidly growing familiar; he and his grandfather both seemed to have the same ticking muscle on their jawlines.

"Ms. Livingston, as I told you before, I own the Boxing N. My grandfather deeded it to me several months ago."

"How soon after he got out of the hospital?"

Josh flinched. "The week after he got out of the rehab center, not that it's any of your concern. He contacted his lawyer without telling anyone in the family what he was doing. Apparently he's had the documents ready since my college graduation."

"And now you're determined to show him who's in command."

"That's ridiculous, but a ranch has to have one boss, and Grandpa has made me legally responsible for everything that goes on here. I've got cowhands quitting because he keeps interfering, yet he no longer has the physical strength to do what needs to be done."

It was a reasonable explanation, especially the part about being legally responsible, but Tara still sympathized with Walt. He'd spent a lifetime running the Boxing N, and giving up control must be difficult.

"At the risk of repeating myself, Walt hired me, not you," she said evenly.

"And, as I said earlier, I'd like to hire you, as well. If you're organizing the records anyway, it makes sense to do the computer work at the same time. Right?"

"I don't care if it makes sense," she declared. "What I do here is up to Walt, and he doesn't want that. Would it hurt you to wait? Or are you trying to force equipment on him that he's never used, hoping to push him out of the way?"

"You don't know anything about it. Whether you like it or not, I'm having a computer delivered this week, along with a scanner and the other equipment needed to move this ranch into the twenty-first century."

"Fine, but my using it depends upon Walt, so that equipment may not get a workout until you hire an office manager and shuffle him into an old folks' home."

"I'm not trying to shuffle him anywhere," Josh hissed. "It isn't any of your business, but for your information, I'm trying to give him some dignity and still keep this place running."

"That isn't what it looks like from my standpoint."

Josh closed his eyes in obvious frustration.

"I'll talk to my grandfather about the computer work," he finally told her.

"Talk or demand?"

His jaw tightened again, but he picked up the armload of horse tackle and headed for the door without saying anything else.

"There's something I don't understand," Tara said before he could leave.

He froze. "What?"

"Walt has a huge amount of experience running a ranch, and caution isn't necessarily a bad thing. Why are you so opposed to learning from him? Has the business really changed that much?"

"You'd be surprised. As for learning from my grandfather, he can be challenging."

She smiled faintly, knowing it would annoy Josh. "Actually, I think he's delightful."

As Josh WENT DOWN the steps of the office, he saw his grandfather coming from the direction of the horse barn.

Delightful? Much as he loved the old guy, *delightful* wasn't the word he'd choose.

"This was in a filing cabinet," he said, indicating the armload he carried. "I'll get rid of it if there's nothing useful."

"I don't give a crap. But I'm telling Tara I want everything computerized since you're so highfalutin sure it's needed."

"I just asked her to do that," Josh returned, all too aware that his request hadn't gone anywhere. Tara was one of the most infuriating women he'd ever met.

"She's working for me, so I'll do the asking."

Why couldn't his grandfather let go of one blessed thing?

Tension crept up Josh's neck. He could have bought a different ranch years ago when a spread south of Schuyler had come up for sale. He'd checked the place out and almost made an offer, but in the end it had felt as if he would be giving up on his heritage.

Josh glanced toward the rolling grassland studded with trees and livestock. His roots were here; the Boxing N had been in his mother's family since the 1800s, and in the distance it gave way to mountains that were strikingly beautiful. Back then the land had been cheap, and his Nelson ancestors had bought a vast section of the lower mountainous region as part of the Boxing N, even though it didn't support many cattle per acre.

Walt was slowly limping toward the office.

Josh sighed and followed. He caught up and endured his grandfather's sour frown as they mounted the three steps. Hellfire, he *wanted* a good relationship with Walt, but few people, if any, had ever gotten close to him. Walt was like the land itself—unyielding, sometimes unforgiving, and oblivious to the changing times.

Inside they found Tara lifting an old hand water pump from a drawer; she glanced up as she dropped it onto the desk. She'd removed her suit jacket and there were smudges of dirt across the breast line of her blouse. Josh swallowed. Tara was bad news from start to finish, and he had no intention of allowing his attraction to her to go anywhere.

"Is something up?" she asked, her face becoming expressionless.

It struck Josh that her reactions generally seemed measured. Even when arguing with him, he'd had the impression her emotions were carefully controlled. He didn't trust that kind of restraint. As a rule the McGregors and Nelsons were passionate people; it might mean extra conflicts along the way, but at least you knew where you stood.

"My grandfather wants to expand your work parameters," he said before Walt could explain.

Walt deserved his dignity, but so did he. He certainly didn't deserve to be treated as if he was thirteen instead of thirty-three.

"I've been thinking about my grandson's la-di-da modern ideas." Walt huffed. "So I've decided you should take care of that computer stuff. Do it whatever way you think it should be done. *You're* the expert." His tone plainly indicated he didn't think Josh possessed expertise of any kind.

"Of course," Tara replied. "Do you also want me to set up a system where bills can be paid online and checks can be printed?"

"Online?" Walt asked.

"Through the internet."

How anyone could be unfamiliar with the concept, Josh didn't know, but he suspected Tara was speaking a foreign language as far as his grandfather was concerned. Josh would have lunged forward with an emphatic yes, but something in her eyes kept him quiet. She'd aligned herself with Walt and would find a way to do things his way, even on the computer. When the time came, Josh was sure he'd have to do a lot of extra work getting things changed to the way he wanted.

"Is that how other ranches do business?" Walt asked.

"I can't speak for other ranches," Tara said, "but I've seen how much time the process saves."

"Okay, do it. Get whatever you need for that inter…online thing."

"Well, it's not quite that simple…"

Behind Walt's back, Josh shook his head and gave her an intense glare, to which she only raised an eyebrow.

"You have to have internet service here at the office," she explained to Walt, "along with a computer, of course."

"Get whatever you need."

"All right."

He limped out, and Josh smiled blandly at Tara. "I already told you that, as the owner, *I* will make the arrangements for whatever is required here at the office."

"Certainly." She returned his smile with one as carefully bland as his own.

He'd always preferred women who were more easygoing, so why did this chilly cucumber make him so aware of her?

"Why didn't you want me to explain the internet to Walt?" she asked.

"Because he's an old-time cattleman and doesn't understand."

"That doesn't mean he *can't* understand, provided the people around him don't treat him as a senile old man. Or as a child, for that matter. He's obviously still sharp."

"I'm *not* treating him that way."

"Ha." She shrugged, and he glanced away, not wanting to watch the movement of the soft fabric of her blouse.

"Incidentally," he said, "you might find jeans and a T-shirt more practical on the Boxing N than silk."

"Thank you *so* much for the advice," she returned with an edge of sarcasm. It was probably deserved; he didn't have any business suggesting what sort of clothing she should wear.

"Just leave the nonoffice items near the door," he said. "I'll get them out of your way later."

"If that's what Walt wants me to do."

Seething with anger, Josh left. At least he was going to get the office and accounts computerized, but he wasn't sure if he'd won or lost the latest skirmish. He didn't even know if winning and losing was the point. If he won, then his grandfather lost. But if things didn't get into shape soon, his reputation would suffer, and the ranch might be hard to keep going.

Josh's trust fund was generous, but he'd quietly used some of it to pay his grandparents' medical bills not covered by insurance. There was also the question of gift taxes on the Boxing N, which he fully expected to pay instead of his grandfather. The remaining principal, while substantial, couldn't support a failing proposition forever.

LAUREN MOVED FROM one patient to another as quickly as possible. If she wasn't careful, she'd end up behind schedule, and that wasn't fair to Tara—her sister was cutting her first day at the Boxing N short so they could spend the afternoon together. They had planned to do it the previous Friday, but the other physician's assistant had called, asking her to trade shifts because his wife was ill.

Her nerves were on edge for fear that Carl might stop by again. It was ironic, because she'd enjoyed her date with him even more than the first ones. After dinner, they'd walked along the river while the sun dropped low in the sky and cast a rosy light over the landscape.

When she'd described the setting to Tara, her sister had made a dry comment about Carl devising the ideal romantic moment, only to quickly apologize. They hadn't discussed men that much, but Lauren suspected that neither of them had a stellar record.

"I heard that you and Sheriff Stanfield went out this weekend," Ethel Carter commented as Lauren took her blood pressure.

The nurse had taken it earlier, but the first check was always high. Mrs. Carter got stressed when she walked into the clinic, a case of white-coat syndrome, as it was called. Some medical professionals discounted the condition, but Lauren was a believer.

"Where did you hear that?" she asked, trying to sound casual.

"Virginia was at the senior center exercise group this morning. Her daughter lives in Windy Bluffs and saw you at the Mexican restaurant. It's nice that you're still going out together."

Great. Gossip was the last thing Lauren needed. Emily had warned her when she'd moved to Schuyler that it was the most popular form of entertainment in town.

"We're friends," Lauren said as though it didn't matter very much. It was true. She and Carl *were* friends. "Are you taking your blood pressure medicine every day?"

"Whenever I remember."

"It's important to be consistent, okay? We can talk about ways to make that easier at your next appointment."

"Of course, dear. Did you and the sheriff have a nice evening together?"

"La Bonita is a terrific restaurant, and their fresh salsa is fantastic. I'm going to take my sister there soon."

Ethel looked disappointed and might have tried probing further, but Lauren patted her shoulder and handed over several prescription refills.

"Keep up the exercise," she instructed. "It's obviously doing you good."

Ethel's face creased into a smile. "I only started because you kept urging me to try. I *do* feel better. The arthritis doesn't hurt as much, and I have more energy."

"That's wonderful."

Lauren went on to her next patient, hoping she wouldn't have to field more questions about her and Carl Stanfield. It could get really old, really fast.

TARA SPENT THE remainder of the morning cleaning out the rest of the file cabinets and emptying cupboards of equipment that had nothing to do with office work. Most of it couldn't have been used in decades, and she couldn't even tell what some items were. She recognized spurs, of course, and rusted samples of barbed wire. The rest was pretty strange, reminiscent of medieval torture implements she'd seen in museums across Europe.

She mentioned it when Walt came in and he chuckled. "The animals might have agreed. We're a little more modern with our methods now, but I gotta admit that I still don't enjoy branding time. If I'd ever found those sapphires in the mountains, I might have even given up on cattle ranching and stuck with horse breeding."

"Sapphires?" Tara exclaimed, her imagination stirring. "I didn't know they had any in Montana."

"They do, and my grandpa used to say his dad

once found some on the Boxing N. As a kid I searched plenty and finally gave up."

"A treasure hunt. Exciting."

"True. It was great fun." The old man's eyes gleamed with the memories.

Walt had brought her more boxes, and when he'd left again she began filling them, taking digital photos of each item. If she could have identified everything with a name, she would have merely logged them, but this was the only way she knew how to keep track. Walt probably didn't care, but in light of the contentious relationship he had with his grandson, she wanted to keep a record of everything she did in the office.

At noon she tidied up and stepped out to the small porch, looking around for Walt. He wasn't there, so she headed for the main house and knocked.

"Is there something you need?" Josh's voice came from behind, startling her.

Tara turned. "Not exactly. I'm leaving and didn't know whether the office should be locked."

"You're leaving? It's only noon."

She gave him a tight smile. "I set my own hours. And need I remind you that it isn't any of your business?"

"I see."

"It doesn't matter whether you see or not. Walt knows my hours will vary depending upon my sister's schedule and my other commitments."

"You don't have to work here at all," he offered quickly.

"Yeah, I understood that the first time you mentioned it," she returned. "Now, should the office door be locked or not?"

"I'll lock it and have a key made for you."

"Thank you."

To the left of where they stood, the porch was secluded, the view of the ranch obscured by a blooming vine that released a lovely scent, teasing Tara's senses. She could see how it might be hard to find a private outdoor space, even out in the country, and this was the kind of quiet spot where a husband and wife could steal a moment together.

Josh cocked his head. "What are you thinking about?" he asked, curiosity in his eyes.

"Oh." She gestured at the corner of the porch. "I was just thinking how the vines must have given your grandparents a nice place to share a kiss in the middle of the day. You know, where no one else was likely to see."

She'd made the comment specific to his grandparents, uncomfortable with the thought that *any couple* might find it a pleasant place for intimacies. The scent of the flowers was evocative, making her mind conjure images that didn't belong there. After all, she wasn't good at physical intimacy. Or any form of intimacy, for that matter.

"Nice thought, but off base, I'm afraid," Josh

responded quietly. "My grandparents led some-what separate lives. They had little in common. Grandma came from the city, and city girls don't adjust well to Montana ranches. I'm sure they cared for each other, but I doubt their marriage would have lasted in today's world."

Tara hid her shock at Josh's blunt statement. It seemed at odds with Walt's painful declaration about his wife earlier that morning. What had he said…that he'd have done anything for her?

Josh gave her a narrow look. "I'm only telling you because if you have a sentimental belief that Grandpa is desperately pining for his wife and needs your support, you can relax."

"No worries," she answered evenly. "Thanks for being original this time. Were you hoping I'd lose sympathy for Walt and want to leave?"

"That isn't what I was doing," he insisted, though the faint chagrin in his face told her dif-ferently. "I meant to ask before, what about all those boxes I saw my grandfather bringing to the office?" It was an obvious effort to changes the subject.

"They were for the nonoffice items. Walt is going to store them somewhere else. I couldn't catalog the contents since I didn't recognize most of the stuff, but I took pictures so there would be a record."

"Isn't that overkill?"

"It seemed best under the circumstances. Uh…

Walt told me there might be sapphires on the Boxing N."

"That's a family myth. I ordered a survey ten years ago, and there's nothing here."

"Surveys can be wrong. Walt was so energized when he told me about searching for them as a kid, it occurred to me that another search might give him a new purpose."

Josh's eyes flared. "The last thing he needs is to get revved up about something utterly pointless."

"I thought you'd prefer getting him interested in something other than the ranch."

"That wouldn't stop his interfering—it would just add a new layer of complication."

"Well, I think you're wrong, and I'm going to talk with Walt about it."

She went to her rental car, refusing to look back to see if Josh was watching.

It was only in the car that she glanced at the rearview mirror. While Josh was still standing in front of the large house, it was hard to know if he was looking her way or at one of the nearby barns.

Not that it mattered. She wasn't interested in him as a man. With that reminder, Tara started her sedan and drove steadily down the gravel road.

CHAPTER FIVE

JOSH DIDN'T SLEEP WELL; he was too frustrated over the way Tara was making his life even more of a challenge. Sapphire hunting was fine for children to dream about, but Walt was an old man with disabling injuries. He didn't need to get excited about something he couldn't possibly do. Josh enjoyed rock hunting and polishing as a hobby, though he had little time for it these days. But it had been a long time since he'd wasted his energy on thoughts of finding gemstones.

Despite his lack of rest, Josh was out before dawn the next morning so he could deal with the boxes Tara had packed. He'd wanted to do it the previous afternoon, but there hadn't been time after a series of panicked calls from one of the young cowhands he'd finally managed to employ.

"I wouldn't have hired such a kid," Walt had snorted.

"He was the best of the applicants," Josh had returned as politely as possible. He didn't want to explain that word had gotten around about Walt's behavior and experienced hands were avoiding the Boxing N. With a little luck, that would begin changing soon. In the meantime he was trying to pair the new guys with ones who'd been around longer.

Fortunately his grandfather had been kept too busy in the foaling barn to think about anything else—hired hands, boxes *or* sapphires. Walt had two mares on the verge of foaling and tended to baby them. Otherwise he probably would have moved the boxes himself. At the very least he would have tried, but there were times when he barely managed to keep himself upright; the last thing he needed was to fall under a heavy load. Several surgeries had saved his leg, but it didn't have the strength to do much.

Josh stacked the boxes in the foreman's house; he'd go through them when he had a chance, although it was unlikely they contained much of value.

After a quick breakfast, he went out to give orders to the ranch hands; at least they'd all shown up for work and nobody had quit for several days. Perhaps he should be grateful for small blessings.

He returned to the office, hoping that Walt wouldn't decide to go, as well. But his grandfather was already there, glaring at the empty space next to the door.

"What did you do with everything?" he demanded.

"Hauled it out."

"I was going to do that."

"Now you don't have to," Josh told him. Grandpa's doctor had told him to avoid heavy lifting, but he had trouble accepting limitations.

Tara arrived with two cartons of file folders in her arms.

"Good morning," she said cheerily. "You know, Walt, I keep wondering about those sapphires you mentioned."

Josh ground his teeth when she glanced at him with an innocent expression.

Walt grunted. "What do you mean?"

"There are all these old records here in the office. Could there be anything more specific about the location?"

"Don't know, but it's worth checking. Keep your eyes peeled," Walt urged. "Right now I've gotta go check on Belle."

Trying to control his temper, Josh waited until he and Tara were alone, then he started looking through a stack of papers on the desk. Obviously there was no point debating the sapphire issue; Tara was clearly determined to do the opposite of what he wanted.

"The men's paychecks are overdue," Josh said shortly. "I need everything available on payroll records."

"Oh." She frowned. "I'll make that a priority."

He was tempted to ask why she wasn't insisting on first talking to his grandfather, then realized it affected her, as well. Unless things were sorted out, she wouldn't get paid, either.

Taking a key on a ring from his back pocket, he tossed it onto the desk. "That's for the office. The computer should be delivered later today, along with a combo printer/scanner/fax machine. The technician will work with the phone company to make sure the internet is up and running. Are you working another half day again?"

Her eyes narrowed. "No, not that it's your business."

"I just wanted to know if you'll be here when everything arrives."

"Yeah, right," she replied with a hint of sarcasm.

He went around the desk to avoid sliding too closely past Tara's slim figure as he left. She was wearing another outfit more suited to the city than Montana—she'd been warned, so it wasn't his concern if she wanted to risk destroying her expensive clothes at the Boxing N's office.

CARL COULDN'T RESIST stopping at the clinic as he passed it early Tuesday morning.

"Is there any chance that Lauren is between patients?" he asked the receptionist.

"You're in luck," Karen said. "Go on back to her office."

He smiled, pleased. It was the second time in less than a week that he'd been able to catch Lauren at the clinic. On earlier visits he hadn't had much success.

At Lauren's door, he watched her standing at a work counter, studying a page in a thick book and making notes on a pad of paper.

"Hey," he said softly, trying not to startle her.

Lauren looked up. "Good morning, Carl. Something up?"

"I just stopped to say hello."

"That's nice. Thanks again for dinner."

"How about trying one of the other places in Windy Bluffs?"

"I don't want to plan much until Tara gets her schedule in place." Lauren's face grew wistful. "Once her visit is over, I won't get to see her that often. It's anyone's guess where she'll be living next."

Carl nodded. "At least it's easier to keep in touch now than in the old days. There's always Skype and email."

"It still isn't the same as being with someone in person. I don't want to miss out on time with her."

He hesitated, once again getting the feeling that Lauren was stalling for reasons that went beyond what she was saying.

But why?

They'd had a great time after she'd first arrived in Schuyler, going to various community functions, eating out and seeing movies together. Then she began putting him off.

Carl tried to think if he'd done anything wrong. Could it be the time he'd gotten an emergency call? It wasn't as if he'd dragged her into the middle of a bank robbery, and Lauren had never suggested she was concerned about getting involved with someone in law enforcement. If she had, he would have respected her feelings and backed off.

He'd finally decided to cool it for a while. Now they'd had another terrific date and she was putting him off again.

"Surely you aren't planning to spend *all* your free time with Tara," he said finally.

"I just want things to go well. I'm worried that she might decide… I don't know…that family isn't very important to her."

"Isn't she the one who found you?"

Lauren's blue eyes darkened. "Yes, though I'm not certain why she started searching. She's very self-sufficient."

Carl reached out and squeezed Lauren's hand. "I can't imagine her being anything except delighted to have you as a sister. Tell you what, I'll check back in a few days to see if a good time opens up for us to get together."

"Okay." She glanced through the open office door before continuing in a low voice. "Carl, there's another thing. We were seen at the restaurant by someone who recognized us. Gossip had finally died down, and now I'm getting comments again. Treating patients is much harder if they're asking about my personal life."

Relief went through Carl. It made sense that Lauren wanted to avoid gossip. She was such a conscientious PA, she'd naturally be concerned that a patient's curiosity could affect their care.

He replied just as quietly. "Don't worry. We can go even farther than Windy Bluffs, if necessary. Or eat a picnic out in the country."

Her smile was strained, and he realized he'd pushed too hard—one of his faults. He tended to go full steam ahead in everything, which wasn't necessarily the best strategy with a woman like Lauren. Besides, she *did* have a lot going on in her life right now. It couldn't be easy getting to know a perfect stranger who was also your sister, and it hadn't been that long since she'd changed jobs and moved to a new state.

"Th-thanks," she replied.

"No problem. Have a nice day."

"You, too."

Karen said goodbye on his way out, and another man offered a greeting at they passed each other at the front door. Carl winced. He didn't want to become grist in Schuyler's gossip mill, either. Obviously coming to the clinic was a bad idea. That had to be part of what Lauren had tried to say, but she was too nice to be blunt. So, unless they officially became a couple, he should phone or run by her apartment.

For once in his life, he would have to take things slow.

As much as Tara had wanted to goad Josh about finding him in the ranch office, she'd restrained herself. It was a serious matter if the ranch hands weren't getting paid on time. They shouldn't have to suffer financially because their employer and his grandfather couldn't get along.

"Is it all right with you if I look for information on the current payroll and give it to your grandson?" she asked Walt when he returned.

"Guess so," he mumbled, looking embarrassed. "I s'pose I haven't been as good at keeping that up as I should have been. Maybe Josh should just start signing the regular payroll checks like he wants. But I'm still paying you, not him." He immediately stomped out, and Tara got angry all over again at Josh. Whether it was reasonable or not, she intended to support Walt and thought it was unfair to have his shortcomings thrown in his face.

From her initial survey of the office, Tara remembered seeing a few payroll records stuffed inside a large book. Now she searched and found it had been moved to a shelf, with other books piled on top.

For the next several hours she pieced together as much information as possible. She respected Walt, but his records were in an even greater tangle than she'd originally thought. She'd heard him called an old-time cattleman and she suspected that meant lots of hours in the saddle, a fair amount of his life battling the elements, with an undying hatred for paperwork.

At noon she absently took a container of yogurt from her bag and ate while finishing her notes. The one relatively modern amenity in the office was a small copier, so she made duplicates for Josh, planning to leave them on his porch.

She stepped outside and looked around. Past the barns was a long, low house that Walt had mentioned was normally the foreman's home. Apparently his grandson had decided to move in there rather than the central ranch house...a choice that plainly didn't sit well with the old gentleman.

Stretching her legs felt good, and she quickly reached the foreman's home. It was picturesque, but unlike the main ranch house, there were signs of deferred maintenance, including a torn screen. She set the copies she'd made on a small table. A breeze ruffled the pages, and she glanced around for something to weigh them down.

Josh stepped out of the door as she found a small rock.

"Can I help you?" he asked.

"I made preliminary notes on the payroll after I spoke to Walt about your request," she told him, to make it clear that his grandfather had been informed. She pointed to the table. "They might help get your cowhands paid."

"Really."

His voice was skeptical, but she decided not to

challenge him on it. Turning *everything* into a battle wouldn't help them coexist.

Tara tilted her head back. "Yes. So, the new owner of the ranch lives in the foreman's house. Where does the foreman live?"

"Grandpa could never keep a foreman. He was too determined to run every aspect of the ranch himself. Because of that, the house has usually been empty, except when family needed a place to stay. I decided to move in when I came back from Texas so I could have some privacy."

The need for privacy was something she understood. But she frowned. "Aren't you doing the same thing?" she asked.

"What do you mean?"

"Well, you haven't hired a foreman, either. I understand you bossed a big ranch down in Texas, so maybe you don't need a second in command, but it sounds as if you and your grandfather have the same management style."

The muscle ticked again in Josh's jaw, then a thoughtful look entered his eyes.

"That might be something to think about."

His reasonableness was surprising; it didn't seem in character, given what she'd seen of him so far.

Tara returned to the office, and soon afterward the computer arrived. She had already cleared a space for the new equipment and continued sorting documents while an employee from Schuyler Office Supply set up the system.

"Wow," the woman said finally, looking around as she ran a printer test. "Don't tell me it's your job to deal with this disaster area."

"'Fraid so," Tara replied cheerfully. The prospect of hard work didn't bother her. She was enjoying her time on the Boxing N, despite the complications Josh McGregor kept presenting.

Another hour passed before she saw Walt again. He limped into the office and dropped into an easy chair shortly after two. His face was weary and lined with pain.

"Hi," she greeted. "I have a pot of coffee going. Would you like a cup?"

"Uh, sure." He started to get up, but she waved him down.

"Cream or sugar?" she asked.

"Black as pitch."

"I probably don't make it Montana style," she explained as she handed him a mug.

He swallowed some and waved the mug in the air. "This is good. Don't bother with Montana style."

Tara grinned. "Glad you like it."

He settled back with a sigh. "I've mostly been in the foaling barn since yesterday afternoon. My favorite mare, Belle, had a hard delivery, and the foal wasn't doing well at first."

"How are they now?"

"Much better." He smiled tiredly, almost dreamily, and she suspected he'd taken a pain pill. "Evelyn and I celebrated whenever a new colt or filly came along. We were only blessed with Sarah, so the foals became the other children we couldn't have. I remember the day Belle was born. Evelyn and I spent the night in the barn and danced in the rain the next morning. Evelyn was so beautiful... hair all wet and her blue eyes shining like cornflowers..."

Walt's voice trailed off, and his eyelids drooped. Tara gently took the mug and set it on the table. He mumbled something and relaxed into sleep, something she figured he badly needed.

Yet as she returned to the paperwork she was sorting by the year, she was puzzled anew by the devotion Walt expressed for his wife. Josh believed his grandparents' marriage had been less than happy, however civil it might have been. But what she kept hearing from Walt told a very different story. Of course, he might be idealizing Evelyn now that she was gone. On the other hand, grandsons couldn't possibly know everything about their grandparents.

The wastebasket filled for the third time that day, and she took it out to the metal barrel behind the office. Walt had explained they didn't have garbage service this far out of Schuyler, so they burned everything combustible and one of the ranch hands took a load to the town landfill every week or two.

"You weren't supposed to throw any papers away until I'd checked them," Josh said out of the blue.

Startled, her arm jerked and most of the wastebasket's contents fell outside the barrel.

"Thanks loads," she yelped, grabbing for the paper sailing away in the afternoon breeze.

It took several minutes and long dashes in different directions before everything was stuffed back into the wastebasket.

"Okay," she hissed, breathing hard with the effort. "Since you don't trust me to tell the difference between a record and trash, you can go through every scrap. I'm sure Walt won't mind *that*." She pulled a handful out and handed it to him.

His face was expressionless as he glanced at the doodles and stray figures that had no meaning or reference.

"Walt told me to get rid of this kind of thing," she continued, "along with old newspapers and advertising flyers, which I'm finding everywhere. But you know best, so you really ought to micromanage the entire trash detail. By the way, I brought two other loads out earlier, so check carefully." She kicked the heavy metal drum.

Josh took the wastebasket, emptied it into the

barrel and replaced the heavy lid. "Sorry, I over-reacted."

"That seems to be your favorite activity. Have you made any more emergency trips to the medical clinic?"

Tight-lipped, he wheeled around and marched away without responding.

Suddenly tired, Tara went back into the office. Walt was awake again, blinking sleepily.

"I thought you'd left," he grumbled.

"Not until you introduce me to your new foal."

His face brightened. "Let's go." He struggled to his feet, and Tara debated whether to offer assistance. *Perhaps not.* The old guy was proud and must hate appearing weak in front of anybody.

Walt limped toward the barns. At one of the well-kept structures, he turned into an open door and led her to a large stall. Josh was there with a cowhand who seemed to regard Walt with apprehension.

"Tara wants to see the foal," Walt announced brusquely.

Josh's eyes narrowed, whether from irritation or something else she didn't know. Walt stepped into the stall, and his face softened as he murmured to the mare and her baby.

Tara didn't know much about equine bloodlines, but clearly Belle was special. She had a dark coat, almost black, with a hint of red. Her head arched high and proud while her eyes seemed unusually intelligent. And watchful. Though she showed pleasure at seeing Walt, she kept a close watch on the stranger he'd brought.

The newborn stood close to its mother's side, teetering on legs that looked too thin to hold it up. Except for a white blaze on its nose, it was a perfect miniature of Belle.

The cowhand tipped his hat to Tara in a gesture that was quickly becoming familiar, and hurried away, no doubt uncomfortable with the tension between the new ranch owner and the former one.

The mare whinnied nervously.

"Whoa, Belle, honey," Walt murmured to soothe her. His old hands caught her halter and he waved at Tara to come closer.

"Be careful where you step," Josh warned. "You aren't wearing boots."

It was good advice, though delivered in a mocking tone. She was wearing a favorite pair of Italian sandals and would hate to ruin them. So Tara moved carefully into the stall. The foal's gaze met hers, and she felt a sense of wonder akin to what she'd felt upon seeing her first kangaroo in the wild.

"What is it, male or female?" she asked.

"It's a filly. That means it's a female," Josh said as if she was simpleminded.

"I'm sure she knows that, but even if she doesn't, you don't need to be condescending," Walt admonished. "Tara has never been on a ranch before, so we can't expect her to know what we take for granted. Your grandma didn't have a clue in the beginning, and she learned."

The hostility between them seemed to intensify again, so Tara smiled at Walt. "It's a beautiful baby. Have you picked a name?"

"What would you call her?" Walt asked.

"I don't know what names are good for horses," she admitted. "How many are born on the ranch each year?"

"Around twelve," Walt said. "Folks like our horses real well, even if we don't have one of those fancy breeding programs."

He threw a challenging stare at Josh and Tara understood why the ranch hands would be uneasy in their presence. Did their relationship disintegrate after Josh became the owner of the Boxing N, or had it always been this bad?

"I'm going to call this little one Tara," Walt announced. "We've never had a Tara on the Boxing N."

From the corner of Tara's eye, she saw the usual muscle in Josh's jaw tighten. His uptight expression was as predictable as the sun coming up in the morning.

"That's flattering," she told Walt, "but I won't feel bad if you change your mind and call her something else."

"Nope, Tara it is." His head cocked. "It's always

good to have a story to go along with a name. Why did your folks call you Tara?"

Though she smiled, she winced inside. "I'm afraid I don't know. I never knew my parents."

"That's a shame. Our daughter used to love hearing us tell how Evelyn and I met in San Francisco, down in Chinatown, while I was visiting the West Coast. She called me a bullheaded cowboy whose brains were in his boots, but married me anyhow."

"I can see how your daughter would have enjoyed that. As for me, I grew up in foster homes," she explained quietly.

"Don't you remember, Grandpa?" Josh asked in a louder voice. "Tara is Lauren Spencer's twin sister. They were separated as babies and met for the first time last year. They visited at the hospital when Alaina was having her baby."

"Of course I remember talking to Tara at the hospital—that's how I knew what kind of work she does," Walt answered testily.

"I'd better leave now," Tara interjected. "Thanks for showing me your new filly, Walt." She turned, glared at Josh and carefully picked her way out of the barn.

JOSH FOLLOWED AS Tara headed for the ranch office. He had to hustle because she could walk quickly in those ridiculous sandals. Ridiculous, that was, for a ranch. They looked insanely sexy on her, as well.

"What's your problem now?" he demanded.

"About what?"

"You seemed upset back there. I apologized for overreacting about the trash. Are you still holding a grudge?"

"No more than *you're* holding one because I didn't take your advice about what clothes to wear."

Josh sighed. Tara's clothing bothered him because he was attracted to her and didn't want to be. Hell, she was a city woman with an annoying personality. The puzzle was how she managed to get along so well with his grandfather when he could barely get Walt to share a civil conversation. Their relationship had never been great; now it was lousy.

"Why did you leave the barn in a huff?" he asked again.

"It wasn't a huff. I just don't appreciate hearing you imply that Walt is having memory problems."

"I didn't," Josh denied, only to question whether it might have sounded that way. The doctor had warned the family to keep a watchful eye, and it was hard to figure out what his grandfather knew and didn't know. Sometimes Josh even wondered if Walt was covering a memory lapse with his irascible behavior. "Grandpa has issues and I'm trying to gauge how serious they might be. You must have noticed how he ducked the question about you and your sister."

He didn't want to admit that Dr. Taylor was

worried his grandfather could be suffering from depression. It wouldn't be unusual in light of his injuries and the dramatic changes to his world.

Tara's face grew thoughtful. "Strong medication might cause lapses in memory. And when you think about it, being unable to remember the situation with me and Lauren isn't remarkable. Walt has far more important things to deal with right now."

"True. We've had a hard time getting him to use the proper dosage until the pain gets out of control, then I suspect he takes too much." Josh hesitated. "The two of you seem to be getting along. Is there any chance you could encourage him to participate in a pain-management program? Dr. Taylor has mentioned it, but Grandpa called it 'la-di-da nonsense.'"

"That sounds like him. I'll think about it, but don't get your hopes up. He might fire me on the spot...or is that why you suggested it?" The tiniest smile gleamed in Tara's blue eyes.

"Definitely not. At least this time."

She grinned more widely. "I'll take your word for it...this time."

Josh chuckled. Maybe there *was* a reason his grandfather enjoyed Tara's company so much. She had a sharp wit and didn't back down. Walt had never liked quitters and wouldn't respect anyone who wasn't willing take it on the chin for something they believed in.

"Is there anything else you want?" Tara asked.

"Uh, yeah. Thanks for the information you put together this morning. Has the computer been delivered?"

"Yes, and Desiree, the employee from Schuyler Office Supplies, installed the payroll program. It shouldn't take long to get the process functional. But you'll have to wait to print checks off the system. I asked if the store had blank check stock, and Desiree said they'd need to put in a special order."

He nodded. "Thanks for jumping on it right way. I'm sure you're interested in getting paid, as well."

The humor in Tara's face vanished. "That isn't why I made it a priority. Walt is my employer, so the ranch's payroll records have nothing to do with me," she explained with exaggerated patience.

"There's no need to get touchy again. I just don't want the Boxing N to become known for tardy payments. Integrity is important."

She let out a long breath. "I'm glad you value integrity, but you haven't lived paycheck to paycheck without your family's wealth to keep you secure. I grew up in neighborhoods where an overdue check meant a family couldn't eat or pay the rent. Some of the Boxing N's ranch hands may be in the same boat. That's more important than your reputation."

Heat crept up Josh's neck. "I know that. What kind of person do you think I am?"

Tara lifted her shoulders. The gesture was elegant, and he couldn't help thinking that she'd look more at home at a French château than in Montana. "All I know is what I've seen between you and Walt, and the way you acted at the clinic," she said. "Oh, and the way you've done your level best to get rid of me. It hasn't been impressive. Now, if you'll excuse me, I need to get my things. I've had a long day."

He watched her go into the office and then come out again and leave in her car.

She had a point. He'd never expected things to turn out like this. Sometimes he didn't recognize himself when he was arguing with Walt or agonizing over a cowhand quitting.

As for Tara?

On one matter they totally agreed: they didn't care for each other. That was okay, though he was fighting an undeniable attraction to her, a response that was purely chemical. She had masses of honey-gold hair and her eyes were amazing, blue with copper flecks. Her figure was slim in the right places and nicely curved everywhere else.

The mystery was why he didn't feel the same response to her twin sister. Although he wasn't interested in a relationship, Lauren was someone who fit in Montana, whereas Tara was standing in the way of his goals, right along with Walt.

Sometimes Josh wanted to tear his hair out when he and his grandfather argued in front of the ranch hands. Clear lines of authority were needed on a ranch, but he couldn't blame the hands for being uncertain about who was in charge. It would get even worse once the Boxing N employees figured out the person working in the ranch's business office didn't work for him.

He pictured Tara in his mind. Silk and linen clothing despite his warnings. An air of sophistication and hints of an accent in her voice that showed how long she'd worked outside the United States. In one of his grandfather's less irascible moments, he'd mentioned her love for travel and living in different countries. While it was clear she'd never fit in in Schuyler, it seemed equally clear she didn't *want* to fit in. Not that he'd known that when they first met. His instincts had simply told him she was a very beautiful, attractive woman who was utterly *impossible*.

CHAPTER SIX

TARA INVITED LAUREN over for dinner on Sunday, and when her sister arrived, she insisted on helping. Unsure of the proper social convention under the circumstances, Tara gave her salad makings and continued with the spicy Thai chicken dish she was concocting.

Normally cooking soothed her, but her thoughts kept wandering to the Boxing N. It was her favorite business contract, and she had to admit that her encounters with Josh added a certain spark to working there, though she'd rather not be so attracted to him. The guy was intensely annoying, but he radiated sex appeal.

Everything else was terrific.

She'd learned Boxing N mares were bred so they gave birth in the mid- to late spring, and that Walt had a reputation for pampering his mothers-to-be. But now that this season's last foal had arrived, he was spending more time in the office.

He often asked about her travels and seemed wistful when she answered briefly. So she began describing the things she'd seen and done, while with another part of her brain, she continued untangling decades of the ranch's financial records. So far she hadn't encountered any major tax errors other than Walt's apparent aversion to claiming expenses on his returns.

"How are things going at the Boxing N?" Lauren asked.

The out-of-the-blue question startled Tara. Had her sister read her mind or was it just an idle inquiry? Maybe they were tapping into a latent telepathy, she thought wryly.

"Um, everything is fine. Walt Nelson is great."

"It's nice you're getting along. He has a reputation for being difficult." Lauren ate a piece of the radish she was slicing. "How about your problems with Josh? I hope he isn't still trying to make you quit."

"Who knows with that guy?" Tara wasn't sure if Josh's foul temper came from his desire to drive her away or if it was part of his natural-born, ornery nature.

Ornery?

She almost laughed. It wasn't a word she'd ever used, so maybe Montana was rubbing off on her. The only other place where she'd seen such wide-open country was in the Australian outback. She'd visited a couple of cattle stations down under, but while there were similarities, the Boxing N was in a class of its own.

"Josh McGregor doesn't like me, but since I don't like him, either, we're even," she admitted.

"I'm surprised at him. He should be grateful for everything you're doing to help his grandfather and the ranch," Lauren returned indignantly. "There aren't many world-class accountants available around here. And most people in town have never even *heard* of a records management specialist."

Lauren's wholehearted support was endearing, though Tara wasn't accustomed to receiving it outside her professional arena. The company she worked for showed their appreciation with their eagerness to keep her under contract, along with generous bonuses, stock options and escalating pay and benefits. But Lauren didn't have any reason to believe her sister was world-class other than the genetic bond they shared.

"I'll work it out with Josh, one way or the other," Tara said lightly. "We've even managed to have a civil discussion. At least part of it was civil. Say, have you seen Carl Stanfield lately?"

Lauren's cheeks turned pink. "Er, yeah. He came by the clinic the other day. I thought I'd told you."

"You haven't mentioned it. He seems nice."

"He is, but we don't really click. I doubt we'll go out anymore."

Tara's eyebrows shot upward. She wasn't an expert on chemistry, but she would have sworn there were plenty of clicks between her twin and the tall sheriff.

"Does he agree?"

"I'm sure he'll figure it out. Besides, I've already discovered it can be awkward dating someone in such a small town. People come into the clinic and ask about it when they should be focusing on their medical needs."

"Wouldn't they get used to it and stop asking?"

"Maybe. But they didn't the first time Carl and I were going out. It wasn't until they stopped seeing us together that the talk quieted down."

Lauren busied herself cutting a cucumber and Tara decided to temporarily back off. Having family was a new thing and she wasn't sure how much to say, or when to say it. She wasn't even sure *how* cozy she wanted to be, just that it would be nice to have someone.

"I hope you like my version of Thai food," she said. "I almost made curry."

"I'm sure the Thai will be good. I don't know what's in this dish, but the turmeric in many curries is good for you. I've always been interested in foods and how they affect health and healing. It was hard deciding whether to become a physician's assistant or a dietitian."

"You never considered being a doctor?" Tara asked.

"For a while, but that level of schooling is expensive, and I didn't want to graduate with too much debt. My folks helped as much as possible, but that was way beyond their finances. Ultimately I decided I didn't need the title to help people."

"Everybody I've talked to says they'd rather see you than one of the clinic doctors. They say you really listen to them."

Lauren's face turned pink again. "That's nice. Small towns are like that."

"I don't think the size of a town matters. Patients prefer seeing somebody who genuinely cares. A woman I know in Paris goes to great lengths to see a specialist she thinks is more understanding about her arthritis."

"You've lived so many places. Doesn't it scare you to go to a country where they don't speak English and you're so far away from home?"

Tara shrugged. "Usually there are *some* English speakers around, and it's the business language at the sites where I've worked. Besides, it's an adventure going somewhere new and exploring the differences between one culture and another."

What she didn't add was that, to her, "home" was a hollow concept. She remembered at least seven foster placements in her childhood, and none of them had been a home the way other people defined it. Some kids had terrific foster parents and kept contact after leaving for work or school; she hadn't been so fortunate.

Maybe it was her fault; she just couldn't let people get close. On the other hand, the constant moves from one home to another were part of the reason she'd become cautious about relationships, so what was the chicken and what was the egg? It was one of the ways where she and Lauren were radically different. People liked Lauren and knew she cared about them.

Perhaps Pierre had been right. A year ago their relationship had come to an abrupt halt when he'd declared he would rather take a cold halibut to bed.

Tara pushed the memories away and ate a bite of chicken. The pungent flavor slid over her tongue. Mmm. She loved the different cuisines she'd sampled in her travels. Exploring the world would have to take the place of romance in her life.

LAUREN THOROUGHLY ENJOYED the meal Tara had prepared. They both liked spices, which was something else they had in common. Nevertheless, Tara's personality was radically different from her own. Her sister was extraordinarily bold. She'd lived all over the world and done things that Lauren knew she would never try. Climb a mountain? Go scuba diving? Live in one country after another? *Never*.

"Is it hard to move every couple of years?" she asked. "As much as I wanted to live in Schuyler, it was tough leaving Southern California. It helped that my best friend was here already, but I had to leave my other friends and coworkers, along with my parents, though we talk on Skype every week. Separately, of course, since they're divorced."

"It isn't that difficult for me," Tara admitted. "My acquaintances are pretty casual. I lived in so many different foster homes when I was growing up that I learned not to get close to anyone. I mean, what's the point when you'll be moved before long and never see them again?"

Lauren wondered how her twin could be so nonchalant. It would be awful not to have anyone who genuinely cared what happened to you. She lifted her chin. No matter what had occurred in the past, Tara had family now.

"Isn't there a man in your life?" she asked.

"No one special." Tara grinned. "Someone who travels fast has to travel light. A guy would tie me down."

A familiar concern went through Lauren. She might be determined to keep in touch and be the family her sister hadn't had, but some of it depended on Tara. "Don't you want to get married and have kids?"

"I'll leave that to you. Speaking of which, I... um, don't completely agree about the sheriff. He seemed quite interested."

"Oh." Lauren swallowed. "It's just that I think he needs someone bolder."

"Trust me, anyone who can lecture Josh McGregor is bold enough for Sheriff Stanfield."

"I didn't lecture Josh."

Tara snickered. "That wasn't how he saw it. Perhaps you should give Carl a few more chances."

Lauren smiled and concentrated on her food. Her sister didn't understand; she thought nothing of challenging Josh. But it wasn't that easy for someone who'd grown up in a household of endless arguments, sullen silences and disagreements over the smallest things.

Lauren had finally gotten her dream of a family of her own, only to have the dream constantly threatened. So she'd become a peacemaker with an aversion to rocking the boat or confronting anyone. She did what was necessary at work because it was important for her patients' welfare, but she struggled in her personal life.

"By the way, my parents hope to meet you as soon as possible," she said, determined not to think about Carl any longer. "They want you to know they would have adopted both of us if they'd known I had a twin."

Tara's smile flickered with an odd emotion. "I wonder how our lives might have turned out if that had happened."

"I think it would have been wonderful."

"Well, I'm glad you had a family. Maybe you'll have one of your own someday and I'll be Aunt Tara."

It was a wonderful image, and Lauren imagined the excitement of her children when Aunt Tara came for a visit, full of stories about faraway places.

She wanted to fall in love and have kids, but she didn't want a marriage that would fall apart the way her parents' relationship had crumbled. That wasn't even taking Carl's dangerous line of work into consideration—and why did her thoughts always circle back to him?

Keeping her distance from Carl was the best strategy, even though she got a sinking feeling in her stomach at the prospect.

TARA WAS RAPIDLY entering figures into the computer on Tuesday when Walt leaned forward in his easy chair. "You said at the hospital that you've ridden before. Do you want to go riding with me sometime?"

She almost said yes before her brain did a double take. Was he able to do something so physically demanding? Yet surely being able to do something he loved would be good for Walt. Wasn't pain worse when you were unhappy?

"I, uh, don't want to be rude, but does your leg agree with your yen for horseback riding?" she asked finally.

Rather than getting angry, Walt chuckled. "I've been secretly mounting a horse for the past three weeks. My leg isn't thrilled, but it's making peace with the process." He grinned. "I want to be ready to go after those sapphires."

Tara hesitated another moment before deciding Walt was a responsible adult and she couldn't make decisions for him. "In that case, count me in."

"Then how about tomorrow afternoon, around three?"

"Sounds good."

THE NEXT MORNING she brought suitable clothing and changed shortly before the time they'd arranged. Josh was nowhere to be seen, and she suspected Walt had planned the outing so his grandson wouldn't know what they were doing.

Things had been interesting with Josh the past few days. They still clashed, but he hadn't gone out of his way to chase her off the property.

Walt picked out a mellow gelding named Ringo as her mount and they rode northwest. Before long all signs of civilization fell away, and there was nothing except rolling land around them.

She loved seeing the ranch through Walt's eyes. He'd been born on the Boxing N, and his father had begun teaching him about cattle and horses before he could remember. Every tree and hillock had a story, and some of the unhappiness in his eyes seemed to recede as he recounted tales from the early days of life in Montana and how his family had come to Schuyler.

He also spoke of his wife with a longing that tugged at Tara's heart. Despite everything Josh had said about his grandparents, the picture she kept getting was of two people passionately in love and deeply committed to each other.

"We'll keep it short," Walt commented after a while, "on behalf of my leg and your greenhorn muscles."

She laughed, knowing how sore muscles could be if pushed too hard on a horse. Walt might be susceptible, as well. Though he rode as if born in the saddle, it had been over six months since he'd been active.

They returned to the horse barn, and since a groom had always taken over when she'd ridden elsewhere, Walt showed her the basics of equine grooming. It was hard work, but Ringo obviously appreciated the brushing, nudging her affectionately as she ran a soft cloth over his face.

Walt tried grooming his own horse, but his leg was obviously bothering him. He declined her offer to help and finally muttered something about getting a ranch hand to finish for him. Tara wrinkled her nose. The ranch hand might mention it to Josh, who'd then learn what his grandfather had been doing…and she wondered if he'd blame *her*.

So what? Josh could just…lump it.

AT THE END OF the week, Josh crouched and examined the damaged fence that one of his employees had found. Fence repairs weren't unusual, but Clyde Hawes had called, saying it appeared to be vandalism. Intentional damage was rare in the area. The days of cattle rustlers and territorial rivalries had largely passed; when they had problems, it was usually a lark, pulled by drunken teenagers.

"What do you think, boss?" Clyde asked. He was one of the older hands on the ranch, and Josh relied on his experience.

"You're right, it looks cut. Take care of the repairs, and I'll give a report to the sheriff."

"Yup."

With no more ado, Clyde set to work.

Josh remounted Lightfoot and headed back to the ranch center, calling the county sheriff's office on his satellite phone as he rode. Carl Stanfield wasn't available, but a deputy took the report and said they'd run extra patrols past the Boxing N. She didn't need to say that catching someone in the act was unlikely.

After tucking the phone back in his pocket, Josh flexed his hand. It was better. Healing had taken a while, especially since he hadn't been able to take it easy the way Lauren Spencer had advised. That was ranching. Hard, unremitting effort. The only reason someone would do it was pure love for the life.

Tara's comments about living paycheck to paycheck crossed Josh's mind, and his mouth tightened. He'd almost protested that he worked just as hard as anyone, but how could he deny that his trust fund set him apart? He didn't live high. His pay as a foreman had more than covered his expenses, but it wouldn't have concerned him if a paycheck was late.

He wished he could push Tara's voice out of his head, but she *had* put a finger on one of his troubles. He was trying to do it all, the same as his grandfather. And he knew better. His experience in Texas had taught him the importance of having a foreman on a large ranch. Instead he'd told himself that he first needed to get the place in better working order. With a small ranch he might have pulled it off, but he had to delegate at the Boxing N.

As he approached the ranch center, Tara rushed through the door of the foaling barn.

"I went to visit the filly," she said, her eyes wide and alarmed. "A cowhand is down in Belle's stall. He's unconscious and there's blood on his forehead. I tried calling nine-one-one, but my cell doesn't have a signal out here."

Josh swung off Lightfoot and dropped the stallion's reins over a post. Andrew Whitlan was lying motionless inside Belle's stall. The mare nickered angrily and stomped the barn floor. She was an exceptionally protective mother and must have believed she was defending her baby.

"Is my grandfather here?" he asked Tara.

"Your mom took him to a doctor's appointment."

Right. Josh had forgotten Walt was scheduled to see the orthopedist in Helena.

"I need to get Belle out of there before we can do anything," he explained.

Murmuring softly, he stepped into the stall. Belle eyed him with a challenge. The mare was one of the finest ever born on the ranch, but she was high-strung and difficult to handle. His grandfather was the only human she completely trusted.

"Whoa, girl, it's okay. You know me." Approaching without making any sudden moves, he sneaked his hand up to the lead on her halter.

Her nostrils flared, and he glanced over his shoulder. Tara had come into the stall as well, and was kneeling beside Andrew.

"Don't move him," he warned in the same soothing voice. "He could have a neck injury."

"I figured as much," she commented drily.

The teenager's eyes fluttered open, and he moaned.

"Don't try to get up," she cautioned.

"I…I'm okay," the kid answered gamely.

"Probably," she agreed, "but remember what ballplayers are told on the field—don't move until the coach says it's okay."

Andrew smiled feebly and remained still.

Tara looked at Josh. "Shall I go call nine-one-one at the office?"

"No, use this." He tossed his satellite phone to her. Belle reared, and he brought her down again. "Whoa, girl." He pulled firmly on the halter, trying to convince her to come with him, but the effort seemed to agitate her more. No way was she leaving without her baby.

After a brief phone conversation, Tara looked up. "The ambulances are tied up on other calls. They asked if you have a neck collar and whether we could transport him. Surely that isn't standard procedure."

"This isn't the city—sometimes we have to do

what's necessary," he returned, only to regret his sharp tone. He needed her cooperation. "Look, we've got a wide range of emergency equipment. Tell them we'll bring him in ourselves."

Tara relayed the information to the dispatcher and pressed the off button. "Now what?"

"Can you get up nice and slow and coax the filly from the stall? Belle won't leave without her."

"Sure."

Tara stood and held her hand out. "Hey, there, baby," she breathed.

Josh's eyes widened as the filly eagerly came to Tara, sniffing and nuzzling her fingers.

"Come on, little one." Tara took a slow step backward, and the filly followed trustingly. As Josh had expected, once her foal was headed toward the exit, Belle was eager to leave, as well.

"There's an empty stall next to this one," he said.

Tara nodded, and a few moments later, both horses were safe inside, with the stall door closed behind them.

Josh ran to the supply room and retrieved a neck collar and backboard. His first aid training had never been more useful as he eased the collar around the kid's neck.

"Andrew, we're also going to put a board under your back," he explained. "That way we can be sure you stay in one position on the way to the hospital."

"Gee, boss, I don't need a hospital," Andrew complained.

"Yeah, that blood on your forehead is just paint and you were taking a nap when I got here."

The boy grinned sheepishly. "I didn't know she'd get so upset if I went into the stall. It's my fault," he added hastily. "I startled her."

Josh finished strapping him onto the backboard and patted his shoulder. Andrew Whitlan definitely had the right stuff. He'd defended the horse instead of himself.

Ironically, Josh had intended to spend the morning working with Andrew before being called away because of the vandalized fencing. He was sure the kid could become a good cowhand with the right guidance.

"I'm awful sorry," Andrew added. "You aren't going to fire me, are you?"

"No way," Josh promised. He looked at Tara. "Can you help lift him into the truck? I'll call one of the hands if you don't think you're strong enough."

"I can do it."

Josh got his pickup and backed it into the barn. Andrew was skinny, and it didn't take long to slide him into the truck bed.

"I'll ride back here with you, okay?" Tara asked.

"That'd be *great*."

The boy's enthusiasm brought a reluctant smile

to Josh's mouth. He remembered what it was like to be a teenager with raging hormones. If a woman with Tara's looks had offered special attention, it would have taken more than a kick in the head to stop him from enjoying every minute.

When Tara was settled next to Andrew, Josh climbed behind the wheel. The distance into town loomed before him ominously. The truck had great suspension, but every bump would be uncomfortable for the teenager. And what if his injuries were more severe than they seemed?

CHAPTER SEVEN

JOSH DROVE OUT on the Boxing N's gravel road, scowling at every jolt. It was smoother once they reached the paved road, and he used Bluetooth to contact Schuyler Memorial Hospital to give them an estimated time of arrival.

A stray thought went through his head as he disconnected… Bluetooth was another one of those "fancy-dancy" inventions his grandfather poohpoohed on a regular basis. It made Josh wonder whether Walt had done the same thing with his wife; Grandma Evelyn had loved modern gadgetry. While he was down in Texas, they'd emailed and Skyped on a regular basis. Josh had wondered what happened to her laptop before realizing it might have been in the car when it crashed.

He pulled into the parking lot at the hospital and saw a medical team was waiting for them outside the emergency room entrance. Schuyler had the best emergency response procedures in the area.

"Hey, Andrew," said the doctor as he jumped into the back of the truck and began a swift examination. "I hear you've acquired a taste for horse hooves."

"Just my dumb-ass luck, Dr. Gonzalez," Andrew replied. "I'd rather have a horse under my butt than in my face."

The doctor chuckled and looked at Tara. "I see you had pleasant company for your ride into town."

"Yep. Makes a kick in the head worthwhile."

Tara's eyes twinkled down at Andrew. "Watch it, or I'll tell your girlfriend you were flirting."

"Ellie wouldn't care. She'd say I need the practice."

Dr. Gonzalez gestured to the orderlies. "Okay, let's bring him inside."

Josh helped slide Andrew onto the waiting gurney, and they followed the group into the hospital.

"We'll check in with you as soon as we know something," the physician advised.

Josh frowned, torn by the desire to stay and his obligation to Tara. "Actually, I'll be back as soon as possible. I need to take Ms. Livingston back to her car."

"Don't be silly," she objected. "I'll wait, too."

"Tara, don't forget to call Ellie," Andrew called as he was wheeled away.

"I'll do it first thing," she assured.

Josh led Tara to the waiting room, where she took out her smartphone, consulted a piece of paper and punched in the numbers. He didn't try to follow the low-voiced conversation.

When she was done, Tara glanced at him. "Andrew's girlfriend is babysitting her brother and sister, so she can't come over right away. I also called his mom on the way into town. Mrs. Whitlan was visiting an aunt in Helena, but she's contacting his father and they'll both be here as quickly as possible."

If possible, Josh felt worse than before. As Andrew's employer, he should have thought to contact the Whitlans earlier. He'd just focused on getting Andrew to the hospital while ignoring the grinding pain in his gut—the whole thing was too reminiscent of the day his grandparents had been hurt in that car crash.

He let out a breath. "I'm sorry you got caught up in this."

"No reason to apologize. I'm glad I was there. Andrew seems to be a nice kid."

"He is." Josh leaned back and brushed his fingers through his hair. "I only hired him this month and haven't had time to do any proper training. Something like this should never have happened."

TARA REGARDED JOSH'S FACE. At times she could barely stand the guy, but she sympathized with his anguish. He obviously cared about his employees and felt responsible for Andrew's injury.

"It was an accident," Tara told him. "You aren't at fault."

"That won't be much comfort if he's seriously hurt."

Josh looked so miserable that Tara felt sorry for him.

"Honestly, don't beat yourself up," she urged. "On the drive into town, Andrew admitted that you'd told him not to go in Belle's stall, but he wanted to impress you with his ability around horses, so he went in to clean it out." She grinned. "I'm not sure why he looks up to you so much, but there's no accounting for taste."

The atmosphere lightened, and Josh returned her smile. "Gee, thanks."

"Don't mention it."

They fell silent as a man came in and spoke to someone at the desk about his wife. It was a long discussion, and Tara watched idly. He appeared worried, but as time went on, she began to doubt his concern was genuine. Finally he stomped off after being told his wife would be admitted to the hospital for tests.

"Not the happiest marriage, I'd guess," Josh commented.

Tara was surprised he'd picked up on the subtle signals, but a stubborn gremlin inside made her say, "Who knows? He might just hate hospitals and red tape."

Silence fell for another few minutes.

"I understand Andrew's father works for one of your brothers," Tara murmured at length.

"Yeah, Trent. Perry Whitlan grew up on a ranch and his father was a top-notch rancher, but Perry decided construction was more his taste, so the ranch got sold before Andrew was born."

"Will Mr. Whitlan be able to leave the job site and come to the hospital?"

"Sure, Trent is a good boss." Josh rubbed the back of his neck. "He owns Big Sky Construction, and one of our sisters is his office manager. Alaina is supposed to be on maternity leave right now, but she's spending lots of time at work, anyhow. She says little Evelyn doesn't care whether she's in a bassinet at home or at the Big Sky office."

Tara remembered that it was Alaina who'd been having a baby the day that she and Lauren had stopped at the hospital.

"Big Sky must be a popular company. I see their sign on construction sites all over town."

Josh chuckled. "It's the biggest in the area. As a matter of fact, Trent is one of the reasons that ranchers around here have a hard time getting good cowhands. He's major competition when it comes to hiring."

"You don't seem to mind."

"Nah. Trent is a good employer, and his success benefits the community. Besides, I enjoy razzing him about it. Though, frankly, he's more fun to tease since he got married. Emily has been good for him."

"Even though she's from the city?"

Josh shrugged. "Time will tell, to quote my mom. City people usually end up returning to the city. We're used to that around here. They come in, buy a place, spend a bundle fixing it up, only to discover they can't stand the quiet."

Cynical, Tara thought. Or maybe realistic. She couldn't imagine living in such a small, remote town herself. It was nice for a visit, but she loved the excitement of cities such as Paris and Tokyo. Then something else occurred to her and she cocked her head.

"Is that what your mother says about Trent and Emily's marriage…that time will tell? It's rather pessimistic."

Josh looked shocked. "Of course not. She thinks Emily practically walks on water. The same with Kayla, my brother Jackson's wife. It's just one of those old phrases that get passed down. Grandma Evelyn used to say it, too."

Awkwardness suddenly filled Tara. Josh had lost his grandmother a few months before, and while he'd mentioned her in several conversations, Tara had never offered condolences. It was one of the social conventions she didn't handle well. She didn't know what it was like to have a grandparent she loved or how it would feel to lose them.

Lauren would understand. She probably said all the right things at all the right moments. Was it simply because she'd grown up with a real family?

Ever since Lauren had mentioned her parents wishing they could have adopted them both, Tara couldn't help thinking how different her life might have been. It was an appealing image. On the other hand, she would be a different person now, and she didn't know if that would be good or bad.

Twenty minutes later, another man rushed up to the emergency room desk. "I'm Perry Whitlan. My wife called and told me our son is here," he gasped. "His name is Andrew."

"I'll check on him."

Josh stood. "Hello, Mr. Whitlan. I brought Andrew in after the accident."

"Is he badly hurt?"

"I'm sorry, I haven't spoken to the doctor yet."

Tara's jaw dropped.

She might be lousy at human relations, but even *she* recognized a lame-ass answer when she heard one.

She stepped forward. "Good afternoon, Mr. Whitlan. I rode into town with Andrew. He talked the whole way and is mostly embarrassed about what happened. His main concern is keeping his job at the Boxing N."

The man's face relaxed. "That sounds like Andrew. I kept telling him that he was just romanticizing the life, but he still wanted to try. Turns out I was wrong and he loves it."

"I understand you grew up in ranching."

"Yeah, only I wanted to build things instead of mucking out stalls and chasing cows. Right now I'm foreman on a construction job over in Cottonwood Bend. That's why it took me a while to get here." He looked at Josh. "My son was thrilled when you hired him. Andrew applied at two other ranches and they wouldn't give him a shot. You'd think with his grandfather's reputation he wouldn't have had so much trouble."

Josh shifted his feet, uncomfortably aware that he wouldn't have hired Andrew, either, if he hadn't been desperate. "He's a good kid and has real potential."

"I'm glad."

A hospital volunteer stepped into the waiting room. "Mr. Whitlan? You can come in and see your son."

Josh glanced at Tara when they were alone again. "Thanks for the way you handled that."

"No problem."

Strangely, the temporary absence of tension between them made her uneasy. She didn't want to become friendly with Josh. It was already hard enough being caught between him and Walt. Work tensions she understood and could deal with as necessary. But in Schuyler she was treading on new ground; somehow the Boxing N was becoming more than a place of employment and Walt more than a boss. She didn't need the added complication of being attracted to Josh. It was annoying. She wanted to ignore her response to him, but it wasn't that easy.

Still, it wasn't as if she was moving to Montana, and she'd learned a long time ago how to get through difficult situations. So she squared her shoulders and sat down, determined to get through this one, one step at a time.

JOSH WAS PUZZLED by the shifting emotions on Tara's face, but right now he could only afford to worry about one thing, and that was whether Andrew was all right.

Half an hour after Perry Whitlan arrived, Andrew's mother hurried in and was escorted to the examination room to see her son. After another twenty minutes, the elder Whitlans came out, relaxed and smiling.

"It was so nice of you to wait, Mr. McGregor," said Mrs. Whitlan. "Andrew is fine. He needed a few stitches and the doctor wants him to stay overnight for observation, but it's mostly a precaution. He says Andrew must have a very hard head, which I could have told him *without* a CAT scan."

Josh's taut nerves began to uncoil. "Terrific," he answered. "Tell him to get better soon and that I'm looking forward to seeing him back at work when he's ready."

"Thank you."

While he shook hands with Perry, Mrs. Whitlan grabbed Tara into a hug. "I'm so glad you were there to help my son."

As Tara stepped back, her cheeks were pink and she seemed distinctly uncomfortable. "I didn't do that much."

"That isn't what Andrew said."

After he and Tara left the hospital, Josh glanced at his watch. "It's nearly two. Have you eaten?"

"No, but I have yogurt back at the office."

Yogurt? Josh shuddered as they walked out to his truck. He helped her into the high seat, distracted enough that he could almost ignore her long, silk-clad legs. "Let's go by the Roundup Café. A good meal is the least I can do to show my appreciation."

"That isn't necessary."

"Come on, I'm sure we're both hungry."

He wasn't sure why he kept pushing, except it seemed appropriate. Tara had helped with a ranch emergency, and he was caught between gratitude for the assistance and frustration that he now owed her.

When he had a moment, he would have to sort everything out in his head and decide how to respond. In the meantime, buying lunch was the civil thing to do…sort of like discharging a debt.

"All right," she agreed slowly.

It was a short drive—nothing in Schuyler was a long way from anything else. Josh parked in front of the café and went to open the passenger door. He put a hand out, once again trying not to look at her legs; sometimes being a gentleman was a challenge.

He swallowed as she hiked up her skirt and extended her leg to the ground. Ordinarily he wasn't a leg man, but hers were a treat. And she wasn't even wearing a sexy outfit, just a slim suit that was entirely professional...however unsuitable it might be for a ranch.

Inside they were seated quickly.

"Good to see you, Josh," the server said. "Before it slips my mind, folks have been wondering if you're having the big barn dance at the Boxing N this year. I meant to ask the last time you were here and forgot."

Damn.

He'd been ducking the question for several weeks, unsure of the answer. For the past half century the Boxing N had thrown a huge party in the spring. A wave of nostalgia went through him. A whole lot of nice things had happened at those barn dances, including his first kiss.

But the party had always been Grandma Evelyn's special project, and he didn't have time to take care of it himself. His mom had offered, but it wouldn't be fair. She was enjoying her new grandbabies, and working on the party would be a constant reminder that she needed to do it because her mother was gone.

"I don't know, Betty," he said finally, "we may have to skip it. With Grandma gone..." He drew a harsh breath; it was hard to say more. After rushing Andrew to the emergency room, the memories of Grandma Evelyn lying in a hospital bed were sharper than usual. "Next year for sure," he promised.

"I understand. Do you need time to look at the menu?"

"Not for me," Tara told her. "I'll take my usual Cobb salad and iced tea."

"The Roundup chef salad with Roquefort," Josh ordered. "Regular coffee, and lots of it."

"Gotcha." Betty made a note on her pad and headed for the kitchen.

Tara's eyebrows shot upward. "A salad? You're a rancher. Don't you usually eat a slab of beef with a few potatoes on the side? Or at least a burger?"

"That's a stereotype. Humans are omnivores."

"I've known vegans who would disagree."

Vegans weren't common around Schuyler, though they had a few vegetarians. Josh's teenage nephew, Jackson's son, had even gone vegetarian for a while, though Alex had ultimately decided he couldn't give up meat forever...mostly because he missed pepperoni pizza.

"In that case, I suppose your vegan pals are going to open a bunch of petting zoos when they convert everybody," he said before gulping down the cup of coffee Betty had just poured for him. These days he practically lived on coffee, the stronger the better. He refilled his cup from the carafe Betty had left on the table.

Tara squeezed a lemon wedge into her iced tea. "Couldn't cattle survive without humans?"

"You mean out in the wild? Some breeds might, but not all. So if everyone became vegan, there would be a lot of cows needing homes, and they don't make good house pets."

Tara smiled. "Interesting point."

"Will you use it on your vegan friends?"

"They're more acquaintances, and I doubt I'll see them again. I've never gone back to a country where I've worked—there are too many new places to see."

"Don't you stay in touch with the people you know?"

"We exchange an email or two in the beginning, but it doesn't last. We've all got our own lives."

Their meals were delivered, and Josh noticed that Tara's salad came with dressing on the side and a bottle of balsamic vinegar. Apparently she ate here often enough that Betty had remembered her likes and dislikes.

Tara sprinkled vinegar over her plate and began eating, occasionally dipping the edge of her fork into the container of creamy dressing before taking a bite. No doubt it was one of the ways she maintained her alluring figure. As a rule the café served their salads slathered with dressing, but Tara's choice was undoubtedly healthier.

He dug into his own meal, ruefully aware that it was almost the same as a slab of meat with so much turkey, beef and bacon, piled on top—not to mention sliced eggs and various kinds of cheese. The owner of the Roundup Café was known for telling his short-order cooks that if a customer could see lettuce, there wasn't enough meat on top.

"You're obviously familiar with the Roundup Café," he commented after they'd eaten awhile in silence.

"It's a quick place to come when Lauren is on her lunch hour," she explained. "Of course, we don't get here as often now that I'm working at the Boxing N and other sites."

Josh hesitated. The story of twins being separated was unusual—and intriguing—but it wasn't any of his business. Still, he didn't know what else to talk about.

"How is it that you and Lauren were raised separately?" he asked.

"Our parents died in an accident when we were babies, and the foster care system wasn't able to keep us together."

"The day Alaina had her baby, I heard you tell my niece about Lauren being adopted and having her name changed. Did your adoptive parents change your name, too?"

"Actually, I was never adopted," Tara said matter-of-factly. "Livingston is my birth name, and I grew up in foster care."

He frowned. "If you were infants when your folks died, why weren't you both adopted? I thought people preferred babies."

"There was a question about whether we had

family somewhere. By the time the legalities were resolved, we weren't babies any longer."

Josh frowned again. He wasn't an expert on social services and foster care systems, but something didn't make sense. "Why didn't they keep you together if they were trying to find your relatives?"

Tara didn't answer for a long moment and he had the oddest notion that she was getting hostile, but she finally shrugged. "One of my foster mothers told me that I'd been a cranky baby with colic. She said I was passed from home to home whenever they got worn out taking care of me. My guess is that Lauren was easier to handle and they decided to leave her in one place."

Even Josh's nearest and dearest wouldn't call him insightful, but he got the sense that Tara felt responsible for the way she and her twin had been separated. But it was hardly her fault. A baby couldn't be blamed for having colic or being temperamental.

"So who found who?" he asked, hoping to get into less sensitive territory.

"We found each other, I suppose. She was old enough to remember her birth name when she was adopted, which helped. I put my name in one of those registries that help people find their birth families. When she did the same thing, we were able to connect."

Tara's face was smooth and cool, as if she was

talking about two other people. Josh had more questions, but he didn't think it was smart to ask them. After all, they were strangers who'd spent most of their brief acquaintance sparring with each other, so intimate conversation was awkward.

At any rate, he didn't want to get better acquainted. Tara didn't belong in Schuyler, and by her own admission, she wasn't even good at staying in contact with the people she'd left behind. Neither quality made her someone he'd want as a friend *or* a lover. Now he just had to convince his body that those were excellent reasons to keep his distance.

"THANKS FOR THE UPDATE, Edith," Carl said into his radio. "I'll check in later."

He drove by the medical clinic and resisted the temptation to stop. As a rule he didn't suffer from self-doubt—he might even be improved by a bigger dose of humility—but Lauren's behavior continued to nag him at odd moments.

With any other woman, he would have said the mixed messages weren't worth the trouble. Lauren was different, though. She had a sweet vulnerability and compassion that had utterly charmed him from the beginning.

It was when he passed the Roundup Café and saw Josh McGregor and Tara Livingston sitting at a window table that he got an idea... Tara might be able to offer insight to her twin. At any rate, he ought to touch base with Josh about his report to the sheriff's office. A sabotaged fence was a serious matter in cattle country.

Carl made a U-turn, parked in the café's lot and went into the restaurant.

"Hey, Josh. Afternoon, Tara," he greeted as he approached their table. "Good to see you."

Tara grinned, and Carl noted it was quite different from Lauren's gentle smile. Interesting. The two women were physically identical in almost every way and Tara possessed a sophisticated appeal, but he found Lauren far more desirable.

"Did you get my report about vandalism at the Boxing N?" Josh asked.

"Yup. Do you have any missing cows?"

A grim expression crossed the rancher's face. "It's difficult to do a quick count on a big ranch, particularly since we're shorthanded, but I'm going to give it a shot in the morning. How much help a visual survey will be is another question. I'm still checking Grandpa's stock records against the herds to determine our actual numbers."

"Let me know if you come up with anything," Carl advised carefully. He didn't want to get involved in the conflict between Josh and his grandfather. It was hardly a secret—a few weeks ago the two men had gotten into a rip-roaring argument in front of the blacksmith shop. Cowhands who'd quit the Boxing N were also telling tales, saying they were worse than a pair of snarling bears fighting for food after hibernation.

Carl turned to Josh's lunch companion. "Tara, is there any chance we could get together to talk? When it's convenient, of course."

She nodded. "I'd say now, but Josh is taking me back to the ranch to pick up my car, and I don't want to hold him up. Another time would be fine."

"I'll be happy to give you a lift," Carl volunteered.

"That's great." Tara immediately got to her feet. "Josh has an order to get at the feed store. We were just discussing how long it would take to stop and load everything."

Carl was almost gleeful, which he tried to hide as a sober, responsible law enforcement officer. "Then this works out just right."

Tara nodded. "Josh, thanks for lunch, though it wasn't necessary."

"I figured I should feed you."

She raised an eyebrow. "That makes me sound like a cow at a feedlot."

"It was just to thank you for the help with Andrew," he returned stiffly. He turned to Carl. "One of my hands had an accident. He's fine, but Tara assisted with getting him to the hospital."

Carl restrained a laugh. He had the impression that Josh McGregor took after his grandfather, and being under an obligation wouldn't sit comfortably with Walt Nelson, either.

He escorted Tara to his cruiser but wasn't sure how to start the conversation. Instead he began telling her about an upcoming fund-raiser for the fire department.

"So, what's up?" she asked after they'd turned onto the Boxing N's gravel road. "I'm sure you didn't offer to drive me out here to talk about fund-raising."

He cleared his throat. "Right. Actually, I've been thinking about Lauren and wonder if you could point me in the right direction. I'm not making much progress with her."

Tara chuckled wryly. "I suspected that's what you had in mind."

"Do you think she's interested? I'll back off if that's what she really wants, but I'm having trouble reading the signals. They're rather mixed."

"I'm not sure I'm the one to ask. Lauren and I are still getting to know each other," Tara explained. "Even so, I think she likes you."

"Lauren likes everyone. I was hoping for more."

"Then don't give up. Maybe you just need to try something new."

Carl drew to a stop beside the car parked near the office. He'd been out to the Boxing N a few times, so he knew his way around. "I suppose sisters have to be loyal to each other. Especially twins."

"Honestly, this isn't about confidentiality. I'm

too new to having family to know what I should or shouldn't say. I just don't have any tips to offer."

Carl gazed at her curiously. After all, if he and Lauren ever got together, Tara Livingston could become his sister-in-law. It was a big *if*, but he couldn't help considering the possibility.

"Lauren mentioned you grew up in foster homes while she was adopted. She feels guilty because she was the fortunate one."

"There's no need," Tara answered firmly. "It's just the luck of the draw, and I don't believe in whining about circumstances. I decided a long time ago to get on with my life."

He grinned. "Healthy attitude. I can't tell you how many criminals blame their actions on a terrible childhood."

"Annoying, isn't it? We could all find excuses if we wanted them."

"Sure. Well, thanks for the encouragement. I think Lauren is pretty special."

"Me, too," Tara agreed, sounding a little surprised. "I want her to be happy, so if you're serious about her, you'd better be a good guy. You don't want to tangle with me—I'm a tough cookie."

He held up his hand. "Scout's honor."

"Great. Look, I don't know if it will help, but I know Lauren is particularly fond of pansies. You might try sending her a basket of plants in bloom."

It was a terrific idea. "Thanks, I'll give it a shot."

Tara slid out of the car, smiled in a friendly way and went into the office building.

Whistling, Carl headed back to town. He hadn't gotten everything he'd been hoping for, but he'd heard enough to come up with a new approach. He'd considered ordering roses or lilies for Lauren, but it had seemed boringly prosaic. Pansies fit Lauren much better.

If the florist in Windy Bluffs didn't have any plants, he'd buy them at the garden center and pay the florist to arrange them in a basket. That way Lauren should be able to avoid awkward questions at the clinic by saying they were from a grateful patient. It would be true, in a sense, since he'd seen the doctor there for his annual physical. Of course, sending flowers to Dr. Clinite had never occurred to him, but Bill Clinite didn't look anything like Lauren Spencer.

CHAPTER EIGHT

SO MUCH HAD HAPPENED over the past few hours, the silence in the Boxing N office almost took Tara by surprise.

She glanced at her watch, wondering if Walt had returned from his doctor's appointment. Sarah McGregor had explained the orthopedic specialist was in Helena, almost two hours away. They might even spend the night.

Though it was after four, Tara decided she had enough time to print the payroll checks. The check stock had arrived that morning, and since she'd already set up the computer program, it should be easy to finish the job.

Soon she had the checks printed for Josh's signature and walked to the foreman's house to put a note on his door so he'd know they were ready.

The conversation with Sheriff Stanfield kept going through her mind as she returned to the office. Considering her poor romantic past, it was ironic that he'd asked her for advice about her twin. She only hoped she'd done the right thing. Lauren had appeared wistful when talking about Carl, however much she'd insisted they didn't click. It seemed equally clear that things had clicked on Carl's end.

Maybe Lauren just wasn't ready; she'd mentioned ending a long-term relationship in California, though she hadn't explained why. Hopefully it wasn't the reason she was putting the brakes on with Carl. The sheriff seemed to be a nice guy, and it was a mark in his favor that he was willing to back off if his attentions were unwanted.

Shortly after five Walt came into the office.

She smiled. "Hi, how was the drive to Helena?" she asked, knowing he probably wouldn't want to talk about seeing the doctor.

"Long."

"Yeah, I have to go back soon and exchange my rental car. The company I used only lets you have one for a month at a time."

"I've got a pickup you can use," Walt proposed eagerly. "Free of charge."

"That's generous, but I've never driven something that big. I'd better stick with a sedan."

He looked crestfallen. "I understand, but remember it's available if you need it."

"Thanks. By the way, you should know that one of the ranch hands went into Belle's stall earlier and it didn't go well. Mama and baby are fine," Tara added hastily, seeing the elderly rancher's eyes fill with alarm, "but Andrew needed a few stitches and they're keeping him overnight at the hospital, just to be safe."

Walt glared fiercely and slammed his right fist into his left palm. "I'll have the boy's head. None of the hands are allowed in there."

Tara wasn't worried about Andrew. She'd already realized that Walt was more bluster than hurricane. "I'm sure he meant well and has learned his lesson. As for having his head, Belle took care of that for you."

He snorted. "I'd better go check on her. Are you staying longer? There's something I want to speak to you about."

Tara was meeting Lauren for dinner, but she had some time. "I can stay for a while."

Walt made his way out the door, limping worse than usual. After the trip to Helena and back and being examined by the orthopedist, he had to be exhausted.

A few minutes later, he returned and sat down again. He was silent for a long moment, and Tara kept working. She'd decided that sometimes he needed to gather his thoughts—not memory loss, just a struggle to figure out exactly what to say and how to say it.

"My daughter has been asking about the dance we've always held at the Boxing N," he said finally. "About whether I want to have it or not. She brought it up again on the drive home."

Tara leaned forward. "Someone mentioned it at the Roundup Café this afternoon. It sounds like a big deal."

"I'm not fond of parties, but it was real important to Evelyn," Walt muttered. "She experimented with recipes and made sure everything was exactly the way she wanted. I didn't figure we'd have it with her gone…just wouldn't be the same."

Tara thought about Josh's face when Betty had mentioned the barn dance—warm nostalgia, with a hint of sorrow. Walt looked the same.

"Now I keep thinking how disappointed she'd be," Walt continued. "There isn't much time left, so I wondered if you'd help me get it together."

"Uh, sure." The idea of planning a town barn dance was mind-boggling to Tara—she'd never even thrown a dinner party—but how could she turn him down?

"Keep track of your hours and let me know."

"Don't be ridiculous. This is for fun."

She sat on a nearby chair with a notebook and carefully began listing everything Walt thought was important, adding numbers from the phone book for the contacts they'd need to make.

"Evelyn always cooked up a storm," Walt told her, "but we'll have the deli deliver food. I'd considered doing that anyhow, before the… I mean… so it wouldn't be so much work for her. Not that we've ever provided all the eats. It's sort of a community potluck. Everyone brings something."

Together they called the deli and got on the catering schedule. The owner was thrilled to hear the annual event was being held after all and promised to do everything possible to help make it a success.

"Tomorrow we'll decide on a menu," Walt said after hanging up.

"Then I can email it to them," Tara offered.

He rubbed the side of his face. "I suppose that internet thing isn't so bad. Evelyn told me I was being as stubborn as a mule about it."

"I had the impression you didn't have a computer here on the ranch," Tara said.

"Just Evelyn's... Haven't been able to face going in her little office at the house. She, uh, didn't have any ranch records on it, only personal things. Guess it's useful for that, but it seems as if everybody spends so much time staring at a computer screen, they aren't going out and living."

It was a valid point. Tara had known people who'd worked all day at a computer station, only to go home and spend the evening on Facebook and Twitter.

"The internet has its drawbacks," she admitted, "but it speeds up a lot of stuff, and the amount of information you can get is amazing."

"I guess."

At six thirty, she stood. "Sorry, I need to get going. I'm having dinner with my sister."

"See you tomorrow."

When she saw Lauren, Tara didn't say anything about Carl; she just chatted about her day and listened to what her twin had to say in return. It was weird. People expected them to have a normal sisterly connection, even though they'd only known each other for a short time. Lauren was clearly eager for their relationship to progress faster as well, but Tara doubted she understood how difficult it was for her to let down her guard.

WALT WAS WAITING when Tara arrived at the Boxing N the next morning.

"I heard you got more involved in the emergency yesterday than you told me," he said gruffly. "If my grandson hired more experienced hands, accidents like that wouldn't happen."

She smiled noncommittally. "What matters is that Andrew will be all right."

"Humph. Are you going to make coffee?" Walt asked hopefully. He'd gotten into the habit of sharing a pot with her every day.

"You bet."

While the coffee brewed, they worked out additional details for the community barn dance, including sending Walt's order to the deli. Since the event was a long-standing tradition, it mostly required determining what jobs Evelyn had done personally and hiring someone to take over. The other tasks, such as preparing the nearby pastures for parking and sports would be assigned, as usual, to the Boxing N cowhands.

When Walt finally settled back with his third cup, Tara started sorting another stack of papers.

She found the ranch records fascinating, although it was clear where Walt's heart lay. Anything to do with the cattle was haphazard and cryptic, liable to be tucked in any corner of the office. On the other hand, his horse-breeding records were neatly kept in a ledger with an embossed leather cover.

The Boxing N office promised to occupy a fair amount of her time in Schuyler, but she didn't mind. It was the only large job she'd committed to; the rest were quite a bit smaller...things like auditing a small business's previous year's accounts and helping a dentist set up a better filing system. She'd gotten offers to take on additional local contracts, but at the moment, she was enjoying the pace of her life. Besides, her time at the Boxing N didn't feel like work. It was different than anything she'd done before, and where else would she be able to go horseback riding in the middle of the day?

Tara was especially looking forward to sorting out the truly *old* Boxing N documents, along with the historic editions of the *Schuyler Outpost* newspaper she kept finding. She'd seen enough yellowed deeds, geological reports, ancient breeding records and bills of sale from over a century ago to get excited. Of course, the further back in time she went, the fewer papers and records she expected to find, a reminder that her career was a necessity of the modern age. She suspected an old cigar box had once been the primary storage facility for many businesses.

And it was in the older records that any sapphire information might be found, but Walt had reluctantly told her to concentrate first on what was needed for current operations.

She brewed another pot of coffee and poured Walt his fourth mug.

"Mighty good," he grunted. He eyed her cup. "How can you drink it with cream and sugar? It covers up the flavor."

She smiled. "How can you drink it black? Cream and sugar bring out the flavor."

Walt's eyes gleamed. Tara had discovered he liked it when she gave him a sassy response. The old guy had plenty of edges, but they got along well, possibly because she had her fair share of edges, too.

They chatted and had several spirited debates over the next few hours. Then he left, saying something about having another "danged appointment." Presumably this one was in Schuyler, since otherwise Sarah McGregor would surely have insisted they stay in Helena for the night.

It wasn't a huge surprise when Josh came to the office soon after Sarah had picked up her father. He seemed to avoid his grandfather whenever possible.

"Hi," he said. "I, uh, wanted to thank you again for yesterday. Also for getting the payroll straightened out. Do you know when you'll have online bill-paying established?"

"Soon. I've been checking in to who offers it as a service and what they require."

"Great. Prompt payment is important for a rancher's reputation. Unfortunately, that will be something new for the Boxing N."

Although she'd seen enough to know he wasn't wrong about Walt's haphazard approach to the ranch's business, she wanted to defend the old man.

"Your grandfather seems to be respected in town," she returned stiffly.

"Merchants know they'll get paid, just not when."

"Surely that's true of many ranchers. I understand it can be a marginal business, especially now that people aren't eating as much red meat."

"Grandpa and his brother did okay, despite changes to the market. But that might be what prompted them to decide what to do with their ranches when I was a kid. They wanted to be sure the Boxing N and Crazy Horse would stay in the family, so when I was eight, they made a plan to give one to Jackson and the other to me."

Tara's brow furrowed in concentration. "I don't understand. Lauren told me you had a sister, Madison, who is younger than you. There was no plan for her?"

"She wasn't interested in ranching."

"Really? How old was she when the decision was made? Three or four? It's rather patriarchal to decide she wasn't interested in ranching before she's even started school," Tara observed in a dry tone.

Josh's face tensed. "Maddie was in preschool. Grandpa and Uncle Mitch established an additional trust fund for her, along with ones for Trent and Alaina after they were adopted. It's an equitable distribution."

"I understand Trent wanted to work in construction from a young age, but it's sexist to assume Madison and Alaina wouldn't fall in love with ranching while growing up."

"They didn't," Josh emphasized. "But if they change their minds, they can buy ranches with their trust funds."

"That isn't the same as owning the historic family ranch, as you well know." It wasn't Tara's business, so she wasn't sure why she was yanking Josh's chain. Maybe she just wanted to see what would happen if she provoked him.

"Don't ask me to justify their decision. I was a kid, so obviously I wasn't involved. Besides, Uncle Mitch and my grandfather have put all of us in their wills." Josh was clearly becoming irate. "Nobody is getting overlooked for *any* reason."

"Good for them. It's nice to know the McGregors and Nelsons have carefully mapped out the lives of the next generation."

His jaw tightened further, making the angles of his face even more striking. And the way his eyes flared made her think he was aroused in another way, as well. Interesting… She might not have a passionate nature, but that didn't mean she wasn't curious. What would happen if she kept pushing?

"Parents are *supposed* to influence their kids, but no one has controlled anybody," he ground out. "We're all doing what we want to do."

"Why didn't you work here on the ranch instead of in Texas before your grandpa retired?"

"I told you before that Walt was challenging. I tried coming here during my first college break, and Grandpa treated me worse than the greenest cowhand. Even my mother said it might be best to go somewhere else."

Tara cocked her head. "All right, there's something else I don't get. If the Boxing N is so important to Walt that he couldn't bear to retire, why didn't he just plan to leave it to Sarah? Is it because she's a woman, or because she married the Boxing N's biggest rival?"

"Hell," Josh snarled.

He clenched his teeth, breathing hard, plainly trying to keep his composure. Tara didn't know exactly why she kept pushing, just that something inside wanted to provoke him. She lifted her chin in challenge. His control snapped as he reached out and yanked her close.

Her body yielded against his work-hardened muscles as his mouth claimed hers, firm and demanding, in a way that made every other kiss she'd shared pale in comparison. But comparisons were forgotten as the embrace softened, his lips becoming sensuous, gently opening hers.

At the same time, his hands moved over her hips, tugging her lower body close, leaving no doubt of his desire. It was intoxicating, and Tara felt an urge to throw caution to the wind. But a habit of self-protection quickly reasserted itself and she knew she shouldn't have provoked him. After all, she wasn't a seductress… Maybe hormones had simply made her crazy.

She stiffened and pulled back a fraction of an inch. It took only seconds before Josh's grip eased, though his arms remained loosely around her as his breathing evened, then they dropped as well, and he stepped back.

"I'd better go," he muttered.

He stalked from the office, and Tara stood motionless for a moment. The previous day Josh had pointedly informed the sheriff that their lunch was merely a thank-you for her help, as if he didn't want her, or anyone else, to think they'd gone out for social reasons. Still, that kiss showed that *something* was going on behind his grim exterior. It had been as hot as a kiss could get.

Taking out her purse, Tara looked into a small mirror she kept in her wallet. She smoothed her hair and renewed her lip gloss, yet it was Josh McGregor's face that she kept seeing in her mind. He was pure, sexy heat.

Pushing the thought from her head, she focused

on her work again. She'd enjoyed kissing Josh, but it was an anomaly, not to be repeated.

AT LUNCHTIME LAUREN sank into her office chair with relief. They'd had a spate of sprained ankles, wrenched shoulders, bumped heads and feet that had stepped on nails, requiring tetanus shots. Schuyler wasn't much different than Los Angeles in that respect—it was late spring and people were taking fitness shortcuts, hoping to get in shape for summer.

Some were optimistic; one patient had wriggled into a tight bathing suit and had been scared to use the scissors on her own. Lauren had suspected pregnancy after a thorough exam.

"I shouldn't have forced it on," Carolyn had declared in embarrassment. "I *knew* I'd gained weight, but I'm so hungry these days. I can't seem to stop eating."

"Mmm. When was your last period?"

Carolyn had looked dumbstruck. "Uh…four months ago. But I *can't* be pregnant. I mean, I thought I started menopause early."

"We'll do a test, but you may not want to be wearing a bikini this year."

"Who cares?"

The pure delight on Carolyn's face had been great, but she'd used the visit to encourage Lauren to go on a date with her brother-in-law.

"He's a good guy," Carolyn had declared, "and he isn't a goofball like my husband."

"I'm concentrating on spending time with my sister right now." Lauren had demurred. Her patients' matchmaking attempts continued unabated, possibly with the hope of cementing their newest physician's assistant's presence in the community.

A knock sounded on her office door now, and Karen came in, carrying a lovely basket of pansies.

"Another thank-you from a patient, I guess," Karen said, setting it on the desk and rushing out when the phone rang.

Her face brightening, Lauren pulled the card out; she'd received a number of bouquets. It was nice that Schuyler was so intent on keeping her in town, and the bouquets were far more welcome than matchmaking. Best of all, this particular offering was pansies. She loved pansies; they were such homey, bright little blossoms.

But when she opened the card, she bit her lip. The basket was from Carl Stanfield.

Lauren, I saw these and couldn't resist sending them to you. Would you have dinner with me tomorrow? Give me a quick call when you have the opportunity. I hope you can come. I'm taking a few days off, and eating dinner with a friend would be a pleasant way to begin my break.
—Carl

Lauren clutched the note tightly and wished she felt free to accept Carl's invitation without any angst or second thoughts. Still, why shouldn't she go? He'd described it as spending time with a friend, and pansies weren't exactly a romantic flower. So maybe it would be all right.

Sitting forward, she grabbed the phone and dialed his home number before she chickened out. As expected, she got his voice mail, which might be a little cowardly, but it was easier to inject the right tone that way.

"Hi, Carl," she said, her voice light and casual. "Thanks for the flowers. Dinner tomorrow would be great, but I can't stay out late because I have to work on Saturday. How about coming over between four thirty and five? Or if you prefer, I can meet you somewhere. Bye."

Putting the receiver down, she realized her heart was pounding and she hadn't taken a breath.

She needed to calm down. There was no way she could call back and say she'd changed her mind; that would make her look like a dithering idiot.

It would be all right. Wouldn't it?

AFTER LEAVING THE Boxing N office, Josh busted his butt, moving loads of hay, grooming the horses and cleaning out the stalls. He couldn't believe he'd given in to his attraction for Tara. What an utterly asinine move. And what if it made her think he was interested in starting something with her?

He shuddered. *As if.* However beautiful she was, Tara was also a city woman and far too stubborn and sharp tongued. More than that, she was an international traveler who planned to spend her life hopping from one country to another. She'd be wrong for him even if she did something totally out of character and decided to stay in Schuyler. She was a woman who wore silk shirts, didn't care about ranching and seemed to delight in making his life difficult.

Damn. He didn't want to even *think* about Tara.

Josh was working in the big barn when Andrew arrived, saying he'd been approved for light activity.

"You shouldn't rush it," Josh told him, thinking that "light" activity was too ambiguous for his taste. Light work on a ranch might be strenuous to an office worker.

"Don't knock it, boss," Clyde Hawes advised. He'd been working alongside Josh, helping with the maintenance and repairs that had been neglected in the months since Grandpa's accident. "I appreciate a man who doesn't let anything get in the way of working hard."

Andrew's chin rose higher. There was a bandage on his forehead and he had a black eye, but he seemed able. "Honest, the doctor said it was okay to come back—claims I have a head like a rock."

"Clyde, why don't you take Andrew out to ride fences for a couple of hours?" Josh asked. Riding fence lines was his favorite chore on the ranch, but he couldn't do it all. "Show him how to handle any issues, but don't let him overdo it."

"Sure thing."

"Find me before you leave for the day," Josh added. "There's something I'd like to discuss."

Clyde nodded. Much to Andrew's disgust, he insisted on saddling both horses, and they rode out with the teenager still protesting that nobody had to babysit him.

The corner of Josh's mouth twitched as he finished repairing a broken hinge on one of the stalls. Andrew was eager. He hoped to buy his own ranch someday and wanted to learn everything possible from hands-on, daily effort. In some ways he was mature beyond his years; in others he was a typical hormone-driven eighteen-year-old male.

As for Clyde Hawes?

He would be a good choice for the Boxing N's foreman. Clyde was the most experienced of the hands and wasn't overly concerned about the often conflicting orders he got. He'd give Walt a nod of respect, talk to him about the old days of ranching and quietly do whatever Josh had asked him to do in the first place.

Josh decided he'd offer Clyde the foreman's job and make an effort to step out of his way. Owner and foreman were two different roles, and he had to learn to be an owner. He just wished it hadn't been Tara Livingston who'd identified the problem.

Josh wiped the sweat from his forehead and dropped his tools into the box.

Perhaps he should talk to Tara and make sure there weren't any misunderstandings between them. Her car was still parked near the office and he'd prefer to handle it as soon as possible. What's more, it wasn't a conversation he wanted to have with his grandfather around, and Walt would be at his physical therapy appointment until late afternoon.

Once Clyde and Andrew had ridden out of sight, he went straight to the office.

"Hey, Tara," he announced as he came through the door, "there's something we need to clarify."

She lifted an eyebrow. "Yes?"

"It's about earlier. I want to get things out in the open. That kiss shouldn't have happened and I want you to know that I wasn't trying to start anything. That is, I'm not interested in a long-term relationship right now. I simply can't afford the distraction."

"Oh, really?" she asked in a sugary tone. "What made you think I was hunting for a husband or that I'd want to stay in Montana with someone who considers a relationship to be an unwelcome distraction?"

Josh winced, realizing how arrogant he must have sounded. He'd made more than his share of blunders lately. His mouth was running ahead of his brain so much it was surprising that anyone in his family or the town was willing to talk with him. He should have just said he wasn't interested in dating.

Tara continued crisply, "I've had offers from men in other parts of the world and I haven't accepted any of them. Now you think I'm yearning for happily-ever-after with an obnoxious rancher? Considering the size of your ego, it's a good thing you live in Montana—a smaller state wouldn't have room for it."

"I apologize," he said stiffly. "I didn't consider my words carefully enough."

"That's a serious understatement."

Josh wheeled and marched out, furious that he'd stuck his foot in his mouth yet again.

It was ironic that despite his large family, he felt isolated. He couldn't discuss the problems with his grandfather with anyone in the family, but especially not with his parents. His mom was still grieving and didn't need to listen to his complaints about her father. And while he'd always been close to Jackson, he hadn't been comfortable talking it over with him, either. Their circumstances were different. Great-Uncle Mitch had happily retired when the time came, with no attempts to keep running the Crazy Horse Ranch.

The truth was that he hadn't spent much time with any of his family since returning to Montana. Instead, he'd been consumed by the Boxing N.

In the corral Josh saddled Lightfoot and rode

out, eyeing the cattle scattered across the landscape. That morning he'd done his best to determine if any were missing, but the numbers seemed all right. Clyde and the other hands agreed. So the cut fence might have been simple vandalism, not theft.

Whenever his thoughts drifted to his problems with Walt, Josh slapped himself. He didn't believe in self-pity. Besides, with hard work and careful management, he could keep the Boxing N going. It would be terrible if the Nelson ranch had to be sold, and Josh was going to make sure that didn't happen.

CHAPTER NINE

TARA WANTED TO LAUGH whenever she thought about Josh stomping away.

How wrong could a guy get? Men had always complained that she was difficult to approach, never offering encouragement, and now Josh McGregor had assumed she was interested in him?

While she found Josh attractive and *had* provoked him, that didn't mean she was interested in a relationship, especially after her experience with Pierre.

Tara's humor fled at the memory, and she flinched. She'd actually considered marrying Pierre until that last night—or rather, the morning after, when he'd compared her sexual prowess to a fish. She'd told him to drop dead.

Restless, Tara got up and walked around the office. The expansive views made it an enticing place to work. Walt had told her that when he'd moved into the building he'd expanded the existing windows to provide vistas of both the ranch and the garden where his wife spent so much time in the summer.

Lord.

Tara rested her forehead on a cool pane of glass

and wished she understood why some people were lucky in love and others ended up with someone like Pierre. Was she somehow undeserving? After all, she'd been pushing people away since infancy.

The thought was dismal, and it didn't bode well for her having a relationship with anyone, much less her sister. Lauren could ultimately decide it wasn't worth trying to get close to someone who had so much trouble with intimacy.

Tara didn't know why she'd told Josh about her childhood. He couldn't possibly understand what it had been like and might even look down on her because of it. Growing up she'd discovered that a lot of people were suspicious about children in foster care, as if they'd come from questionable backgrounds.

With a sigh she sat down at the desk again, looking at a document she'd found earlier. It was an old survey of the Boxing N Ranch. The number of acres seemed huge. She didn't know the usual size of ranches in Montana, although she'd heard that the McGregor holdings were equally large.

It was interesting. People in town didn't speak about either family as if they were out of the ordinary. She'd known folks who either resented or sucked up to those with financial success. But in Schuyler, both the McGregors and Nelsons seemed to be respected for hardworking values and old ranching traditions.

Walt limped into the office about four o'clock

and sank into his favorite easy chair. He didn't say anything for more than an hour, so Tara quietly kept working until he started talking. As usual it was less a conversation than a monologue. Starting with family history, he roamed over a century and a half of Montana ranching.

Once in a while he said something about his wife. Tara was always careful not to look closely at him when he mentioned Evelyn; it was as if his sorrow made him feel exposed and vulnerable.

"I messed up," he said at one point. "I was supposed to retire and we were going to go visit all the places we'd dreamed of exploring. But I kept putting it off and then it was too late."

"I'm sure she understood."

"Perhaps." He squared his shoulders. "Have you decided where you're going next?"

"Basically I've narrowed it down to Berlin, Rome or Madrid. I've visited all of them and want to see more."

His face grew more melancholy again. "Evelyn especially wanted to visit Italy. She was an art major in college and loved the Renaissance masters."

"Perhaps you could go in her memory?"

"No," he returned brusquely. "It wouldn't be the same without her. I only have the ranch left, and I can't even handle the Boxing N without Josh. I'm a useless old man."

"Ridiculous," Tara shot back. "You're only in

your seventies. You have a brother in his eighties who's still going strong. From what I hear, Mitch Nelson manages to *thoroughly* enjoy life. In fact, according to Lauren, he's a favorite with the widows in town."

Walt chuckled. "True enough." He pushed himself to his feet. "Did you know it's past six?"

Tara checked her watch and laughed. "No, I lost track of the time."

"We have plenty of daylight left. How about a short ride?"

"Sure. Just give me a chance to change my clothes."

"I'll get the horses saddled."

As Walt left she turned off the computer and stretched. She didn't know when she'd come to care so much about the lonely old man who missed his wife more than his family seemed to realize. Not that she'd heard that from anyone except Josh, but nothing suggested his family saw things differently. Though all things considered, Josh was hardly going to confide in *her*.

Walt's grief tugged at her heart. What would it be like to love someone so much that it was a struggle to find meaning in life without them? Was the joy of the years together worth risking the pain of losing them? At some point she might be able to ask Walt those questions, but his wounds were too raw, and she'd probably leave Schuyler before he'd healed enough.

Of course, there was no reason she couldn't visit him whenever she came back to see Lauren. It was nice to think she'd have a second reason to return to Schuyler. And with a little luck, she could avoid Josh on those visits.

Grimacing, Tara went into the bathroom and changed into her riding clothes. Walt had suggested she keep some at the office, and they'd gone out riding whenever possible. She enjoyed it, even when she found it difficult to put Josh out of her mind.

It might not have been the smartest thing to set herself up as Walt's ally against his grandson, but that was what she wanted to be. At the same time, she had to admit that Josh was clearly caught between two painful positions—he cared about his grandfather, but he also needed to be his own man, running the Boxing N.

She'd also seen enough of the ranch's finances to know it had to start turning a profit. Right now the Boxing N was losing money. Maybe the Nelsons and McGregors were wealthy enough to carry it for a while, but as an accountant, she found it unnerving to see a business in the red.

Not that she was going to admit any of that to Josh.

TARA GOT INTO her car an hour later. She'd enjoyed the ride with Walt, but memories of kissing Josh returned, and she fastened her seat belt in frustration. It was like the difference between smelling chocolate and actually having the dark, rich flavor sliding over her tongue.

At the same time, she agreed that it shouldn't be repeated…probably the *only* thing she and Josh agreed about.

Regrettably, her resolve didn't cool the heat she felt whenever she thought about him. It just went to show that you didn't have to like a man to find him sexy.

There was no justice in wanting to crawl into a hayloft with the guy, however tempting it might be to discover if sex could be better than her experience suggested. But even if she tried, it would probably come to nothing. And ultimately, she wasn't willing to try again, however great the temptation.

CARL WAS DELIGHTED when he found Lauren's message on his voice mail. The suggestion of pansies and another approach must have been right on target. He'd have to thank Tara again.

The next afternoon he arrived at Lauren's door at exactly four forty-five. She opened when he knocked, and he gazed at her in admiration. The soft blue dress showed off her figure, the skirt flowing around her hips to below her knees. She looked sweet and feminine and incredibly attractive.

"Hi," he said, resisting the urge to kiss her on the cheek. After all, he'd promised himself to take it slower this time around.

"Hi, Carl," she replied with a smile. "You didn't mention where we were going. Is this okay?" She brushed a hand over her dress.

"You look terrific. I thought we could check out the Italian place in Windy Bluff since we had Mexican the last time."

"That's nice."

They drove to the nearby town, chatting about Schuyler's upcoming Independence Day celebration. It was still over six weeks away, but the town was revving up for it with a lot of energy.

"It's wonderful to live in a place with so much community spirit," she said.

"Yeah, Schuyler keeps us busy during the summer, with both big and small events. I just learned the Nelsons will be holding their annual dance after all. There's also a rodeo and the volunteer fire department's barbecue. I'm thinking of entering the chili cook-off that's part of rodeo week."

Lauren smiled. "You cook?"

"I'm not bad, but my chili is fantastic, even if it's immodest to say so."

She laughed and he enjoyed the way it sounded… definitely something he could get used to hearing often.

"Spicy chili or mild?" she asked.

"I'll make it whichever way you like it best," he told her as he parked at the restaurant.

"Oh."

Carl thought her cheeks colored slightly and she bit her lip, as though uncertain or uncomfortable.

"Don't bother trying to make it according to my preferences," she added and he was again unsure what she was trying to tell him.

Inside the restaurant, the maître d' nodded at him. Carl had driven over at lunchtime to ensure everything would be just right.

They were led to a secluded table where a small basket of blue and yellow pansies sat in the middle. Lauren looked apprehensive.

"Is something wrong?" he asked.

"Uh, no. It's just that pansies aren't usual for a restaurant, especially an Italian place."

"I ordered them for tonight."

"That was…um, thoughtful." Her voice had a hesitant edge, and she seemed to grow more nervous.

"Tell me more about yourself," he said after they had ordered. "What was it like to learn you had a twin sister?"

"Strange. I thought we'd be instantly close, only we're too different. But I think it's getting better. When we first met in Paris it was really awkward."

Carl nodded. "I like Tara, though she *does* seem challenging to get to know well. Still, she's the one who told me that you like pansies."

"I don't remember mentioning it, but she never forgets anything. Even the smallest detail."

They continued talking, sharing some of their

history. She seemed surprised he'd grown up in Maryland.

"You're such a fan of the St. Louis Cardinals, I thought you were born and raised in Missouri. You never supported the Orioles?"

"When I was little, sure. They're a good team, but I always liked the Cardinals." Carl stopped and cleared his throat, recalling the way he'd gone on and on about his team's baseball stats and season prospects during their first date, months earlier. "Anyhow, I kind of adopted St. Louis as my hometown when I moved."

"When did you decide to go into law enforcement?"

"When I was five—mostly because my dad was a cop."

Lauren laughed. "Did you ever think about anything else?"

"Naturally. A year later I decided to be an astronaut, followed by a fervent desire to become a major league pitcher."

"What happened?"

"I realized it required the ability to throw a ball straight, so I thought being president of the United States would do instead. What were your dreams?"

Another strained expression crossed her face, but she answered lightly. "Typical, I suppose. A ballerina. For a while I wanted to be an astronaut, too, and when I was *really* little, I wanted to be a professional kitten holder."

"Then you must like cats," he said eagerly, pleased to find something else in common.

"What's not to like? They're rotten little monsters who purr."

He grinned. Lauren was *definitely* a cat person.

She stirred restlessly and glanced around the restaurant. "If you don't mind, I'm going to freshen up."

"Sure."

He watched her walk between the tables, the soft fabric of her dress swishing around her curves. Heat flickered through him, and he reminded himself to go slow.

LAUREN WENT INTO the ladies' room with a sigh of relief. The evening wasn't going the way she'd anticipated. Carl wasn't acting as if the evening was dinner between friends—he'd ordered flowers for the table and he kept smiling at her in a way that seemed more romantic than friendly.

She should have known better. In fact, she *had* known better—she'd just wanted to spend more time with him. That had been her problem when they first started dating. She'd realized they weren't suited and kept justifying accepting invitations because she liked him.

"Is something wrong?" a voice inquired and she swung around to see a woman with a pleasant face surrounded by silvery hair.

"Uh, no. I mean, it's complicated."

"I noticed you're here with a very handsome young man. Is he the complication?"

Lauren shrugged, not sure how much she should say. Windy Bluffs was close enough to Schuyler that it wasn't unusual for gossip to pass between the two communities. It had happened the last time she'd eaten there with Carl, after all. Still, she longed to discuss the situation with someone.

"You look very nice together," the older woman added helpfully.

"We… Um, it isn't like that. We're just friends."

The lady chuckled. "Is that what you want?"

No. That was the worst of it. Lauren might have tried to fool herself, but she'd known Carl was still interested. She even *wanted* him to pursue her, while the scared, uncertain child inside knew it was a bad idea.

"I guess not," she admitted.

"In that case, good luck, dear. Me and my Harry, we've been together fifty-seven years today, though I never thought we'd make it past our third date."

"Congratulations. I hope you have a wonderful anniversary celebration," Lauren said.

Once she was alone, Lauren washed her hands and stared at herself in the mirror.

"You're an idiot," she told herself, "but you'd better find the courage to do the right thing."

CARL WAS SURPRISED when an elderly lady smiled and winked at him as she walked past the table.

But Lauren came soon after and he stood to pull out her chair.

"It isn't necessary," she protested.

"My grandfather would never forgive me if I didn't behave as a gentleman," he answered. "He has very strict ideas."

"That's nice."

"My grandparents will be coming out to visit Schuyler in a few months and I'm sure you'll meet them."

"Oh, I hope they won't need to visit the clinic."

"I meant that I want to introduce them to you."

The uncertainty in her face seemed to grow. "I always enjoy meeting people."

"What led you into medicine instead of ballet?" Carl asked, deciding to change the subject.

"I wanted a career that helped people, and I enjoy science. Medicine seemed to be a good combination. How did you circle back to law enforcement from your dreams of the presidency?"

He grinned. "At five it was about being the hero."

"And later?" she asked.

"Same as you, I wanted to help people, except I decided to do it by protecting them from the bad guys." He sighed. "But after years in various cities dealing with some of the worst that the world has to offer, I started getting cynical."

"You've never seemed cynical to me."

"That's good to hear. Basically, I didn't like

the kind of person I was turning into and made a change. It's a good thing we didn't meet while I was cop in St. Louis. You probably wouldn't have liked me."

Lauren didn't reply for a minute, then leaned forward, looking resolute. "Carl, you're a great guy and a terrific sheriff. Everyone says they feel safer now you're here. But I…I'm just not the right person for you to…"

Carl waited while she stopped. He had a feeling he wasn't going to enjoy what she had to say.

"On your note you wrote that you wanted to go out as friends," she finally continued. "But now you're acting as if you're interested in a different kind of relationship."

Carl was chagrined. Even when he was determined to restrain himself, he hadn't managed to do it. "I am."

"It's flattering. But the thing is…with your job and who you are…you need to be with someone who has more guts. I don't have what you need. If you think about it, I couldn't even tell you that when we were dating a few months ago."

Stillness settled over Carl. He'd been right—Lauren *had* been trying to warn him away again. He just hadn't wanted to accept it. It wasn't the first time. He'd dated more than one woman who'd decided they couldn't handle his work. But with Lauren it was far harder to be philosophical.

"I understand. In that case, friends it is," he said, forcing a smile.

She looked relieved. "Absolutely."

They ordered and the conversation flowed, Lauren more relaxed now. He'd never push her into something she didn't think she could handle. It was tough enough to make a relationship work and even harder for a law enforcement officer. His own parents were evidence enough of that. After all, they'd gotten divorced because of it.

SINCE HER SISTER was working Saturday morning, Tara went out to the ranch to visit Walt and do more planning for the dance.

Josh met her as she got out of the car, and she hoped he wasn't going to launch another discussion of why they shouldn't have kissed. Once was bad enough—a second time would be downright insulting.

"Grandpa told me you're working on the Boxing N dance," he said brusquely.

It sounded like an accusation, and Tara raised her chin. "Yes. He said your mother has been asking about it, but he needed help making the arrangements, especially since there wasn't much time left to put it together."

"I see." Josh's face had its usual uptight expression.

"Let me guess. It's your ranch and your land, so you're upset that no one asked permission to hold a dance." Yet as soon as Tara spoke, she knew it wasn't fair. Walt *should* have talked to his grandson about the dance; she just didn't want to acknowledge that to Josh.

"Not at all," he returned stiffly. "But you were hired to organize the office, not plan social events. Are you expanding your résumé?"

"I'm doing it because Walt asked and he's a… That is, I just wanted to help." Tara had stopped herself from saying that Walt was a friend, but it was true. She'd come to care about him and knew he felt the same for her.

It was a peculiar revelation. She'd done things many people would call exotic and unique, odd or amazing, but to her, being able to call someone a friend was out of the ordinary, and warmth curled inside her at the thought.

Tara's chin shot higher. Her arrangements with his grandfather weren't Josh's concern. "So what is your problem?"

He sighed. "Nothing, I guess. It's just that the dance was something Grandma loved, and it almost seems wrong to have it so soon. She hasn't even been gone for eight months."

Tara's exasperation vanished. How could she possibly understand how it felt to lose someone she loved as much as Josh had loved his grandmother?

"Wouldn't she want the event to continue?" she asked carefully. "Walt told me it was special to her."

Josh released a heavy breath. "Yes, that's why

I told Betty at the Roundup Café that we'd have it next year."

"The dance is in two weeks," Tara murmured. "If you prefer, you could help your grandfather instead of me."

Josh instantly looked alarmed. Yet a curious thought came to her... Both men cherished Evelyn's memory. Wasn't *that* the most important common ground between them...not the Boxing N Ranch?

"I think Grandpa would prefer working with you," Josh said, "but I'd like to be the one who pays for the time you spend on making the party arrangements."

Though anger welled in Tara, she tried not to let it take control.

"The other day I saw an article from something called the *Schuyler Outpost*, dated August 20, 1892," she commented casually. "It talked about hoof-and-mouth disease."

Josh's eyebrows drew together in confusion. "The *Outpost* was the town newspaper back then. Luckily we've never had an outbreak of hoof-and-mouth in the area."

"I disagree... I think *you* have a raging infection right now. You have a lot of nerve trying to pay me for doing Walt a favor. He's my friend and I'm glad to work with him on this." She spoke more loudly than she'd intended.

A dull red crept up Josh's neck. "I wasn't trying to insult you."

"Maybe so, but stop making assumptions about me and everyone else," she advised tightly.

With that, she turned and unlocked the office door to wait for Walt.

LAUREN FINISHED HER SHIFT at the clinic and walked back to her apartment. She was unbelievably tired. Now that the workday was over, her depression came rushing back, along with exhaustion. It was amazing how much energy it had required to push her feelings aside and focus on patients.

She'd done what was necessary and told Carl to find someone who was strong enough to stand by his side and be a true partner. He didn't need a wimp who'd panic because he was in danger or couldn't even voice her opinion if she disagreed with him.

Sometimes doing the right thing was a real "pain in the neck traveling south," as Tara sometimes described it.

Her sister was sitting in the grassy area in front of the apartment, reading a book. Despite everything on her mind, it made Lauren feel good that her sister would simply drop by for a visit.

"Hey."

"Hey, back." Tara cocked her head and frowned. "What's up? You look as if something is wrong."

Lauren's eyes widened. She'd become an expert at hiding unpleasant feelings from people in case they rocked the boat. How had Tara guessed something was going on beneath the mask?

"I..." She bit her lip and blinked back a threatening tear. Part of her wanted to pour everything out to her sister, and another part still worried that Tara would think less of her.

Tara stood and tucked her book in a bag. "Maybe we should go inside to talk."

Mutely Lauren nodded. She unlocked her door, and they went into the apartment. Sinking into the couch, she tucked her legs under her and watched as Tara took the chair opposite.

"Okay," she said, "what's wrong?"

"It's truly silly." Lauren gulped. "It isn't as if I broke up with Carl. We weren't even going out, not really."

Tara winced. "I'm afraid this is my fault. In spite of what you said about not clicking, I thought you liked him. So when he asked for advice, I thought he should give it another try. I'm so sorry."

"Don't blame yourself. I don't want to like him, but I do," Lauren admitted.

"Then what happened?"

"Nothing. I just told him that anything other than friendship was out of the question."

"Is this about you thinking you aren't bold enough?"

Lauren nodded miserably. "Yes, though it's also partly because his work is so dangerous. He could get hurt or killed whenever he goes on duty. Even when he isn't on duty, he's on duty. You should have seen him break up a fistfight one time when we were at the movies. But it's a lot more than that. I'm scared of arguments," she admitted in a rush. "Even when people have small disagreements I get cold chills."

"Why does conflict bother you so much?" Tara asked gently.

"My folks. It was wonderful when they adopted me, but their marriage was in trouble, even then. They argued constantly, and it got to the point that I cringed if anyone raised their voice or got upset. It always felt as if everything was about to get ripped away."

Instead of scorn, Lauren saw sympathy in Tara's eyes. "That must have been awful. You've never said anything about it."

"I...didn't want to tell you because...well, I didn't want you to think I was stupid. Not to mention it seems selfish to complain about my family when you never got adopted. So here we are— you're brave and I'm nothing but a coward."

She was stunned when Tara laughed. "Good grief, Lauren. In some ways you're braver than me. I would *never* have the nerve to give someone a shot or stitch up an injury. But it doesn't matter, anyhow. You're my sister. I've got my own hang-ups from childhood, and yours aren't any worse than mine."

Lauren slowly let the air out of her lungs. "Except you're always confident and put together."

"I learned early not to show weakness. That way nobody can hurt you, because they can't find anything to exploit."

It made Lauren sad, perhaps because Tara sounded so calm and matter-of-fact. For herself, she only remembered living in one foster home before being adopted. Children had come and gone in the Baxter household, and while they had made it clear they were guardians, not real parents, they'd been kind people.

"What did Carl say when you told him you just wanted friendship?" Tara asked.

"He was nice. I mean, he didn't get upset or anything."

Curiously, Lauren knew she might feel better if Carl had pushed harder, but he'd accepted her decision without protest. She supposed that deep down, a lot of women wanted someone who would fight for them, no matter how many barriers were put in their way.

Her spirits lifted marginally as she and Tara ate dinner together. They *were* growing closer. Tara had even recognized she was upset. Before, Emily was the only person who would have seen how she was really feeling.

It was something she could hug to herself when she tried to sleep that night.

JOSH SAT ON THE porch of the foreman's house late into the evening, staring toward his grandparents' home. At some point he'd have to either build his own place or build another one for the foreman. It was okay for now. Clyde and his wife were buying a home in Schuyler and didn't want to move out to the Boxing N. Josh could cover any emergencies that came up at night, and Clyde could always be reached by phone if needed.

At the moment there were other issues to consider.

The annual party had become a well-established tradition, starting with his grandparents' marriage, though the Boxing N had hosted community barn dances for over a hundred years. And it seemed as if everyone had been sad that it might not take place.

But Josh's frustration had mounted that morning when one of the hands mentioned he was supposed to mow the pasture for the event and fill the gopher holes. Once more, things were happening on the ranch without his permission, even without his knowledge. Then he'd learned that Tara was involved, and it had almost felt as if she was taking Grandma Evelyn's place.

Why hadn't Walt asked his daughter to help? Sarah McGregor should be the one planning and organizing, not a prickly city woman.

Suddenly realizing his mom might be upset about it, Josh called her. But before he could say anything about the party, she thanked him for talking his grandfather into holding it, refusing to believe he hadn't been involved in Walt's decision. She felt it was a good sign that he was taking matters into his own hands.

And it was.

When the call was over, Josh took a deep breath and stood. He'd acted like an ass. Unfortunately it wasn't the first time, and it probably wouldn't be thc last.

CHAPTER TEN

THE NEXT SATURDAY MORNING Josh was busy dressing a wound on a cow brought in by Patch Standish. Range cattle didn't enjoy being corralled, and this one was turning a relatively minor case of first aid into a rodeo.

Dodging another kick, Josh saw Tara and his grandfather ride past.

What the devil is going on?

The moment of inattention cost him; the cow landed a hoof in his stomach. Patch snickered. They'd tied the animal well, so it wasn't able to do significant damage, but it had still put some oomph into its indignant kick. They would keep her confined until they were sure she was healing without infection, but in the meantime she was a very cranky gal.

When Josh had finished disinfecting the gash, he quickly went to the horse corral and saddled Lightfoot.

A cold sweat broke out on his brow as he rode in the direction Walt and Tara had gone. He'd stayed away from them both over the past week, but he couldn't ignore it when Walt was doing something unsafe.

What if Grandpa lost control of his horse? He could fall trying to dismount. His slowly healing ligaments and muscles could even be reinjured simply by mounting and stretching his leg over the saddle.

Josh urged his stallion along, praying he wouldn't find a disaster ahead of him.

At length he halted Lightfoot on a rise, gazing in every direction before finally spotting two figures. They seemed to have stopped beneath the shade of a black cottonwood tree and were looking toward the mountains.

Not wanting to thunder up and spook the other horses, Josh slowed Lightfoot to a walk when he got close. Through the rustling of leaves in the breeze, he heard Tara's low, sultry laugh.

Walt must have heard his grandson's approach, because he turned his head.

"Hey, Grandpa," Josh called. Now that he could see everything was all right, he wondered if he'd overreacted. *Again.* "I was concerned when I saw you ride out. I didn't know the doctor had okayed you to ride."

Irritation crossed the old man's face. "I don't need a babysitter. Anyway, I brought Tara along for company."

"I see." Josh knew his tone was dry. Despite the assistance Tara had given with Andrew, it was hard to think of her as adequate support in case of emergency. She probably couldn't even find her way back to the house.

"I'm perfectly all right," Walt emphasized.

Josh hadn't missed that his grandfather was sidestepping the question about the doctor. "Didn't the orthopedist say to take it easy?"

"You don't see me roping cattle or branding them, do you?"

"Riding can be strenuous."

"How? I'm on the finest fence-riding horse on the ranch."

"Zelda is a sweetheart," Josh admitted.

His grandfather *had* chosen well—Zelda was an unflappable mare with a sweet, even gait. Josh sighed, recalling what Tara had said about not treating Walt as if he was a child. It was all too easy to fudge on important things like dignity and pride, though his grandfather was equally guilty on that issue.

"Besides, Tara and I've gone out several times and nothing has happened," Walt announced, his glare daring Josh to say something.

Several times?

How had he missed that? Josh glanced at Tara, but her face remained expressionless. His frustration flared again; it was unlikely his grandfather would have attempted to go riding if she hadn't been there.

"Do you mind if I join you?" he asked.

Walt shrugged, and she shook her head. They started moving again.

The silence was awkward, but Josh ignored it and kept a discreet watch on his grandfather. The tension on Walt's face suggested pain, though it could also stem from annoyance that he'd been caught doing something that would worry the family. It didn't take a psychologist to understand why he'd chosen Tara as his riding companion. After all, she wasn't as invested in keeping his activities within bounds the way his daughter and grandchildren were.

As Tara twisted in the saddle to look at something, Josh reined in his body's response. Her snug jeans and T-shirt revealed curves that reminded him of the minutes they had spent kissing.

Damn it all. He wanted to pound his head on a rock.

As little as he'd wanted her there, he couldn't deny that order was emerging from the chaos in the ranch office. The paychecks were going out regularly, and he'd stopped getting polite calls to remind him about unpaid bills—bills he hadn't known were due because Walt had put them aside to "deal with later."

The efficiency with which online bill paying had been established was amazing. Some of the companies in Schuyler had complicated processes, but Tara had gotten it done, even going in person to pick up authorization forms for him to sign. He'd heard that several were now offering her contracts.

It was hard to admit, but she had better skills for the job than anyone he could have hired locally. She'd even suggested looking into direct deposit for the cowhands' pay, which would save everyone time and money. She was very good at the technical end...if only she wasn't so determined to thwart him in every other way.

"Tara, what do you think of Montana?" he asked when the silence had continued for over a mile.

"As a tourist?" she asked. "Or as someone who doesn't love ranching as much as you?"

Josh clenched his jaw at the dig. "I'm asking your impressions as someone who has spent most of her adult life in foreign cities taking taxis," he returned.

"I've gone into the countryside whenever I could," she said. "The Australian outback is even vaster than Montana. It's compelling."

"You took a tour?"

"Actually, I went on walkabout with an old Aborigine I met on vacation. I really had to join with the land. He sometimes went days without saying a word. But when he did speak, it was always to say something worth hearing. He's one of the wisest people I've ever met."

"I'm surprised he'd take you."

Tara nodded. "So was I, but it was a priceless three weeks. Eventually I had to get back to work, while he continued on his way." She paused before adding reflectively, "I never did learn his name."

Josh tried to picture such a cool, sophisticated woman spending weeks in the rugged circumstances that would have been part of an Aboriginal walkabout. His imagination failed him.

"That still doesn't tell me what you think of Montana."

"It's a beautiful part of the United States. I understand why Lauren decided to move here after coming to Emily's wedding."

It was a reminder that one of his sisters-in-law was close friends with Tara's newfound sister. He'd have to guard his tongue around the family. Their patience with him was already strained.

"I'm surprised you went riding today," he commented. "I thought spending time with your sister was your top priority."

Walt sent him a sour glance but remained silent.

Tara just smiled faintly. "It is, but Lauren is helping at the bloodmobile."

Something on a fence caught Josh's eye. He hesitated before riding down to investigate. A wire had come loose. He dismounted—same as the ranch hands, he carried tools in his saddlebag, and it didn't take long to handle the repairs.

Clyde had just started as foreman, but no matter how good he might be, there would be times when a fence was down or something else had happened. Anyway, the first task Josh had given him was recruiting ranch hands to replace the ones who'd quit. Sad to say, but Clyde would probably be more successful at it than Josh had been.

Mounting again, he urged Lightfoot to trot in Walt and Tara's direction. When he caught up, Tara was alone and his grandfather was some forty feet away, gazing into the distance.

"Is something wrong?" he asked.

"No, he just wanted to be alone for a while."

"I stopped to mend a fence," Josh explained unnecessarily.

"Right."

"I promoted Clyde Hawes to foreman, so things are getting better. I, uh, should thank you for that. Until you pointed it out, I hadn't realized that I was trying to wear too many hats."

Tara fingered Ringo's reins. "I'm sure you would have figured out what you needed to do before long."

"It's nice you aren't rubbing it in."

She laughed and Josh decided he should stop beating himself up for finding such a gorgeous woman attractive. The key was controlling how he handled it. Basically, while a no-strings affair would be pleasant, he doubted Tara was willing, and it probably wasn't a good idea in any case. He should just privately acknowledge his response to her and accept that nothing could come of it.

"The Boxing N is probably one of the largest ranches in Montana, though a lot of the acreage doesn't support many cattle," he said, deciding to stick to something concrete. "We need a fair number of hands just to keep an eye on fence lines."

Tara held up a hand. "Josh, we're riding on a beautiful day through a stunning piece of land. Do you ever just stop and enjoy what you're doing?"

It was a valid question, but she didn't understand. "Look, I've been waiting a long time for this. I have goals for the ranch, which include raising cattle for the organic market. It takes years to get certified and earn a reputation, and I'm already behind the curve."

"There's more to life than ranching."

Sighing, he gazed across the rolling grassland, the more rugged high country rising above it. This section had never been heavily utilized, and never for wintering cattle. Basically, it meant nonorganic feed had never been hauled in for the stock to eat. It was perfect for what he wanted, and in his mind's eye, he saw herds grazing within well-maintained fences. The dividing fences would be necessary to keep organic stock inside, though it was possible the entire ranch could eventually become certified. He'd even designed a special brand for his organic herd.

If he could just get started, in ten years, Boxing N cattle might become a market leader.

Might?

There wasn't any "might" about it. *Nothing* was going to stop him from making it a reality.

TARA SAT QUIETLY in her saddle, recognizing that Josh was lost in his vision for the future. Although she had goaded him about it, she respected his goals, and they sounded financially viable.

Her goals were important to her, as well. In addition to her travels, she wanted to work hard, helping companies organize their record-keeping in accordance with regulations. It was a challenge she enjoyed. Perhaps it wasn't as lofty as growing healthy food, but her work could help people…perhaps a senior citizen with her life savings invested in a company's stock, or a customer who relied on a product for their livelihood.

Yet unlike Josh, she wanted to explore the world along the way.

Tara glanced from Walt to his grandson. The two men were more alike than either of them could admit. Josh was fixated on the future, planning to devote his life to building the kind of ranch he'd dreamed of owning. She wasn't sure he really even saw the beautiful view, only the number of cattle it would support. As for Walt? He was fixated on the past. He'd spent his entire life focused on the Boxing N instead of his family, and now he deeply regretted each of his lost opportunities.

She'd never realized how things could get passed down in families, including mistakes.

Maybe it was a good thing that Josh expected to wait on having a family. From what she'd picked up both from him and from things Walt had said, if he ever *did* get married it would be to a woman who shared his goals. Ultimately, that just meant there'd be another wife who got put last. If she loved ranching, perhaps she wouldn't mind.

With no real experience of what family meant, Tara didn't know what was right and what was wrong. It was hard enough figuring out how to be a sister to Lauren, so she didn't have a prayer of understanding the complicated dynamics of extended clans such as the Nelsons and McGregors.

Tara's mount snorted and tossed his head. "It's okay, Ringo," she soothed, "we're just waiting for Walt."

Josh glanced at her. "Did Grandpa say why he wanted to be alone?"

She bent and patted Ringo's neck, trying to decide what to say. It seemed certain that Walt was thinking about his wife, but Josh probably wouldn't believe her. The irony struck her. For once in her life she'd gotten insight into someone, and she couldn't do anything to help. She was convinced the two men could meet on common ground—their love for Evelyn Nelson. But saying something about it would just make Josh more stubborn.

"Walt has gone through major changes in the last few months," she said carefully. "I'm sure both the past and future are on his mind."

"He could think about those things at home. He's alone there, too, and it's safer."

"Maybe too alone," she said, despite her resolution.

Josh's sober expression seemed to dismiss the possibility. She didn't get it. How could his opinion about his grandparents' marriage be so different from her own?

"Why do you think your grandparents weren't close?" she asked curiously.

"Any number of reasons. They never kissed or held hands. They didn't talk with each other in a way that two people might if they were in love."

"Which way is that?"

Josh looked at Walt, his face sad. "I'm not sure how to explain. Everyone could tell my oldest brother's first marriage was hopeless from the beginning. But it's different with Kayla. I'm sure they argue and have to work things out, but even after a couple of years, they still look at each other as if they've won the grand prize."

Tara wasn't sure if that was the only measure of a good marriage, especially for a man from Walt's generation and upbringing as a tough, close-to-the-land rancher. "Some people are more public about their feelings."

"Yeah, but Trent is the same with Emily, and Alaina is obviously crazy about her husband, Mike." Josh laughed ruefully. "It's annoying sometimes—they're incredibly happy, so Mom is on a marriage kick, figuring my sister Maddie and I should find someone and skip down the aisle, as well. But I'm not interested, and I doubt Maddie is, either."

The way Josh described his siblings' marriages sounded terrific, but if Tara had learned anything in her travels, it was that you couldn't judge by appearances.

"What kind of marriage do your parents have?" she asked.

Josh looked taken aback. "I've never thought that much about it. I'm not sure I know," he murmured as if to himself. "I can tell they're good friends, but I couldn't even say that much about my grandparents. They seemed to live separate lives. Grandma would be tending the garden or painting while Grandpa was out working, either on the ranch or in his office."

He dismounted, and Tara concentrated on the landscape instead of his muscles as he moved.

"There's a spring nearby," Josh told her. "The water is as clear and pure as it gets. Are you thirsty?"

"Um, sure." She swung off her own mount and led Ringo as he headed toward a small rise.

"We shouldn't get out of sight," she urged. "Walt will worry."

"That's okay, it isn't far."

Josh tethered the horses to a branch. Beyond him, Tara saw a small spring bubbling joyously from a rocky opening. The water flowed down the hillside, with wildflowers blooming along the wandering channel.

"How lovely," she exclaimed. It had been a long time since she'd believed in fairy tales, but this was like something out of a storybook.

Josh shrugged. "It's useful. This particular spring has never been known to go dry, even in drought."

She knelt to scoop water into her mouth. In Australia she'd drunk water in the wild while on walkabout, but it had never been this cold and pure.

"Don't you want some?" she asked, standing and looking at Josh.

"Yeah." He turned abruptly, bent and drank heavily.

Walt had ridden closer. "Fill my canteen, will you?" he called. "This is much better than the water at the house."

He tossed the canteen to Tara, who emptied the contents and handed it to Josh. Once it was filled, she carried it back to Walt.

"Mmm," he murmured after taking a long swallow. "That's the best water on the ranch." He gestured to the meandering waterway. "Evelyn threw wildflower seeds out here every fall. I suppose nobody will do it now."

Tara glanced around to see if Josh had heard, but he was still by the spring and she had a feeling Walt hadn't intended him to hear.

She pushed the thought away and decided to

get another drink. Walt was right—it was the best water she'd ever tasted.

JOSH TRIED TO LOOK away from Tara as she drank from the spring again, but her figure was too nicely displayed to make it easy.

Damnation, he didn't want his libido controlling his actions.

To make things worse, his grandfather was watching him with a knowing eye.

"What do you say we head back to the barn?" he asked when Tara had finished and was walking toward them. The sunlight glinted off her honey-gold hair and highlighted her blue eyes.

Walt grunted in agreement. This time Josh was certain that the lines in his face were from pain. He obviously hadn't dared dismount to get a drink.

Tara mounted Ringo and they started off, Walt leading the way, side by side with her. Josh rode fifteen feet behind. He told himself it was to give Walt and Tara space, but the view of her backside was also a powerful incentive.

She appeared to be an excellent rider, managing Ringo with no difficulty.

"When did the Nelsons first come to Montana?" she was asking Walt.

"In 1872. We were the first. The McGregors didn't come until a couple years later, and even then they spent part of their time in Oklahoma."

Josh smiled. The rivalry between his parents'

families would never be forgotten as long as Walt was around. Of course, his McGregor grandparents were also guilty of dredging up the subject. They disputed the date of their arrival, claiming it was a year before the Nelsons. However, at any gatherings where both families were in attendance, the subject was politely avoided.

"What was in Oklahoma?" Tara asked.

"Land and cattle. And later, oil."

"I'll bet there were plenty of people who wished they'd held on to their land once oil became so important."

"Yeah, the McGregors just got lucky. The Nelsons earned their stake another way."

"How was that?"

"It's a family secret."

Josh stared at his grandfather's back in surprise. Was there a part of the Nelson history he didn't know, or was Walt just spinning a story for Tara?

She chuckled, the husky sound making Josh shift uncomfortably. "Let me guess," she said, "you don't know the secret, either."

Walt laughed outright, leaving Josh more stunned than he could remember. Had he *ever* heard his grandfather laugh so heartily?

"You're too smart, young lady," Walt told her. "You're also right. My great-grandfather kept changing the story, and I never got the skinny on it. When I was a lad, I had visions of daring bootleggers, but the money predates Prohibition, so it wouldn't have been profitable enough for a stake in the 1800s."

Josh grew envious as the two continued chatting. He loved his grandfather, but the old guy wasn't the easiest person to know. Grandma Evelyn was the grandparent he'd been close to, and he'd always wondered how a woman with her natural warmth and charm had ended up with Walter Nelson.

When he'd gotten older and understood how it could be between a man and a woman, it had seemed a terrible loss. Evelyn must have been capable of great passion, something that had appeared lacking in her marriage. Nonetheless, she'd been the sort of person who made the best of things, getting active in community affairs and devoting herself to her daughter and grandchildren.

And all the while Walt had been there, putting the ranch first and everything else dead last.

So how had Tara gotten through to Grandpa? It didn't make sense.

Josh regretted the thought as soon as it formed, because he was instantly riveted on her jeans and the way she filled them out. While he'd decided it was okay to be attracted to Tara, provided he didn't do anything about it, it could be a difficult decision to keep.

CHAPTER ELEVEN

TARA WAS BUSY every possible minute over the next week, which was the way she liked to be.

Between party preparations, she finished shifting boxes and other miscellaneous stacks in her search for current paperwork. It was amazing the spots she found things tucked out of sight, old mixed with new. Of course, the most intriguing items were the documents and ledgers from over a hundred years ago, including a Bible with a singed cover. Walt's eyes had gleamed when she'd told him what she'd found so far.

"I wonder if my great-grandfather's journal is around anyplace," he'd mused. "My mother thought it was lost when the first house burned."

Tara had winced, thinking of the history that might have gone up in flames, but she was eager to explore whatever had survived. Both she and Walt had discussed whether they'd find information about the sapphires and what to do if they did.

By Saturday everything was in good shape for the big event. Huge tents had been erected, and the largest barn would be used for dancing. In addition to the pasture prepped for parking, another had a softball field laid out in it. Horseshoes, croquet and volleyball were also available, along with portable bleachers for people who just wanted to watch the various athletics.

Lauren hadn't wanted to go, but Tara convinced her to attend. They arrived before the official starting time, and her sister's eyes widened as they wandered around. The serving tables in the food tent were weighed down with platters and bowls from the caterer and partygoers, the barn was strung with Japanese lanterns, and a country band was already playing.

Tara grinned at her sister's wide-eyed surprise. "Pretty good, isn't it, to get this together in such a short time?"

"No wonder you were busy."

"To be honest, everyone was so enthusiastic about this event, there was practically a stampede of people getting involved."

A tall cowboy immediately claimed Lauren for a dance, and Tara went looking for Walt, only to see Josh talking with a couple of women. She instantly turned the other direction and found Walt sitting with his daughter along the barn wall.

He struggled to his feet. "Here's the gal who pulled this all together," he announced.

"Nonsense," Tara declared. "I simply did what you said. Everyone else was just waiting for the okay."

Sarah McGregor pulled her into a huge hug, and

Tara caught her breath; it was warm and sincere, and for a split second it was the way she'd always imagined a mother's embrace might feel. It was a foolish, sentimental fancy, something she usually avoided.

"Thank you," Sarah murmured. "You've been good for Dad."

Unexpected emotion filled Tara's throat, but before she could say anything, Sarah straightened and waved at her son approaching them.

"Josh, take Tara for a dance. She deserves it after all her hard work."

"That's what I came to do."

Tara couldn't tell whether he was sincere or if a hint of sarcasm tinged his voice.

Together they joined the crowd of couples.

"You don't need to dance with me," she said, trying not to remember how strong and hard his arms had been when they'd kissed. "I'm sure you have other women you want to ask."

"Why do you say that?"

"I saw you chatting them up when I got here, two of them, anyhow."

He frowned. "Chatting them up?"

"Did I get the idiom wrong? I've spent so long working with people who speak English as a second language, I sometimes get mixed up myself."

"No, I just don't appreciate sounding like a guy on the prowl."

"Isn't *every* single man on the prowl?" Tara asked lightly.

"Not necessarily."

"Don't tell me you live as a monk."

His mouth tightened. "I haven't done much socializing since I moved back to Schuyler—I've been too busy. But that won't last. I enjoy dating as long we understand each other."

"And by 'understand each other,' you mean they need to accept you aren't looking for anything permanent, just a good time."

"I'm not shallow. There's nothing wrong with wanting to stay single."

"I agree. I'm not interested in a relationship, either, though for different reasons. It doesn't mean we're shallow."

Tara hoped that was true. At times she felt terribly limited because she avoided getting too involved with people. But that surely meant she was careful, not shallow.

JOSH TRIED TO QUELL the heat settling in the lower half of his anatomy. Tara was a delicious armful, and she danced remarkably well. In fact, as the music picked up, they whirled and did a number of fancy steps he rarely got a chance to try.

His eyes were fixed on hers, and they could have been doing the tango with all the steam they were generating.

Slowly he became aware that most of the dancers had left the floor and were just watching them. With only a few bars left of the song, he swung Tara around and they finished to the sound of applause.

"Nice footwork," Walt declared as they returned to where he was seated. His eyes had that knowing look again, but Josh ignored it. Walt might suspect his grandson was attracted to Tara, but he was sorely mistaken if he thought anything would come of it.

"Thank you, Tara," Josh said formally before turning to his mother. "How about a whirl around the barn floor?" Asking her to dance had been his original intention...along with wanting to hear what Tara might be saying to her and Walt.

"I'd love to."

His mother had been the one who'd taught Josh to dance, so they made a good showing on the floor as well, though he realized that Tara was more striking in her vibrant aqua dress and long, blond hair. Something about her drew attention.

"Tara looks lovely tonight," Sarah said as if reading his thoughts.

Josh shrugged, knowing his mother's matchmaking tendencies.

"She must have gone shopping in Schuyler," he said casually. "Candy McCoy is wearing the same dress."

He'd been talking to Candy and her friend Marie when Tara had come into the barn. He wasn't a fashion aficionado and wouldn't have realized the dresses were similar if it hadn't been for Candy's reaction. Her eyes had flared with anger while she muttered to Marie that the store had promised no one else had bought that style.

While Tara might have gotten the dress after Candy, the shop would have been technically correct in any case. Tara's gown was a rich aqua, while Candy's was neon red and a size too small, possibly to draw attention to her generous bust.

"Candy certainly enjoys standing out in a crowd," Sarah commented, and from her tone Josh realized his mother didn't like the youngest McCoy sister any better than his sisters did. Ordinarily Mom liked everyone.

"She succeeded tonight," Josh said lightly, hoping to give the impression that neither woman was important to him.

"I don't think so. Haven't you noticed that most people are watching Tara?"

"Probably because she's new in town and they're intrigued by the separated-twins story. Say, did you know Grandpa has been going riding lately?"

Sarah made a face. "He told me that's what he planned to do."

"Didn't you try to stop him?"

She gazed at him with loving, exasperated eyes. "Of course I tried, all the while knowing it wouldn't do a lick of good. Your grandfather has his faculties intact, and I'm not ready to treat him as if he's in his dotage."

"Okay, okay." He twirled her across the floor, hoping to forestall further discussion about his grandfather *or* Tara.

LAUREN WAS ENJOYING herself more than she'd expected…as long as she wasn't paying attention to Carl Stanfield as he danced with the local girls. Some of them were quite attractive, too.

She didn't lack dance partners herself, but it was strange. She and Tara were identical twins, yet it felt to her as if Tara was the truly pretty one. Mostly it was because Tara carried herself with confidence and knew how to accessorize properly. Emily had the knack, too, though she rarely bothered with her appearance. Well…that wasn't true any longer. After meeting Trent, Emily had adopted a sexier style.

Lauren scrunched her nose. She and Tara had bought their dresses at the same store in Schuyler, yet her sister managed to look as if she'd stepped out of a Paris fashion show. It was a puzzle how they could be so much alike and yet so different.

The band was playing a lively tune she didn't recognize. According to Lauren's dance partner, Grayson Welch, it had been written by a local musician over a hundred years ago. As the song ended, Grayson whirled her around in a flourish, right in front of Carl.

"May I claim the next one…as a friend?" Carl asked after Grayson had thanked her for the dance.

That was nice. He was making it clear that he wouldn't press for anything else.

"Um, sure," she said.

The band started playing another classic, "Make the World Go Away." *Of course.* It was like teasing an addict with the drug they craved, in her case, with one of her favorite romantic songs, filled with yearning, regret and hope.

Carl's strong arms swung her among the other dancers, making her tingle. She closed her eyes, losing herself in the music and sensations cascading through her body.

"Hey," he whispered, guiding her toward the edge of the dance floor. "Are you light-headed? It's warm—maybe we should go out for some fresh air."

Lauren almost declined, but his protectiveness filled her with guilty pleasure. Besides, it *was* warm in the barn, and the area outside was beautiful.

They exited at the far end, away from the food tent and other activities, and walked toward a stand of trees. In the distance the crack of a bat hitting a softball sounded through the evening, followed by faint cheers, but on this side there were few people.

A cooling breeze ruffled the grass, and everything was bathed in the long rays of the sun.

"Mmm," she murmured. "It's lovely out here. The air tastes golden."

Carl nodded. "This is my favorite time of day. At the risk of sounding poetic—which I'm not—it's sort of magical."

Lauren shot him a quick glance. It would be wonderful if he'd escorted her outside to sneak a kiss, but he was obviously too honorable. Her contradictory desires were frustrating. One minute she was glad he'd backed off, the next she was wishing he hadn't.

A flash of irritation went through Lauren. Her ex-boyfriend had crashed through her reservations and fears with the subtlety of a bull in heat. Carl could have done the same, but no, he was a gentleman. If he'd persisted, she probably would have succumbed eventually.

Suddenly it struck her that *wishing* Carl had persisted was another form of the cowardice she despised.

She lifted her hand and touched his face, moving closer. His eyes darkened.

"Lauren?"

"Magic moments can be outside of time, can't they?" she whispered.

"Yes."

The next thing she knew, his lips were on hers.

Seduced by the enchantment of the light and the moment, she kissed him back wholeheartedly.

When his arms loosened, Lauren pressed closer, not wanting the magic to end. Obligingly, he tightened his grip again, exploring the depths of her mouth with his tongue.

It was only when voices in the distance intruded that he drew back, took her hand and headed toward the barn as though nothing had happened. But he was breathing raggedly and through his fingers she could feel the rapid pace of his pulse.

"I'm sorry," he said.

"Hey, we decided it was a moment out of time," Lauren reminded him. She didn't want to regret her impulsive behavior; it represented a brief conquest of courage over fear.

"You're right," Carl agreed. "But we'd better go inside now, or I'll be in the doghouse with all the men who were waiting to ask you for a dance."

She fixed a neutral smile on her face, and as they entered the barn again, Roger Dean arrived to invite her onto the floor. "Sorry, Sheriff, even a guy with a gun and a badge can't monopolize one of the prettiest women around," he said with a wink at Carl.

"My loss—I didn't think to bring either with me," Carl answered easily.

Roger was a good dancer, and Lauren loved the song the band was playing, but nothing tingled as he swung her in a circle.

Because Walt wasn't easily mobile, Tara divided her time between the dance floor and checking on the food tent and other areas.

"I feel guilty," Sarah McGregor told her when they crossed paths again close to nine in the evening. There was still a glow in the sky, but the pastures being used for sports were already brightly lit with the lights Walt had rented. "I should be looking after everything instead of you being stuck with it."

"Don't worry, I'm happiest when I stay busy."

Sarah laughed merrily. "You're sweet. Truthfully, I've never had any responsibilities at the Nelson dance. My parents took care of everything while I was growing up, and when I was an adult it was pleasant to attend the party just as a guest. My mother encouraged it. Looking back, I wonder if she was protecting her position as hostess."

"Or maybe she wanted to give you a chance to relax," Tara suggested. "Walt told me you often entertain out at your ranch and that your husband has elevated barbecuing to an art form."

"Yes, Dad has finally managed to recognize a *few* good qualities in Parker McGregor." Sarah's eyes twinkled. "It was at the annual Boxing N party that Parker and I fell in love. I was a senior in high school and only seventeen, because I'd skipped a year. We were married that July. Mom was concerned about my age, but she was happy for me and Dad didn't seem to mind *too* much."

Tara was tempted to ask Sarah about her parents' marriage but worried it would be intrusive and might make her sad. Even now her expression shifted between pleasure and reflection, with hints of sorrow.

A man Tara remembered seeing at the hospital waved from across the tent, and Sarah waved back. "That's Parker reminding me that I've got to go out to the softball field," she explained. "I'm going to cuddle my grandbabies while their parents play ball."

"Have a good time." Tara snagged a cookie and started back to the barn. To her surprise, Josh stopped her on the way.

"Tara, I want to apologize."

"For what?" she asked. They'd barely crossed paths over the past week. "You didn't step on my toe while we were dancing and haven't insulted me in days."

His jaw tensed then relaxed. "I deserve that, but I'm talking about the way I reacted when I learned about the party. I was frustrated because something else was happening on the ranch and no one had consulted me about it. It wasn't fair to put that on you."

Josh was exhibiting something Tara admired— the ability to admit when he was wrong and apologize sincerely—but it made her uncomfortable. She was reluctant to see his better side, although she didn't want to examine her reasons for that reluctance too closely.

She was, however, able to understand his frustration.

"That's all right. It must be difficult in these circumstances."

"Even so, I'd like to think I haven't been acting completely in character since the, um…accident."

His voice had become choked, and Tara sympathized. The loss of his grandmother had obviously been hard on the whole family, especially the way it had happened. Having to then face the situation on the ranch must have made it more of a struggle. Even she knew that life had to continue after a painful loss, however difficult it might be.

"Are you claiming you've never lost your temper before?" she asked with a teasing smile, hoping to lighten the atmosphere. She was good at idle chitchat and quick repartee; it was when things got emotional that she struggled.

"Of course not," he replied in a similar tone. "I'm a veritable saint."

"Doesn't sainthood get boring?"

"Not at all. When I'm bored, I just polish my halo."

"It's nice to know you keep yourself occupied."

"Uncle Josh," a voice called. "Can I talk to you?"

"On my way," he called back.

Tara slipped past him into the barn, only to run into Andrew Whitlan. The young ranch hand's black eye had nearly disappeared, and he sported a red scar where Belle's hoof had struck his forehead.

"Hi, Andrew. You're looking better."

"I'm doing great. Come with me a second, I want to introduce you to my girlfriend."

Andrew steered her over to a young girl standing next to an older couple. "This is Ellie. Ellie, this is Tara."

"Hi, Ellie," Tara said. "Now I have a face to go with your voice."

Ellie grinned. "Thanks for helping take care of Andrew. He says you helped lift him into the truck and everything. And you were so nice when you called to tell me about him being hurt."

Tara smiled back. "I was happy to do whatever I could."

"I saw you earlier, with Josh McGregor. Jeez, you're a good dancer."

After they chatted a few minutes, Tara circled the edge of the dance floor to find Walt. He was seated in the same place as before, leaning forward.

"I was wondering if you were going to ignore me for the rest of the evening," he said gruffly.

"Only half of it," she returned.

He sat back in his chair and sighed. "In days past, Evelyn and I got applause on the dance floor, too. Guess my dancing days are over."

"Hey, don't be so pessimistic," she chided. "It's

a slow number right now. Why don't we give it a shot?"

His face brightened, and he pushed himself to his feet. "Why not?"

As they joined the others in a waltz, Tara saw Josh come back inside and watch them. His expression was impossible to read.

CARL MADE SURE he partnered with a wide variety of women—young, old, in between, married and single. All the while he was mentally kicking himself for giving in to temptation.

He had deeper feelings for Lauren than he'd ever experienced in the past, but he couldn't push her into something that would make them both miserable.

His father's job had ultimately driven his parents apart, his mother unable to deal with the stress of being married to a cop. He understood, in a way. It had to be hard to know the person you loved could leave for work and never come home again.

Ironically, now that his father was retired, they'd remarried. Yet they would never get back the lost years. Nor was his mother thrilled that her son had chosen law enforcement as a career instead of medicine like his sister.

He still remembered his mother's expression when she'd talked to him after his graduation from the police academy. Her words were practically burned into his brain.

You've made your decision, and I'm trying to respect it. But when you choose a wife, make sure she can accept your career. Your dad and I married right out of high school, and he decided during college to become a police officer. In a way, I never forgave him for it.

Curiously, when his father had been shot after the divorce, his mother had rushed to the hospital, staying at his bedside until the danger had passed. It had been surreal to see her skillfully manage the physicians and nurses, refusing to let them get away with vague answers or comforting platitudes. She'd dealt with it so well that he'd always wondered why she hadn't been able to handle the marriage.

Whatever the explanation for his parents' divorce, Carl knew all too well that it took a particular kind of personality to handle being a law enforcement wife.

Of course, it didn't mean Lauren couldn't work it out. She'd warned him off, but it was possible she would change her mind. He'd had more than one colleague whose girlfriend was initially resistant and then came to understand and be willing to accept the challenge.

On the other hand, he didn't want to hurt Lauren and had told her they could just be friends. He'd fudged on the note sent with the pansies. It had been an unconscious duplicity that he regretted, so now it would be up to her to change the conditions of their relationship. Of course, *she'd* kissed *him*...mixed signals again, and he wasn't sure what he was supposed to do.

Josh was restless. The Boxing N community party had always been his favorite social occasion, but his feelings were still mixed about having the event less than a year after losing Grandma Evelyn.

He'd danced, eaten, played softball on a family team formed by his nephew, but memories of his grandmother still filled his head.

When he returned to the barn after the game, the sight of Tara and his grandfather instantly grabbed his attention. They were waltzing. Slowly, to be sure, but dancing. Why did she *do* things like that? She had to realize how much pain it caused Grandpa.

More than that, it was a reminder of how everything had changed. The dance floor was a place where Walt and Evelyn had seemed to connect, and it had always been a treat to see them out there. Now Grandma was gone and Walt was dragging his leg where only a year before, he'd danced the night away.

Going over to them, Josh tapped his grandfather's shoulder. "May I cut in?"

A speculative gleam entered Walt's eyes before he nodded and relinquished Tara.

"People are going to talk," she said when Walt was seated again. "Doesn't more than one dance with the same woman constitute a long-term commitment in your book?"

"Very amusing."

"You didn't need to rescue your grandfather," Tara continued, showing she'd understood his motives for cutting in. "Walt is capable of making up his own mind."

"He shouldn't be dancing," Josh gritted through his teeth.

"Right. He shouldn't be dancing, he shouldn't be riding and he shouldn't be making any decisions. In other words, he shouldn't be living."

Josh was appalled. "I never thought that."

"I didn't mean you wanted him to stop breathing," she returned. "In fact, you're desperate to protect him from physical harm so he'll *keep* breathing. But Walt is obviously the kind of man who needs a reason to live."

"You barely know him. He has a family who loves him and needs him. He knows that."

She turned her copper-flecked eyes up to him. "I'm talking about quality of life."

"Do we have to go over this again? Walt's life has always been about the ranch," Josh murmured. "But he can't run it alone or do a fraction of the work needed to keep the place afloat. He just won't accept it."

"Now we're back to whether *you* run the ranch or not."

"Everything is connected."

"No doubt."

The song ended, with Josh ensuring they were on the opposite side of the barn from where his grandfather was sitting.

They muttered polite, insincere platitudes, and Tara walked away, the soft fabric of her dress shifting and flowing around her figure.

Josh sighed, wondering if his nephew wanted to play another softball game. That was one option. The other was running to his house for a cold shower.

CHAPTER TWELVE

A FEW DAYS AFTER the Boxing N party, Tara blinked at the yellowed sheaf of papers she'd unearthed from an old bureau in the back room of the office. She'd planned to put it with the rest of the historical records for future review, but something had caught her attention—the word *sapphires*.

The pages were loose, but had once been part of an ancient record book. They'd fallen behind one of the drawers and must have gone unnoticed for an undetermined length of time.

Sapphires found on south ridge.

Following the notation was a series of numbers and letters that didn't mean anything to Tara but were probably intended as directions or coordinates.

Weeks earlier she'd searched the internet for *sapphires* and *Montana*. Sapphires had been found in Montana during the latter part of the nineteenth century. The various articles were full of descriptions about alluvial deposits and other things that didn't mean much to her.

Trembling with excitement, Tara typed everything from the yellowed pages into the computer and emailed it to the address she'd set up for Walt. Next she scanned the pages and printed additional copies. That way she could be sure the information would be preserved.

Walt was at another doctor's appointment, or she would have gone to tell him immediately.

As she returned to her other work, she couldn't stop thinking about all the questions that had occupied her since she'd first learned there could be sapphires on the Boxing N. Could those be the mysterious source of cash that Walt had mentioned? Yet the Nelsons had arrived in Montana before sapphires had been found in the state.

And would the average rancher of the 1800s have recognized a raw sapphire if he found one? The pictures on the internet didn't look impressive, and it would be hard to determine gemstone quality without proper training.

With the self-discipline she'd learned over the years, Tara forced herself to focus on her work and was startled when Walt came through the door a short while later.

"Walt," she exclaimed, excitement flooding back, "look at what I found today."

She picked up the pages inside their protective sleeves and brought them to him.

Walt sat reading and rereading for several minutes. "Holy cow," he murmured. "You found it. My great-grandfather claimed he'd found sapphires, but he was an old man by then and nobody be-

lieved him. Granddad said his father had written
it all down, but he thought the records were lost
when the old homestead burned."

"Instead they were stuffed behind the bottom
drawer of the old bureau in the back room."

As she'd hoped, there was a sparkle of boyish
enthusiasm in Walt's eyes. He pored over the papers again and again.

"I wasn't sure what all those numbers and letters and so on meant," Tara said.

"I'll have to study the old deeds and plat maps."
He glanced at her. "Let's go through the rest of that
stuff right now."

She collected the two boxes of records from more
than a century ago and sat next to Walt. She slipped
a page into a protective sleeve, handed it to Walt,
did the same with another and started reading.

Hours later, Tara glanced at her watch. "I hate
to say it, but I have to leave. It's past seven and I
promised Lauren I'd come over."

"Can we pick this up first thing in the morning?"

"Absolutely." She grinned. "This is much more
fun than payroll records."

Walt headed for his house while Tara locked up
the office. She half waved at Josh when she saw
him on his porch, and he half waved back at her.
They'd been on stiffly polite terms since the party.
She thought about stopping to tell him about the
journal but decided it was Walt's news to share.

Josh had resisted the sapphire story before, but now they had evidence.

Josh watched Tara's Toyota Camry leave. She'd stayed later than usual, probably because she and his grandfather had been talking together in the office. Tara and Walt had formed an inexplicable friendship and he couldn't understand how a globe-trotting princess had connected with an elderly, self-contained Montana rancher.

Then realization suddenly struck.

Tara had grown up in foster homes without anyone to count on. She was probably looking at Walt as a sort of father or grandfather figure.

The humor was hard to escape. Walt had hardly been a grandfather to his own grandchildren.

Josh shook himself. He was being ungrateful. The old guy was hard to know, but there had been plenty of good times on the Boxing N when Josh was growing up.

The next morning he worked near the office, keeping watch, and was able to meet Tara when she arrived. Her eyes were sparkling.

"Hi," he greeted her. "I guess yesterday was a full day."

"Yes." She seemed to be brimming with some sort of inner delight. "What did you think when Walt told you the news?"

For the first time in ages Josh had gone to bed

early. He hadn't spoken to his grandfather the previous evening.

"We didn't talk last night," Josh explained. "What's up?"

"No, it's his baby." Her face brightened as she glanced at the main house. "Oh, good, here he is."

Josh was surprised his grandfather was already up and around. In days past, he'd begun work by 5:00 a.m., but things had changed since the accident. There must have been something he found exciting to get him out so early.

They waited as Walt slowly made his way from the house to the office. Josh was impatient, wondering what was coming next. Did his grandfather have an idea that would further derail his plans for the ranch? Hell, what if it was something about that sapphire myth?

It didn't help that a fresh, sweet scent was coming from Tara, a faint combination of floral and mint, as though she'd just stepped from the shower with her teeth freshly brushed and her hair wrapped in a towel. It wasn't the most comfortable image for a man who'd been celibate for so long.

Somehow, the thought made Josh feel better. Tara had simply shown up in his life at the moment his libido was waking up and asserting itself again. It explained why he sometimes thought about her in the middle of the night or out riding fences.

"Morning, Josh." Walt flashed a smile at Tara. "Did Tara tell you what she found?"

"She's saving it for you," Josh told him, deciding that staying calm and disinterested was the best approach.

They all stepped inside.

To avoid Tara, Josh hadn't been in the office since signing checks for the last payroll. Now he glanced around in reluctant appreciation. Rather than the familiar magpie's nest of papers and miscellaneous junk, it was clean and organized, clearly a working office. It might even be the first time it had ever looked that way.

Walt settled into an easy chair with a grunt of relief, and Josh sat opposite.

"There's coffee?" Josh asked in surprise, catching the scent of a freshly brewed pot.

"I started setting the timer," Tara explained. She filled three mugs, handing one to Walt and another to Josh. "There's cream and sugar," she told him.

Josh hesitated. The truth was, in the morning he preferred his coffee both sweet and creamy. Walt had always given him a hard time about drinking it that way. But he was an adult now, not a teenager looking for approval.

"Thanks," he said, fixing his mug the way he liked it.

"Tara makes darned good coffee," Walt told him.

Josh took a swallow and had to agree. It was considerably better than the crap *he* brewed each morning.

"Take a look at this," said his grandfather, pulling a sheet of paper from the envelope Tara had removed from a locked file drawer.

It was a photocopy, and Josh read the old-fashioned writing in silence. So it *was* about the sapphire goose chase. "Interesting."

"It's astounding," Walt exclaimed. "We might have sapphires on the Boxing N, just the way my great-grandfather claimed."

"Unlikely. He wrote this after gems were found in other parts of Montana. I'm sure he believed he'd found them, but it was probably wishful thinking. No sapphires have ever been discovered around Schuyler."

Josh didn't repeat that he'd looked into it as a kid, and when he'd gotten old enough to go off on his own, he'd searched the Boxing N from one end to the other. After that he'd focused on collecting less valuable specimens, such as Montana agates and smoky quartz. It would be great to share Walt's excitement, but the chance of there being gems on the ranch was exceptionally slim.

"Just because none have been found, that doesn't mean they don't exist," Walt insisted.

"Sure," Josh agreed, not wanting to argue the point; he didn't want Walt to get his hopes up. "I'll order another geological survey if we ever figure out where your great-grandfather thought he found them. But there's absolutely nothing to go on in the survey from ten years ago."

He glanced at Tara; it wasn't hard to see her

anger on Walt's behalf. A thread of amusement went through Josh. When he got right down to it, her staunch defense of the old man was admirable.

"Believe what you want, which is nothing. I'll believe Granddad's stories about his dad," Walt declared stubbornly.

Tara stood abruptly.

"Do you have something else to show me?" Josh asked.

She regarded him coolly. "It's just time to get my day started. I'm sure you're eager to do the same."

"Yeah." He swallowed the last of his coffee and looked at his grandfather. "We can get geologists to check it out again. Perhaps someone from the university might be interested when classes start this fall."

Walt simply nodded.

Josh thought about Tara and Walt's excitement, and was uneasily aware that he'd been the one to puncture the balloon.

When had he turned into a dull grown-up?

TARA DROVE TO Lauren's apartment that evening, hoping her sister would understand what she wanted to do.

Once Josh had left that morning, Walt had spent hours poring over the old maps and records.

"Let's not wait," she'd said in the midafternoon. "Let's look for the sapphires. Just the two of us."

His face brightened. "I'd like that. I'm sure the spot my great-grandfather described is near where Evelyn and I used to camp. We can bring supplies on pack horses and stay as long as it takes."

Although Tara had suggested the idea weeks earlier, she'd thought they'd go out and look for an afternoon, not take an extended camping trip. But why not? Ultimately, it was no different than exploring the Australian outback or mountain climbing in Switzerland, and she'd enthusiastically pursued *those* undertakings.

Besides, Walt's face had been eager, energized by the prospect, and Tara wanted to support his new interest in life. He'd quickly assured her that he felt able and willing to take on the discomfort of camping.

"I'll go alone, if you can't," he said. "There's no one else I'd want to take."

Having a friend was new to Tara, but she had the feeling this could be the difference between remaining a pleasant companion and something deeper. Even so, she hadn't given him a final agreement, explaining that she needed to discuss it with her sister since the search would be longer than she'd anticipated. After all, getting to know Lauren was the reason she'd come to Schuyler in the first place.

So after dinner, she sat and told the story to Lauren, whose eyes grew wide with amazement and a touch of wonder.

"He says he's going regardless," Tara finished, "but I'm afraid to let him be out there alone."

"You have to go," her sister agreed. "For his sake and yours. It's the kind of thing you love." She laughed. "Actually, I wish I could go with you."

"Walt wouldn't mind. Can you get some time off?"

"Not on such short notice," Lauren said regretfully.

"That's too bad. I'm going to stay in Schuyler longer, to make up for my absence. That way we'll have the full three months together that we'd originally planned."

Lauren looked pleased, but also wistful. "That's nice. I just hate to think of you leaving at all."

"Emily is here," Tara reminded her. "Besides, it's easy to stay in touch these days. And there's all my frequent flyer miles. We can both use them."

The assurances seemed to cheer Lauren, and Tara went home to pull out her rough-terrain clothing, assessing what else she might need for a horseback camping trip into the mountains. Walt wanted to leave in four or five days, so there wasn't much time to get ready.

Josh crossed her mind. There was no question he'd disapprove of what they were doing. But since it would get his grandfather out of the way for a while, maybe he'd take the opportunity to make a few of the changes that were so important to him.

Tara conditioned the leather on her boots. Admittedly, she was starting to sympathize with Josh. He cared about Walt and worried about him. Even so, this trip was Walt's decision, and Josh's potential reaction shouldn't bother her...except it did.

"WHAT DO YOU WANT, an invitation?" Carl snapped at the cat he'd recently adopted.

Samson sat on the floor, tail flicking in disapproval. He couldn't have said it more plainly: *You're lousy company and I'm not sure I want to be near you.*

Carl released a heavy breath. "Okay, buddy, I'm sorry." His temper was wearing thin, mostly because he hadn't slept well since the Boxing N party. He held out a handful of cat treats. "Come on, you deserve 'em, fella."

Carl had already discovered the six-month-old kitten was generally mellow, and unlike some felines, he didn't hold a grudge. Samson also ate voraciously, growing in leaps and bounds.

As Samson gobbled the treats out of his hand, Carl thought about Lauren's childhood desire to be a professional kitten holder. She'd like Samson.

He rubbed behind the cat's huge ears and listened to his rumbling purr, reminiscent of a rusty motorboat. Much as Carl appreciated felines, they weren't a substitute for human company.

Later that afternoon Carl saw Lauren's car in the grocery store parking lot and convinced himself that he needed milk.

They ran into each other in the produce section...after he'd walked around the store to locate her. They chatted about the growing trend toward organic and the fact that Schuyler was slow in joining the movement.

"Emily says organic is considered too 'new age' in Schuyler," Lauren said. "But I can usually find the basics, and the store is great about ordering stuff for me."

"I never thought of asking."

"You should. The manager is quite cooperative."

Carl knew Jeff Browning. Aside from the town's eagerness to make Lauren happy, Jeff was a single man in his thirties with a lively interest in the opposite sex.

"That's good to know," Carl murmured. "I haven't seen your sister for a few days. She hasn't left, has she?"

"She left today to go camping in the mountains with Walt Nelson."

"Really?" Carl was surprised. Walt had a reputation for not getting along with people, so it was hard to imagine him taking anyone camping.

"Yes. Well, it's was nice to see you."

With a polite smile Lauren headed toward the bread aisle while a harsh breath hissed from Carl's lungs. He'd invented an excuse to see her and hadn't even made it meaningful. But after all, they had agreed to be friends and, aside from a slip at the party, they could surely manage it. Friends saw each other from time to time and even did things together.

As he strode from of the store, without any milk, he saw Lauren loading groceries into her car. His automatic reaction was to offer assistance, but he stopped, knowing it was ridiculous; she only had a few bags and would have them loaded by the time he arrived.

Feeling like a lovesick puppy, Carl waved at Lauren and drove out of the parking lot.

JOSH REMOVED A handwritten message that had been taped to his door and stared at it in disbelief.

We've gone to look for the sapphires. Don't go fussing about the payroll checks. Tara put them on the top shelf of the locked cabinct, ready to sign and she says you know what buttons to push for the next set. See you when we get back. Grandpa

We?
His grandfather could only have meant him and Tara.

The paper crumpled in Josh's fist. How could she have agreed to such a thing? Despite everything he'd said, Tara clearly didn't have a clue how fragile his grandfather's health had become. Walt's limp *alone* should have told her it was a bad idea.

Besides, it was a wild-goose chase in the first place.

Thoughts raced through Josh's head. Ten years ago, with Walt's permission, he'd arranged for the geologist's survey and had specifically asked to be notified if there was any potential to the family legend. After finishing, the geologist had said that although nobody could be a hundred percent certain, no evidence of sapphires had been found. Walt had seen the report, so why was he doing such a crazy-ass thing?

And the message didn't say where he and Tara had gone. The ranch was huge. Finding them up in the hills would be difficult. Walt didn't have a satellite phone— that being one of those modern contraptions he despised.

Josh hurried to the barn.

Patch was there and confirmed Walt and Tara's departure several hours earlier.

"Did my grandfather tell you where they were headed?" he asked, trying to keep the edge out of his voice.

"No. Seemed real excited, though, about getting away from doctor's appointments and such. Maybe he left some information at the house."

Josh ground his teeth. Walt should have been specific in his message. Keeping people informed of your whereabouts was simply common sense.

He went to the main house. There was a bulletin board in the kitchen that the family had always used for messages. Nothing current had been posted, though Josh's throat tightened when he saw various notes in his grandmother's writing. A shopping list. A reference to Alaina's pregnancy. Several reminders to call different people.

Why hadn't Grandpa taken them down?

A sick feeling in his stomach, Josh walked through the house. It was surprisingly clean and well dusted, but he found nothing to tell him where his grandfather and Tara had gone.

Maybe they'd left a note with the payroll checks in the ranch office. But there was nothing there, either, nor could he locate the papers with the old coordinates. He checked his emails, hoping for a message from Tara, and absently signed the checks for Clyde to distribute.

The other possibility was Lauren Spencer. He grabbed the phone, only to realize he didn't have her number. A quick call to the phone company revealed it was unlisted. But Emily would have her number and address. He called and tried to keep the inquiry low-key. There was no point upsetting anyone else.

Then he punched in Lauren's number.

"Hello?" Over the phone her voice sounded remarkably similar to her sister's.

"Hey, Lauren, it's Josh McGregor. Listen, did

Tara leave any information with you about her camping trip?"

"Y-yes," Lauren said after a brief silence.

Relief hit him. "Great. I need it."

"Tara told me it was only for emergencies."

"This *is* an emergency."

He heard her quick intake of breath through the phone. "What happened?"

"Grandpa is out there when he should be home. That's what." It wasn't quite a yell, but it came close.

"Oh. I...I don't think that qualifies, Josh. Listen, I'd better go." And she disconnected.

Josh immediately drove into town and knocked on the door of her apartment.

"I had a feeling it was you," Lauren said when she answered.

"Look, I'm sorry I got testy on the phone, but I'm worried about Grandpa." Josh gave her what he hoped was a persuasive smile. "And you *can't* be happy about Tara taking off like this. I need to know where they've gone."

"Tara gave me the information and said it was in case they didn't get back by a certain time."

"Please understand. I know you haven't treated Grandpa at the clinic, but he isn't in good shape. We've already lost Grandma Evelyn, and I don't know what we'd do if something else happened to him."

Josh recognized the sympathy in her eyes. Why

couldn't it have been *Lauren* who'd made friends with his grandfather instead of her impossible sister?

"Okay," she finally agreed.

He waited while she fetched a sheet of paper.

"I made a copy for you," she told him.

"Great."

"Be careful, Josh. You need to think about what you're doing."

It was a gentle repeat of her warnings at the clinic, but this time he suspected she was talking about more than getting into stupid accidents.

"I know. But Grandpa should have thought more about this, too." He didn't add that Tara should have used her brain, as well.

Tara didn't care about Grandpa the way his family did. How could she? She was a friend, not a relative. Yet as soon as the thought formed, Josh knew it was unfair. Tara had connected with Walt in a way he'd needed…a way no one else had been able to do. But it was still reckless to go on a prospecting trip with him.

Josh checked the position of the sun as he hurried back to his truck. Generally he didn't bother wearing a watch, since ranching put him in tune with the rhythms of the land and sky. Now he realized it was later than he'd thought.

First he studied the information Tara had neatly typed out for her sister. On the back was a rough map that showed where they were headed. It was

one of the most rugged sections of the ranch—
Smaug's Mountain—a name the family had given
it decades before when they'd become enamored
with J. R. R. Tolkien's books. It would take several hours of fast riding to get there.

He gave Tara credit for at least telling *someone* where they were going. With the map and
hard work getting supplies together, he'd be able
to leave by sunrise.

CHAPTER THIRTEEN

TARA HUMMED WHILE SHE stirred a pot of stew over the campfire. It didn't smell bad—fresh air and excitement added savor. The food would get less inspiring once the fresh stuff was used up and freeze-dried took over, but Tara had subsisted on far less when needed. Heck, she had a week's worth of food in her pack alone, just with the bags of trail mix she'd brought. With the supplies they'd brought in on the pack horses, they could stay for a couple of months.

"This thing looks ridiculous," Walt proclaimed.

She glanced over to where he was seated in the bright blue plastic air chair she'd brought...though she hadn't told him about it until they'd arrived.

"It looks better with the cloth thrown over it."

"Yeah, well, I guess it's more comfortable than a rock," Walt acknowledged. He'd snorted in disgust upon first seeing it, but when she'd convinced him to give it a try, his attitude had shifted. It had taken even less convincing for him to use the raised air bed she'd sneaked onto one of the pack horses.

His face had been drawn and pale when they'd arrived the previous afternoon, and she'd wondered if he regretted the trip. But his determination while setting up camp had convinced her otherwise. Then he'd introduced her to a pool fed by both hot and cold springs that was sheer heaven; the ache in their muscles had melted away in the swirling mineral water.

"You should have brought a chair for yourself," he said. "That way we could have a proper living room."

She chuckled.

They had spent the morning searching for alluvial deposits. Tara's research had indicated those would be the most likely places to find the gems. Shortly before noon they had staked out a place to dig and then returned to camp to have lunch.

"We should get started right after we eat," Walt told her. "Don't want to waste these long days."

"Nope."

She handed him a bowl and sat on a nearby log with her own.

"Not bad," he said. "Is there a French spin to it?"

"Actually, it's the way an acquaintance in Japan makes her stew."

Once they'd finished eating, Tara did the dishes at one of the hot springs and returned to the campsite. Walt was asleep and she read a book, waiting until he woke naturally.

An hour later he shook himself and yawned. "You shouldn't have let me nod off, but at least this satisfies our bargain for the day."

Tara eyed him. While making plans for the trip, she'd asked him to agree to a nap each afternoon, or she wouldn't go. She suspected he was secretly relieved about the deal they'd struck—he could preserve his pride and still get the rest he needed.

"It wasn't long, but I guess it'll do. Ready to go prospecting?"

"I've been ready since I was a kid listening to Granddad tell his father's story."

Suddenly there were sounds in the distance of heavy animals moving through brush. Walt stood and grabbed his rifle, swinging it to his shoulder with the ease of long practice. Tara had been surprised to see the weapon in their supplies, but he'd explained it was a precaution, in case they encountered a bear or mountain lion. The idea of having to kill such a magnificent creature horrified her, but he claimed it was mostly to scare them off.

Tensely, they waited. A minute later they saw a horse and rider, followed by a pack horse on a lead, coming through a sparsely wooded section to the southeast of them.

It was Josh.

"Holy cow, kid," Walt grumbled when Josh got closer, lowering his rifle. "It isn't safe to creep up on a man that way."

"I was hardly creeping," Josh retorted. "You've had me in your sights for over a hundred feet."

"What are you doing here?" Walt demanded.

"What do you think? I thought you had better sense than to pull a stunt like this."

"I'm a grown man, not a senile fool. I made the choice and I'm the one who has to live with it."

Josh looked at Tara, his eyes sparking in disgust. "I can't believe you, either."

The injustice of it infuriated Tara. She and Walt had taken careful precautions, and they weren't neophytes when it came to living in the rough. Josh knew that, yet he was treating her like an idiot and Walt like a senile old man who couldn't be trusted.

"Apparently it has escaped your notice, Mr. McGregor, but we're perfectly safe in a comfortable campsite," she retorted.

His jaw tightened as he turned back to his grandfather. "We'll head down the mountain in the morning. I just hope Mom won't hear about this and worry herself sick."

"Sarah has already heard about it." Walt's mouth curved in a devilish smile. "I called her before we left and explained what we were doing."

Josh's eyes widened. "She didn't try to stop you?"

"My daughter knows better than that. And by the way, I wasn't asking for her permission. I was just letting her know. I won't be treated like a child. I'm staying here until I'm ready to leave. Right, Tara?"

She grinned. "Absolutely."

As Walt limped out of the clearing with a load

of their prospecting equipment, Tara resisted the temptation to thumb her nose at Josh.

"Tara, would you please—"

"I'm not doing anything except digging for sapphires," she interrupted. Grabbing two shovels and the buckets, she walked away, as well.

Josh had come to fetch them home?

What a jackass.

Josh watched Tara disappear after his grandfather, fighting the sensation that his entire world was standing on its ear. His mother had been told about this crazy stunt and done nothing about it?

Had everyone in his life lost their freaking minds?

With a sigh, he glanced around the campsite. He was relieved to see a raised air bed, presumably for his grandfather's use. The lumpy thing on one side confused him until he investigated. A blow-up chair? It looked ridiculous, but it was probably more comfortable for Walt.

Josh sighed and unloaded his gear. They couldn't leave before morning, anyway. Packing up would take time, and it wasn't safe to travel down the hills at night, even with experienced mounts.

He tethered Lightfoot and his pack horse on long leads so they could graze in the lush grass with the other animals. Walt and Tara's horses were spread out in an open meadow, also tethered, though it was unlikely that any horse Walt had raised would stray. They loved him too much.

Josh laid out his own bedroll on a tarp and headed in the direction the other two had taken. He swiftly covered the ground and found them using shovels to move dirt and rocks, stopping occasionally to examine a stone.

"Have you found the mother lode yet?" he asked.

Tara gave him a chilly look while his grandfather rolled his eyes.

He had to admit they'd organized their search. They were steadily shoveling dirt into small buckets, and once one was full, his grandfather would carry it, dumping the contents in a heap near a creek some forty feet away.

At first Josh was outraged that Tara was letting Walt carry the loaded buckets, only to realize it was an easier task than continually bending and digging.

"Why are you moving the debris so far away?" he asked.

"Because it isn't debris the way you think." Tara took a swallow of water from her canteen. "Sapphires can be found in alluvial deposits—that means gravel or sediment deposited when a river slows down," she said in an exaggerated, condescending tone.

The corners of Josh's mouth twitched as Walt laughed and slapped his leg, no doubt recognizing payback for the times his grandson had acted as if Tara didn't know a cow from a hole in the ground.

"Anyway, you have to wash the gravel and check for gemstones," she continued. "Walt built sieves, boxes with screens on the bottom, to make it easier."

Tara dug the tip of her shovel into the ground again. In the office she'd worn silk suits; at the dance, she'd been sexy and alluring in a dress that had hugged her figure. Now she'd chosen a T-shirt and work jeans. They were snug, with worn patches across her bottom and knees, and yet she managed to look like a fashion model pretending to dig in the ground during a photo shoot.

Unable to bear watching the bending of her hips and the flexing of her shirt against her breasts, Josh grabbed one of the shovels. Tara's curves had given him many sleepless nights and would undoubtedly do so again tonight.

"All right, we'll look for sapphires this afternoon," he announced. "That way you'll see it's hopeless, backbreaking work."

Walt grunted and took another pail toward the debris pile while, unbelievably, Tara stuck her tongue out.

"Stop that," Josh hissed.

"Why not? You're treating us both like children."

He felt a muscle tick in his jaw. "That isn't true."

"It's all a question of perspective." She wiped

her damp forehead. "Why does this bother you so much? I understand wanting to protect your grandfather, but you're worse than everyone else. No one else tried to rescue him from the dance floor or tell him not to go riding."

Josh opened his mouth, but closed it as Walt returned with the empty bucket, and collected the one Tara had finished filling. When he was out of earshot again, Josh leaned forward. "I'm the one living on the ranch and watching what Grandpa does every day, all right?"

She rested her chin on the end of the shovel, her eyes curiously compassionate. "He also gave you the Boxing N. So now you feel even *more* responsible in case something happens. Do you feel guilty that you're young and capable and now own the ranch that means so much to him?"

"Something like that," Josh muttered, startled by Tara's perception.

"Well, I've never been in your position, but I think everyone has to accept risks if they're going to have the life they want."

Over by the creek, Walt dumped some of the debris on one of his homemade sieves and poured water over it.

Josh watched moodily.

Quality of life *was* important, but a fruitless search for sapphires wasn't the only way to have it.

"What do you think is going to happen when his hopes are crushed?" he asked. "Or if he falls?

Grandpa is lucky to still *have* that leg, and who knows what would happen if he breaks it again."

"Walt knows the risks," Tara said, just as softly. "I thought it would just be an afternoon when I suggested going. Then he talked about heading out with pack horses and said he'd do it alone if I didn't go with him."

Pain thumped through Josh's temples. He shouldn't have blamed Tara. They might have knocked heads since her arrival in Montana, but she *had* been good for his grandfather. Besides, while she might have spoken first about hunting for gems, Grandpa would probably have thought of it sooner or later.

"Have you been able to discuss a pain-management program with him?" Josh asked.

"Yes. Walt called it nonsense."

"But in more colorful terms, right?"

Tara grinned wryly. "Definitely. He's very strong willed—how else do you think he's gotten this far?"

"Riding into the mountains couldn't have been easy in his condition," Josh conceded.

She shook her head. "It's more than that. I've never been in daily, unremitting pain, so I can only guess, but getting up each morning and facing everything he feels inside must take more strength than most people possess."

They both fell silent as Walt returned for another bucket.

"Find anything interesting?" Tara asked, gesturing toward the water.

"Not yet. Take a break from digging and we'll go through more together."

"Okay."

Josh grabbed the second bucket, concerned his grandfather would try carrying two loads at once. He hated to hear Walt's breathing become heavier just from carrying a small bucket of soil. Despite the raised air bed, he would have a rough night. Surely he would be eager to go home soon.

THE NEXT MORNING Josh woke to the scent of food cooking. After a night in the open air, he was starving. He rolled over to see Tara bending over a grill on the fire.

She glanced over her shoulder and smiled. How dare she look so fresh and energetic?

Dragging himself to his feet, he stumbled toward the fire. "Any coffee?"

She nodded. "It's been a while since I brewed a pot over a campfire, but Walt says it tastes all right."

"May I have a cup?"

She sent him a wry glance. "I'm tempted to refuse, but I'll be charitable. Sugar and powdered cream are in those containers."

Grateful, Josh accepted a battered enamel mug filled with steaming coffee. He flavored it the way he liked and drank quickly; the caffeine couldn't hit his system fast enough.

Walt returned to camp and hung a small towel on a tree branch. His hair was damp and he was clean shaven.

"Good morning," Josh told him.

"It's good so long as you understand I'm not leaving until I'm ready."

"This has to be hard on you. One night and I feel fifty years older."

"Then you should have brought a comfortable place to sleep and sit," Walt retorted, lowering himself into the inflated chair.

Tara snickered.

"We only have two plates," she said, handing Josh the frying pan, "so you'll need to eat breakfast out of that. Luckily, we have an extra fork, so you won't be doing the caveman thing with your fingers."

She passed a plate to Walt and began eating herself.

Josh forked up a mouthful and chewed thoughtfully. It was tasty, especially for scrambled powdered eggs. Tara had added an herb, along with cheese, making them far more palatable than they might have been.

"How did you learn to cook over a fire?" he asked.

"I told you I've camped before."

True, but Josh wasn't sure he'd believed her. She

was so sophisticated that roughing it didn't fit. Still, the ability to turn out a delectable breakfast in primitive conditions seemed proof enough. He insisted on joining her at the hot spring to wash their dishes, and when they returned, Grandpa was on his feet, leaning on a shovel.

"Have a good ride down the mountain, son," Walt told him. "I'll see you when we get back."

"But—"

"No buts. Tara, are you ready?"

"Sure thing. I'll just get my gloves."

"Wait," Josh said as they started toward their dig site. "I'm not going until you do, Grandpa. I won't leave the two of you alone on the mountain. It isn't safe."

"In that case..." Walt tossed him the shovel. "You'll have to help."

Josh felt helpless as they both grinned at him. But it couldn't be long before they gave up. They'd run out of food—he wasn't going to confess that he'd brought a supply with him—and be ready to head down.

Almost as if his grandfather had read his mind, Walt pointed upward.

"See that?" he asked. "We brought plenty, even for an uninvited third wheel. It's really something how much of that freeze-dried stuff fits on a few pack horses."

Suspended where he hadn't noticed it before,

Josh saw three enormous supply caches in nets, suspended on ropes to keep them safe from animals.

Damn, the old guy was really good.

LAUREN HURRIED DOWN to the café for lunch. She'd phoned in an order earlier to save time. They always offered to deliver to the clinic, but she liked going out; even a little exercise helped freshen her mind for the rest of the day.

Carl was there when she arrived. Lately it seemed as if she kept running into him. In the week since Tara had gone on her sapphire hunt, Lauren had seen Carl at least four times, though not for long and he hadn't asked her for a date or mentioned the kiss they'd shared. It was both disappointing and a relief.

"Hi, Carl," she said, determined not to get imaginative. Schuyler was a small town, unlike Los Angeles. It was unusual to run into someone you knew while shopping in LA. Here, she encountered friends and acquaintances all the time.

"Hey, Lauren. How is everything at the clinic?"

"Great. Another physician's assistant is starting next month."

"Does that mean you won't have to work so many hours?"

"Maybe, but they're also thinking of expanding to being open every Saturday, instead of once a month."

"I'm sure the town would be grateful."

"Yes. The clinic I worked at in Los Angeles was open seven days a week and until ten every night. I know those hours wouldn't be practical here, but Saturdays would be nice."

He nodded. "Is Tara back from her camping trip yet?"

With a hollow sensation in her stomach, Lauren wondered if he'd decided to ask her sister out for a date. After all, he was obviously interested in forming a relationship with someone. It would be nice for Tara—Carl was a great guy—yet she felt a sharp ache at the possibility.

"No, she's still gone." Lauren checked her watch. "Sorry, I'd better get to my lunch."

"Right."

Betty called to Carl as he headed for the door. "Don't forget your food, Sheriff." She handed him a bag and a covered cup.

He looked embarrassed. "Thanks."

Lauren wondered about it as she ate her salad. Carl had ordered takeout but had almost left empty-handed, though he must have prepaid his order. The other day he'd gone into the supermarket but hadn't been carrying any groceries when he left. Of course, he could have purchased something small enough to fit in his pocket, but it still seemed strange.

She sighed, wishing there was someone she could talk to about Carl. But Emily hadn't been feeling well, so she'd been staying home with her feet up. Bothering her with this was out of the question. And Tara wasn't available.

Lauren ate, paying little attention to the food.

Except for their hot kiss at the Boxing N dance, Carl had been friendly, nothing more. She was partially responsible for the embrace and didn't blame him for being reserved since then. After all, she'd told him to find someone else, only to turn around and kiss him a few days later.

Now they kept running into each other and it didn't feel completely accidental. Maybe she just *wanted* to believe there was something more to the casual encounters.

A WEEK AFTER arriving in the high country, Tara was torn between wishing Josh would disappear... and being secretly glad he was there. She still found him annoying and disliked being attracted to the big jerk, but if there was a crisis with Walt, having a strong man available would be handy.

Josh was hard to read. He plainly hadn't changed his mind about the prospecting trip, but he'd stopped saying much about it. Of course, apart from worrying about his grandfather's health, he was probably frustrated about being away from the ranch. His satellite phone helped him stay in contact with his new foreman, but it couldn't be the same as actually being there.

On the eighth morning, she was walking back

from the spring when she overheard Josh talking on the phone.

"…that's right, upgrading the herd will have to wait till next year…yeah, I'm sorry, too…"

At that point Josh looked up, and Tara felt her face get hot. She hadn't deliberately listened, though he probably wouldn't believe her. She hurried on, only to have him catch up within a few steps.

"I meant to tell you before, you're welcome to call your sister whenever you want," he offered, rather than accusing her of eavesdropping.

"That would be nice, mostly to let her know everything is okay. I love the solar unit you brought to charge the phone battery."

"Don't say that to Grandpa… You know how he feels about modern folderol."

Tara chuckled. "Walt and I have agreed to disagree about technology. It must be hard for someone in his generation, trying to hang on to the old ways of ranching, wondering if accepting anything new means something else is being lost."

"The values are the same as they used to be, even though ranching has changed. Maybe it's old-fashioned, but there's a code we follow, and the basics haven't changed since the Nelsons and McGregors settled in Montana."

Tara frowned thoughtfully. She loved cities and technology, but there *was* something to be said for the old ways. As frustrating as Josh might be, she didn't doubt he was an honorable man.

Back at the campsite, her gaze shifted between Walt and his grandson. She hated admitting it, but Josh would probably do a better job running the Boxing N than his grandfather. Still, surely they could work out a compromise for the benefit of everyone.

As for Walt, he was just as difficult to read as his grandson. He appeared amused at times and withdrawn at other moments. Actually, being withdrawn wasn't unusual for Walt, and she suspected those were times he was thinking about Evelyn. But the sly humor he seemed to find in the current situation was puzzling. Perhaps it was simply an aspect of his personality that was beginning to emerge again.

LATER THAT DAY Josh watched his grandfather leave the dig site and return to the campsite.

"Too stubborn to admit how hard this is on him," he muttered. "You're both too stubborn."

Tara's nerves tightened. "For your information, we agreed that he'd rest every afternoon. I didn't tell you about it because I hoped you'd recognize he was being sensible. Yet all you see is frailty."

Josh instantly looked contrite. "I'm sorry."

She sighed. "How many times will you have to say that before you mean it? Do you honestly believe I don't care what happens to him?"

"I know you care. In fact, I've been wondering if…well, I know you grew up in foster homes and never had a dad or a grandfather."

Tara blinked. Josh was suggesting that Walt had become a father figure to her…?

"Walt is a great guy," she said slowly, "but he isn't what I used to imagine a father would be like."

"Which was?"

"A cross between Superman, St. Francis of Assisi and Abraham Lincoln."

"Ah, inhuman strength tempered by gentle wisdom."

"More or less. Anyway, I've always kept my distance from anyone who might embody a realistic parental image."

Jock cocked his head, looking curious. "Why?"

"I'm an adult, and it isn't fair to expect another person to fill that role. My mother and father died when I was a baby. That's just the way it is."

"You deserved parents. All kids do."

"Sure, but not everyone gets them." She stopped and thought for a while. "Walt isn't a father figure, but I admit he crept under my defenses when I wasn't looking. That's unusual for me, but I don't mind. Now I have both Lauren and Walt to care about when I leave."

"You've never had that before?" Josh asked, sounding shocked.

"No. Every time I started letting myself care about a foster family, I got bounced somewhere new, so I learned it's safer to keep a distance. It taught me to be tough, which is helpful in today's world."

It could also be lonely, but that wasn't his business.

"How does Lauren fit into this?"

She shrugged. "I'm still figuring out what it means to have a sister."

"Maybe meeting her helped you open up to my grandfather."

Tara laughed. "Are you trying to psychoanalyze me?"

"Just making conversation."

Tara shrugged and bent over her shovel, thinking Josh's guesses could be closer to the target than he might think.

They'd fallen into a pattern while Walt was resting—they both dug, then sifted through stones and rocks in the sieve boxes. Then they took turns carrying the debris far enough away to prevent it from polluting the waterway more than necessary.

Josh carefully examined a rock he found in the creek bed and then showed it to her. The stone was translucent, with streaks of rust brown and black ribbons floating through its depths. Beautiful, but not the sapphire color she kept hoping to see.

"It's Montana agate," he explained. "They're great for rock tumbling, which is a process for polishing stones. A motor spins a barrel around, with a special grit that slowly takes off the rough outer layers."

"That's nice, but I hope you're concentrating on gems, not rocks in general."

"Why would you say that?"

"I don't know, except that it seems to be your lifestyle, to concentrate on some things and ignore the rest."

He snorted, sounding remarkably like his grandfather. "You don't know what you're talking about."

"Probably," Tara agreed, unsure why she'd said it in the first place. Value was in the eye of the beholder, so maybe Josh just valued things differently than other people. Perhaps a beautiful agate was more important to him than a sapphire.

Still, people made mistakes. The Boxing N had consumed Walt. It didn't mean he'd ignored Evelyn—they'd obviously had a deep and loving relationship—but now he was filled with regret that he hadn't put her first.

Tara handed the agate back to Josh. His fingers brushed hers, sending an electric tingle up her arm.

Gulping, she took an empty bucket to fill. The only reason she was having trouble concentrating was because she hadn't expected Josh to be part of the trip into the mountains. It was high time to figure out the best way to deal with his presence.

CHAPTER FOURTEEN

JOSH WOKE AS the sun was rising.

He rolled onto his back and listened to the birds chattering in the trees. It was nice to be back in the mountains, though he was still concerned about Walt. Once he'd spent a lot of time camping and hiking, sometimes by himself and other times with the family, but it had been a few years since then. When he'd worked in Texas, his time off had been spent in Schuyler—partly to visit the family and partly to gauge how close Walt might be getting to retirement.

At times he'd felt like a vulture. It might have been different if he hadn't grown up being told about the deal that Grandpa and Uncle Mitch had made. *Grandpa is going to retire when you're out of college and you'll own the Boxing N.* It was part of the weaving of his life. Yet when the time came, Grandpa said, "Maybe next fall." Year after year it was the same story.

His whole family agreed that the summer he'd worked with Walt had been an unmitigated disaster. Grandma Evelyn had tried to intervene, without success. "The boy has book learning, but he needs seasoning," Walt would snort before stomping away.

Seasoning? Josh had grown up on a ranch and worked with his father since before he could remember. Even now, after years as a ranch foreman down in Texas, his grandfather often acted as if he didn't know one end of a cow from the other.

"I know it's hard. But remember, you'll be old one day, too," Grandma Evelyn would whisper, squeezing his hand.

Loath as Josh was to admit it, Tara was right about family expectations. If nothing had been said about him being given the Boxing N, he would have just bought a spread with his trust fund. His vision for having a top herd of organic cattle could already be a reality.

Josh dressed inside his bedroll and inched out of the bag. Assorted items he'd emptied from his pockets were collected in his hat, and he shoved them back in his pockets without much thought. There was a natural pool nearby, fed by hot springs, and he wanted to take a plunge before breakfast.

He felt pleasantly nostalgic as he followed the path. The hot springs were why his family called it Smaug's Mountain—Smaug, after all, being a fire-belching dragon. Tara and Walt hadn't chosen the McGregors' usual campsite, but one on the other side of the ridge. Nevertheless, both locations took advantage of the area's geothermal features.

The unceasing flow of warm water was a boon,

since prospecting was a grubby business. Josh also needed to do more laundry than Tara or Walt, since he'd brought fewer changes of clothing. Though he'd hoped to return immediately, he was an experienced outdoorsman and didn't go into the wild without basic supplies.

Hmm. In a couple of days he'd have to make a trip back to the ranch to get the next payroll out. While he was there, he would also pick up some extra clothing, since it was clear that Grandpa wasn't budging until every scrap of food had been consumed.

He entered the clearing around the pool and stopped, transfixed by the sight of Tara floating in the water. At first he thought she was naked—an image that got him hot and hard in a split second—before realizing she wore a scant bikini that blended with her skin.

Her eyes opened lazily, and she gazed at him.

"Come on in," she invited.

Josh hesitated.

"What's wrong?"

"I don't have a suit."

"Wear your boxers. That way you can do some laundry at the same time."

It was true, except the boxers wouldn't hide his arousal, wet *or* dry.

Tara let out a musical chuckle. "If it makes you more comfortable, I promise not to look until you're in the water."

Her eyes closed, and Josh rapidly shucked his outer clothes. A minute later he descended into the churning warmth.

"You can open your eyes," he said.

"Mmm. These springs are pure luxury. Has your family ever considered opening a resort up here?"

"Not a chance—we're cattle ranchers."

Tara raised her head. "Is that why the Nelsons didn't pay much attention to the possibility of sapphires? I understand there are mines nearby that have gems with stunning color."

"That doesn't mean our land has been blessed with them."

"But it isn't impossible."

Sighing, Josh tried to put a few more inches between them. Tara's bikini wasn't racy by some standards, but it revealed entirely too much for his comfort.

"I was interested in the stories as a boy, but now I have to deal with reality," he said. "My great-great-grandfather claimed he found sapphires, but he never produced any as proof."

"Are you sure? It's been a long time since then."

"Of course I'm sure," Josh returned, irritated. "You don't miss something like that lying around. Nevertheless, I commissioned the geological survey ten years ago and specifically asked them to check for gemstones. They found nothing."

Tara's throaty, sexy laugh almost finished him. "Experts miss things all the time. I saw a documentary once about treasure hunters who were looking for emeralds on an old Spanish galleon. In the middle of salvaging the ship, they discovered the rocks they were dumping back in the ocean were really uncut emeralds, each worth thousands of dollars."

"That's different."

"Maybe, maybe not."

Setting his jaw, Josh sank deeper in the water, his frustration only partially due to her stubbornness.

"I…" He swallowed. "Your bikini is unusual. It blends with your skin more than any swimsuit I've seen before."

Tara shrugged. "I visited the Riviera last year with someone who wanted to check out a nude beach. It wasn't my thing, so I compromised with a bikini that wasn't too obvious."

Perhaps it was his imagination, but her voice seemed to get huskier, as if she might be feeling the same heat he felt surging in his groin.

"You didn't object to other people being nude?" he asked.

"To be honest, I couldn't stop wondering if the men were using sunscreen on the vulnerable portions of their anatomy."

The answer was so unexpected that Josh grinned.

"I mean, imagine how uncomfortable it would be getting sunburned down there," Tara added.

"Ouch."

"It sure wouldn't be romantic," she murmured, swimming closer. Her eyes darkened as their legs brushed together.

Slowly he extended his right hand to cup her breast. All the voices of caution in his head were silenced as he slid a finger beneath the thin swimsuit. Her skin was slick with the warm mineral water, and he found the nipple, puckered and firm, nearly driving him insane.

TARA'S BREATHS CAME QUICK and shallow as both of Josh hands grew busy, teasing, coaxing, *demanding* a response. After a few moments, he pressed his lips to hers.

The kiss was even better than the one they'd shared at the ranch office. She swayed closer, his erection hard and insistent against her abdomen.

She reached down for some exploration of her own.

"Be careful," he gasped, "or I'll have the kind of accident I haven't had since high school."

He could have used that line on dozens of women in the past, but at the moment she didn't care. He unfastened the top of her bikini and tossed it onto the grass.

In the water her breasts swayed against his muscular chest while his fingers slipped under the bikini bottom to explore and probe. It was a toss-up as to which part of her body was experiencing the most pleasure. The sensations were torturously exquisite. As he tossed the bottom of the suit after the top, she tugged at the band of his boxer shorts, wanting to lose that barrier, as well.

"I've got protection in my wallet," he gasped.

Tara hiked an eyebrow. "Why did you bring your wallet up the mountain?"

"Habit."

Mutely, she nodded. He lunged out of the pool and fumbled in his back pocket, extracting a small packet.

After he rolled the condom over himself, they tumbled to the grass together. In another moment he was inside her, moving slowly, setting a rhythm. Already acutely aroused, her climax came quickly and he finished soon after.

He lay on top of her, a satisfying weight and a shield against the cool morning air. Nonetheless, Tara quickly wiggled free and returned to the warm water, Josh following close behind. He might have been hoping for a repeat, but she simply washed off bits of grass and leaves before hurriedly dressing. It was time to fix breakfast.

Tara refused to look at Josh, not wanting to invite conversation, even when she tossed his boxers over a bush to dry. The sex had been good for her, and might improve with repetition. But she didn't want to hear *his* evaluation, not when she recalled Pierre's brutal assessment of her ability to please a man. In light of that, she would have stayed well away from Josh if she'd been thinking clearly.

It was bad enough that they spent part of each afternoon alone, digging for sapphires while Walt rested. If Josh had any sense, he'd realize she didn't want to talk about it.

When she reached the campsite, Tara checked to be sure Walt was still asleep.

His breaths were slow and deep, so there was little chance he'd gotten up earlier than usual and witnessed what had happened between her and his grandson. She shuddered at the idea.

They'd come for sapphires, Tara reminded herself. Or more accurately, they'd come for adventure. Sex with Josh had been a different kind of adventure, and it would be silly to regret what had happened, but now it was time to focus on something else.

JOSH FLOATED IN THE warm water, gazing at the sky above him. Tara's swift departure puzzled him. Why had she seemed so detached?

Obviously he didn't understand women any better than other men did. They'd given each other pleasure, and yet she'd immediately behaved as if it hadn't happened. Of course, his actions after they'd kissed a few weeks ago might be the explanation. Tara could be trying to head off another "I'm not interested in a long-term relationship" declaration from him.

He wouldn't dare.

Tara Livingston was a force to be reckoned with,

and she wouldn't hesitate to point out his hypoc-risy. After all, he'd hurried into the mountains for his grandfather's sake, not to have sex…yet he'd brought a wallet stocked with condoms with him. Bringing it *had* been habit, but she still might ques-tion him carrying protection when he'd claimed he wasn't socializing that much.

It wouldn't do any good to argue that he'd faith-fully carried protection ever since his brother had gotten a girl pregnant in high school. Jackson had ensured his younger brother was well supplied with condoms until he was old enough to buy his own—Schuyler being a town where a teenager couldn't purchase them without rampant gossip ensuing.

Still, even though making sure his wallet was stocked was automatic, deep down Josh knew he must have hoped for something at some point with Tara. Nor could he deny wanting a second time… or more; something about Tara had crawled under his skin and made him long for more.

Trying to relax, he closed his eyes and drifted with the eddying currents, letting the minutes flow past.

He'd forgotten how good it was to get away from everything. Perhaps he should build a small cabin here, either on this side of the ridge or the other where his family had usually camped.

Unable to resist, he pictured being alone with

Tara on the mountain, making love in one of the geothermal pools.

Impatiently he shook the image from his head. Before long Tara would be heading for points unknown, and he'd be transforming the Boxing N into a top producer of organic beef. He would have to ignore the way she made him want to forget everything except making love.

A movement caught his eye, and he turned his head. His grandfather stood at the water's edge, his plaid bathrobe looking somewhat absurd in the wild setting.

Walt dropped his robe and waded into the water, clad only in his boxers. It was surprising since he'd preferred bathing alone before now. The network of scars on his leg was still red, though some had begun to fade.

Partway into the warm water, Walt looked up and slapped his thigh. "Don't look if they bother you."

"They don't, not the way you think. I'm just sorry you're still in pain."

Walt shrugged. "It is what it is. Anyhow, my leg isn't what hurts the most."

The buoyancy of the mineral water seemed to soothe his discomfort, and he strode back and forth, bending and lifting his legs in a rhythmic pattern.

"This place is much better than the therapy pool at the rehab center," Walt explained.

"Did you know it was here?" Josh asked.

"A man knows his own land. I deepened the pool and brought your grandma here every fall." Grandpa gestured to where water spilled over a rock dam. It appeared natural, but time would have softened its appearance.

"You took Grandma *camping*?"

Walt's face tightened, and he turned away to continue exercising. His face had closed, an expression Josh was all too familiar with.

Discouraged, he got out and dressed.

Back at the campsite he was greeted by the tempting scent of coffee. He hung his towel on a line they'd rigged and went to the fireplace.

"What's wrong?" Tara asked. No one could have told from her face that they'd made love less than an hour earlier.

"I just got shut out again," Josh told her, following her cue. "Grandpa said something about Grandma Evelyn and I asked more, but he shut me out as usual."

"It's hard for him to talk about her at times," Tara answered quietly. "The pain goes so deep, I think he keeps everyone else out until he feels strong enough to deal with it again."

Josh raised his eyebrows. Tara hadn't seemed the romantic type. "My grandfather—"

"I know what you believe about their marriage," she interrupted. "You probably think it's crazy for someone like me, who knows so little about family and who hasn't known Walt long, to think I know better than you do. But from what I've seen, the thing that hurts Walt the most isn't his limp. It's losing his wife."

Josh focused on his coffee, remembering what Grandpa had said at the hot spring pool about his leg not causing him the most pain... Did he mean his wife's death? The possibility that he'd been wrong about their relationship began to knock at Josh's brain. He wasn't sure what he believed any longer.

He finally looked up at Tara, trying to see beyond the weeks of conflict and frustration between them. From the beginning she'd represented one of his roadblocks to getting the Boxing N in better shape. Sexual attraction had been another complication—Tara wasn't the kind of woman he'd ever desired, or even liked. The McGregors tended to be a passionate, sociable family, while she was coolly sophisticated.

But he'd been wrong about her being a roadblock. Tara's work in the ranch office was unparalleled. He couldn't have done half the job in twice the time, and he knew it.

"I'm not sure about anything right now," he said slowly. "Except that you've been good for Grandpa."

Pink spots appeared on Tara's cheeks. "Thank you." She topped off his coffee cup and sat down with her own, keeping watch on the path to the hot spring pool. "I'm not a people person, but he's a nice man."

"I think you're more of a people person than you think. You knew what to say to Perry Whitlan at the hospital and you did a great job on the party. Folks in town like you."

"They like Lauren," Tara corrected him. "They're nice to me because of her. I mean, I don't make friends, really. It's my fault—I just don't let anyone close…" Her voice trailed off, suggesting a vulnerability he had rarely seen in her before.

"One of those outcomes of childhood?" Josh guessed. "Getting passed around because you were a sick child."

Tara shrugged. "Maybe. What happened when I was a kid definitely had an effect, but I take responsibility for what came after."

The sound of footsteps approaching was probably as much of a relief to her as it was to him. Tara got up and hurriedly checked on their breakfast.

Grandpa came into camp, his limp less noticeable than on some days. He eagerly poured himself a cup of coffee and seemed to have a fair amount of energy.

Although Josh believed the search for sapphires was ridiculous, he was beginning to understand why Tara had thought it was a good idea. Walt had more vitality and his physical recovery seemed to be accelerating. He certainly *looked* stronger and had better color in his face.

Josh swirled the contents of his cup, thinking hard.

He'd accepted that it was too late in the season to initiate a new breeding program; it would have to wait until the following spring. Either way he needed to buy more certified organic cattle. And while there were tasks on the ranch in need of attention, he wouldn't be able to concentrate on them knowing Grandpa was on Smaug's Mountain looking for sapphires. His grandfather might be doing better, but there were still risks. So maybe he should throw himself into the search. He could even bring some more food when he returned from getting the payroll done.

Josh gulped down the rest of his coffee. Life was complicated, especially with Tara Livingston in the mix.

TARA WAS GRATEFUL that Josh hadn't brought up their encounter at the hot spring pool.

They ate breakfast and Walt insisted "we men" do the dishes, so Tara headed for the dig site to sift through more rocks and gravel.

Unfortunately she discovered that peace and quiet couldn't silence the voices in her head, so she determinedly pictured the photos she'd seen of raw sapphires. For the most part they weren't impressive. The advice had been to pay attention to anything translucent, colored or glittery.

Tara sighed, thinking how lovely it would be to find a sapphire. She didn't own much jewelry, mostly a few tasteful pieces appropriate to wear to work. But she had two pairs of utterly indulgent sapphire earrings. One pair were blue solitaires. The others were long drops with stones in a rainbow progression. The jeweler had explained that sapphires came in all colors, even red—but then they were called rubies. Buying those earrings had been an extravagance, because they weren't the sort of thing she wore socially *or* in her professional capacity.

Perhaps she should get them converted into pendants and give one to Lauren on a gold chain. There had to be someone in Schuyler who could do the work. The jeweler in London would likely scream if he knew—he'd claimed that finding two sets of perfectly matched stones in so many colors had been difficult and expensive—but Tara didn't care. What was money if it wasn't used for things that mattered?

"Find anything?" Walt called, startling her. She hadn't heard the two men approaching.

"Not yet." Tara didn't know whether or not she truly expected to find sapphires, but Walt had needed an adventure, and that had been good enough for her.

The morning followed its usual rhythm as they dug, carried and sorted. Walt was optimistic, checking each newly washed set of stones with high expectations, only to cheerfully toss them in the discard pail and turn to the next set.

Amazingly, Josh no longer seemed to be dragging his feet. Sexual satisfaction might account for the change, but probably not after the way she'd shut him out.

Honestly, men were something she'd never understand.

A FEW HOURS after lunch, Walt left for his usual rest back at the campsite. Once he was gone, Tara grew nervous, wondering if Josh would think it was an opportunity to "get things out in the open" the way he'd done the first time they'd kissed. But she didn't want to talk about sex. It wasn't that she was a prude, but she had to admit that deep down she was a little old-fashioned.

"We've got a good pile by the creek," she said when they were alone. "Do you want to wash and sort, or dig and carry?"

"Let's both wash and sort. Midday sunshine is best for checking the stones, and the two of us can resupply the pile when Grandpa gets back."

She'd hoped for separate tasks to help minimize any discussion, only to decide that if Josh was determined to talk, he'd just push until he got his way. Besides, she shouldn't assume he wanted to bring it up at all...

"Sure," she agreed.

She loaded a screen-bottomed box and dunked it under the small waterfall on the creek. Once, twice, three times and the stones seemed clean enough. So she sat on a log and started hunting, often stopping to admire the river-polished rocks. While not sapphires, they were beautiful in their own right.

"What are you smiling about?" Josh asked, balancing his own box on his knee and starting to search.

"I was thinking how beautiful these are, even if they aren't gems."

"True. I've collected several to run through my rock tumbler. But this is the first time since I was a teenager that I've gone looking for anything except in a rock shop."

"A rugged outdoorsman like you? I'd have thought it was natural to dig for your own stuff."

"Too busy. I've been working cattle ever since college."

Tara cocked her head. "I know it didn't pan out when you tried working with Walt, but why Texas?"

"I decided learning a different style of ranching was a good idea," Josh murmured thoughtfully. "My brother worked for years as a ranch hand before getting the Crazy Horse, and it became obvious I should do the same. Of course, it was somewhat different for him. Jackson had to earn his way back from acting like a fool during high school. Great-Uncle Mitch wanted him to prove he was reliable enough to run the Crazy Horse."

"Everyone seems to respect Jackson."

"Yeah, *now*. But he and his first wife got married when they were eighteen because Marcy was pregnant. She was a disaster. Much later Jackson found out that he'd gotten *another* girl pregnant, as well. He and Kayla are married now."

"Kayla is the one with dark auburn hair, right?"

"Right. She's a huge improvement on his first wife, but she has a business in Seattle, so they spend some of their time in the city. That would drive me nuts."

"What a surprise," Tara commented. "Ranching is your one true love."

Josh seemed startled by her description.

"Uh, anyhow," he continued after a pause, "I was offered a job in Texas and thought it would be nice to be someplace where nobody knew me. After a while, I was made foreman."

"It must have felt good doing it all on your own."

"Yeah, it was nice. The Gordons had barely heard of the McGregors or Nelsons, so I had to prove myself the same as anyone else."

"Do you ever regret leaving Texas?"

"Yeah, whenever Grandpa and I get into a fight."

Tara chuckled. "You've had some doozies. I also suspect you have Walt's dry sense of humor. By the way, what did you ask him this morning?"

"Nothing dramatic. He mentioned bringing Grandma up here every fall, and it surprised me. My folks used to take us camping on the other side of the ridge when I was a kid, but not Grandpa.

I always thought he was too busy on the ranch...
wouldn't even take a vacation."

"Doesn't ranch work get quieter in autumn?"

"Some."

Tara fingered one of the Montana agates Josh
had told her about. "I know it didn't go well this
morning, but perhaps you could try asking him
again about Evelyn. When he's in the right mood,
he tells wonderful stories about her."

"Maybe."

Tara knew better than to push, though she wasn't
sure where the conviction had come from.

Josh emptied his rocks into the discard pail. "It's
interesting—for some reason we never came over
on this side of the ridge when we camped up here."

"Then you missed out on the hot springs."

"Nah, there's hot springs over there, just nothing like the pool." Josh's voice dropped. "That's
been a real pleasure."

Tara swallowed, fairly sure he wasn't just talking about warm water.

JOSH WATCHED FAINT COLOR brighten Tara's cheeks.
Her reactions weren't what he'd expected. In his
experience most women were blunt when it came
to sex, or else they were coy. Neither seemed to
fit Tara, and she obviously didn't want to discuss
what had happened.

He looked down at his tray of rocks, though it
was hard to focus on them. A much more attrac-

tive image was the memory of Tara coming up out of the water, a hint of steam rising from her bare skin, his perfect fantasy.

Trying to shake the provocative memories away, he laughed. "Now when I go to sleep at night, this is what I keep seeing—rocks and more rocks."

"Me, too, but at least you can put names to a lot of them. What prompted your interest in geology?"

Josh thought back to when his grandmother had first told him the story of Boxing N sapphires. He'd been eleven and had come into her personal sitting room to find her examining polished stones in a carved wood box.

"It was Grandma Evelyn."

He went on to tell Tara how his grandmother had shown him the stones and told him what each one was called—aventurine, pink quartz, soda-lite, amethyst, jade...dozens and dozens of them. Then Grandma had told him about the sapphires on the Boxing N. Finally she'd said, quite intently, "Josh, there are gems all over this ranch if you know how to see them. Don't confuse them with anything else."

Tara looked at Josh. "She sounds like a wise woman. Maybe she wasn't just talking about sapphires."

Josh shook his head. "Don't get sentimental on me."

"You should know by now that sentiment isn't my strong suit. I'm too practical."

"If you weren't sentimental, you wouldn't have gone looking for family," he retorted. "As for practicality, you didn't know about Lauren, but you still tried, hoping someone out there would be looking for you, too."

"I suppose. But I'm sure your grandmother must have been terribly sentimental."

"Yes and no. She believed in being practical, just like you, but she was also an artist. I swear. Grandma Evelyn was interested in everything. The year before she... Well, I got her a smartphone so she could look up something on the internet whenever she wanted."

Tara was a good listener. She nodded quietly and seemed to be waiting for more, so Josh tried to describe the strong, funny and beautiful woman who'd connected with each of her grandchildren in individual ways. She'd been an artist who illustrated children's books and had painted unique birthday and Christmas cards for every member of her family. Her garden had been like a painting as well, beautifully designed and tended.

"I still have the cards Grandma gave me," Josh said, his throat painfully tight. It still didn't seem possible she was gone.

Tara was silent for a long moment. "It sounds as if she was a second mother to you."

He nodded slowly. "She was. I could always tell her everything."

Tara shifted uncomfortably and finally leaned

forward. "I'm probably going to say this wrong, but I think you're unbelievably fortunate. Not because Evelyn died, but because she was really, really special. Having someone you can grieve for so much... Even the grief seems like a gift."

She dumped the rocks she'd checked into the bucket, then walked away to refill her tray.

Josh watched, his mind churning. Tara was right. He *was* fortunate, and Grandma Evelyn's life was certainly more important than her death.

Then something awful occurred to him... Did Grandpa Walt wonder if he wished Evelyn had lived instead of him? Pain twisted through Josh's midriff. There wasn't any way to reassure Grandpa without making him think it was true.

TARA GAVE THE STONES in her tray an extra washing to allow Josh some time alone. He was a pain in the ass, but his devotion to his grandmother's memory was endearing. A lot of people would've tried to keep those feelings hidden.

Like her.

She sighed. It would be wonderful to stop being the cold fish that Pierre had accused her of being. Perhaps it would be different if she'd had someone in her life like Evelyn Nelson. Evelyn sounded remarkable. Josh's stories dovetailed many of his grandfather's tales.

Tara determinedly focused again on the stones in her box. It would be amazing to find a sapphire, but what were the odds? The mountain was part of the ranch, so Walt's grandfather *could* have found gems in the area while exploring as a boy, and it didn't sound as if he'd needed to dig for them. So if this was where the Nelsons often camped, why hadn't the stones been rediscovered? So far they'd searched without any success. Of course, Josh's ancestor might have gotten any gems that were near the surface, so anything left was deeper down...

Tara mentally groaned. There were too many tail-chasing questions to consider, and the biggest one that she'd tried to answer, over and over, was about Walt. In the end, if they didn't find sapphires, how would he react?

She wanted to believe he saw the adventure as the most important part of their journey into the mountains, but there was no way to know for sure.

CHAPTER FIFTEEN

JOSH STRETCHED, TRYING to loosen the knots in his back. If anyone thought gem prospecting was exciting and romantic, they should try searching for Montana sapphires, especially after sleeping on the ground.

The previous day he'd ridden out early to deal with the ranch payroll but had returned by evening. Though Tara's ability to handle the situation was far greater than he'd given her credit for in the beginning, he still believed it best for him to be there, as well. He kept losing track of the days on the mountain; it had only been the reminder on his phone that had alerted him about another pay period. Despite his decision to support the endeavor, Josh had almost been embarrassed by the load of food he'd hastily gathered to bring back with him—he'd originally gone into the mountains to bring his grandfather home, and now he was finding ways to prolong the interlude.

Josh finished washing his tray of stones in the creek and began looking through them. Walt was sitting nearby, sorting rocks, as well. His physical health had continued to improve, and he was even cooperating occasionally on things that were better for him, such as getting proper rest and not overdoing it.

Tara had gone back to camp to do her laundry and make lunch. In the beginning Josh had dreaded the times she left him alone with his grandfather, but those were improving, too.

"Do you think Tara is disappointed we haven't found anything yet?" he asked, trying to sound casual.

Walt shook his head. "She's worried about me, that's all."

"Is that what she told you?"

"Not in so many words. You have to learn to read Tara's eyes, son. It's all there, no matter how hard she tries to keep it hidden."

Josh tipped his head back to gaze up the mountain, unsure of what his own eyes might reveal. On the upper reaches, a bald eagle took off from a rocky crag, rising higher and higher on the currents of air. The powerful flight of the bird made him hold his breath for what seemed an endless moment.

A sigh from Walt suddenly drew Josh's attention. "Something up, Grandpa?"

"You reminded me of Evelyn just now. She loved eagles, anything wild and free. Sometimes I think she would have preferred being mauled by a mountain lion than having me shoot it to protect her. Luckily I never had to do more than scare one away."

Josh was startled. For a second he saw pain in his grandfather's face, a grief so raw and terrible it made his own seem mild. It was gone quickly, but it made Josh think that Walt might be suffering far more than his family had realized.

"Tara feels the same about wild animals," Walt said in a lighter tone. "You should have seen her face when she learned about the rifle. I told her it was mostly to scare critters off...though it didn't work with you."

The sly joke was so unexpected it took a moment to sink in.

Josh laughed. Tara claimed he shared Grandpa's sense of humor. Maybe she was right about that, as well.

LATER IN THE AFTERNOON, while Walt rested, Josh kept thinking about his new perspective on his grandfather.

Over by the creek, Tara was working doggedly, taking less time than usual to admire the rocks that had washed down from the higher mountains.

Josh finally cleared his throat, and she glanced up.

"I've been thinking about what you said about Grandma and Grandpa," he murmured. "You'll probably say, 'I told you so,' but I'm starting to agree—he misses her more than any of us have realized."

No triumph crossed Tara's face. "I felt funny

saying anything since I haven't known him that long, but when he talks about Evelyn, it's as if he's bleeding."

"I guess we've been too close to see it."

"Don't forget, you've been grieving, too. I'm a stranger, so maybe it's easier for him to talk to me. I don't think he wants you to worry."

"You aren't a stranger any longer, you're his friend."

Her mouth curved in a smile. "And nobody was more surprised than me to realize it."

The sound of footsteps drew both of their attentions; Walt was returning from the campsite.

"I see not much has gotten done. You've been lazy," Walt announced brusquely.

It was the sort of comment that usually rubbed Josh wrong, but Tara grinned, unperturbed. "We just didn't want to find any sapphires without you."

Surprisingly, Walt chuckled, and Josh wondered if he'd learned something else…that his grandfather wasn't always looking for a fight when he said something annoying. Maybe he simply wanted to talk and didn't know how to begin the conversation.

JOSH KEPT THINKING ABOUT his grandparents as they sat around the campfire that night.

"Grandpa, tell me something about Grandma Evelyn that I haven't heard before, okay?" he asked finally. "I'll understand if it's too hard to talk about it, but it would mean a lot."

Walt gazed into the fire for a few minutes. "I don't know what you have and haven't heard. You know we met in San Francisco."

"Yeah, in Chinatown, and she thought you were stubborn."

"Bullheaded," Walt corrected. "Come to think of it, you may not know that I was busy trying to convince an idiot that New Mexico was a state in the union, not a separate country. The idiot was Evelyn's great-uncle. She watched the fireworks between us and then came over to propose to me."

Josh's mouth dropped open. "The day you met?"

"The same hour. It took me longer to decide."

"How long?" Josh asked, his mind reeling.

"Five minutes, but only because I was playing hard to get."

Josh laughed, feeling both joy and sorrow; it was odd how close the two emotions could be.

That was the first of several evening conversations, though he kept losing track of the time passing. When he got a chance, Josh scribbled notes in a notebook, sometimes by firelight after the others had gone to sleep. He carried the notebook to keep records on ranch business, but Grandpa's stories were far more satisfying.

Yet even when Walt laughed, his face alive with memories, Josh began to see the stark pain in his eyes. It was never far away.

One evening Josh finally leaned forward. "Grandpa, wouldn't it be easier if you hadn't loved

Grandma so much?" he asked. "You wouldn't hurt this way now."

Walt stared as if he'd lost his mind. "Boy, you've got it wrong. Having one day with the person you love is worth a lifetime of grief. The only thing I regret is putting off our dreams. We'd planned to travel and explore the world. God knows what I was waiting for, but we were both healthy and it seemed as if we had plenty of time. Now what do I have?"

"The Boxing N," Josh said instantly. He'd give the ranch back to his grandfather if it would help.

"Evelyn was my life, not the ranch. I'm sorry that it's been so hard for me to stop..."

Walt didn't finish, but Josh knew it was probably the only apology he'd ever get for the way things had been the last several months. And in all likelihood, they'd return to their regular life when this trip was finished. Grandpa would fall back into the same old pattern—arguing and interfering, frustrated that things weren't being done the way he'd always done them.

Josh knew he'd have to look for a compromise, something that afforded them both some dignity. In the meantime, he didn't know what else to say.

"We'll work something out," he murmured finally.

Grandpa nodded. Silently he poked the fire with a stick.

Tara didn't look up; she was reading on the other

side of the flickering fire ring. She rarely joined
in the conversation, giving them space to talk. Yet
Josh was beginning to wonder what she thought
about all of it.

A month ago he would have said it was impossible he'd spend weeks on Smaug's Mountain hunting for sapphires…with his grandfather, no less.
Oh, yeah, and a beautiful, stubborn city woman
who'd managed to get through to Walt when no
one else had.

It still boggled his mind that he was here instead
of watching over the ranch—it was critical to get
operations back on track. But that would have to
wait, at least for the moment.

AT TWO THE NEXT AFTERNOON, Walt smiled affably
and left for the campsite for his daily nap. Tara
watched him go, glad that he was moving more
freely, despite the lingering pain in his leg.

"He seems better," Josh said, as if he'd read her
mind. "But how did you get him to agree to that
walking stick? He's refused to use a cane."

"Because a walking stick isn't a cane…and because I brought two, one for each of us. He wasn't
happy about it at first, but I pointed out that they're
popular with hikers of all ages. I found them at your
sister-in-law Emily's gift emporium—apparently
they're hot items."

Tara halfheartedly flicked her finger through
some wet stones. She'd felt moody all day. The

way Walt talked about Evelyn was a reminder that she'd probably never have that kind of love in her own life. She just wasn't the kind of person that people liked much, no matter what Josh claimed.

Josh was different, though, and there was no reason he couldn't have it all. It was insane that he had put love on a schedule—something he'd contemplate *after* achieving success on the ranch. When would enough be enough? If he wasn't careful he'd turn into an old man, watching his siblings with their children and grandchildren, wondering had happened to the years.

In a way, he was exactly the same as Walt, putting the Boxing N ahead of everything else. Walt's plans to travel with Evelyn could never happen now, but at least he had other memories. What would Josh have?

Still, he had chosen to join in with the sapphire hunt. It would be nice to think he might be learning *something*, for his own sake.

By the creek Josh shifted so his shadow wouldn't cover the stones he was sorting. "I can't believe how much Grandpa has opened up about Grandma Evelyn. I've always assumed he was closed and distant, but you never thought so, did you?"

"It's different for me. You're filtering everything through a lifetime of experiences."

"Maybe. He almost talks about the ranch as if he hates it now, but he hasn't been able to let go, either."

"I don't think it's as simple as loving or hating the Boxing N."

"I suppose."

Tara wondered if Josh truly understood what his grandfather was trying to say about priorities. Walt didn't think ranching was a bad thing. He loved the Boxing N. It produced good beef cattle and fine horses and provided employment for a large number of people.

But Walt also knew he could have given the ranch to Josh a long time ago. He and Evelyn could have been traveling the world on the day of the accident; instead they'd been hit by a drunk driver less than a mile from the Boxing N gate.

Walt Nelson had learned his lesson at a terrible cost. Tara suspected he wanted his grandson to learn it without the high price tag.

CARL EYED THE drunken rowdies at Ryan's Roadhouse. He'd responded to a 911 call from the bartender, saying three out-of-towners were trashing the place.

"Okay, fellas, I'm Sheriff Stanfield. What's going on?"

"None of yer frickin' business, buddy boy," shouted one of them, every word slurred. With no more ado, he lunged forward and threw a wild punch, too drunk to know what he was doing.

Carl ducked easily and brought the guy to the ground, only to be struck from the side.

He turned and saw a twenty-something biker wannabe dancing around with a knife.

City fellow, Carl decided, *probably stuck in a dead-end job and looking for a little vacation excitement.* The thought alone nearly made him smile—he'd come a long way since moving to Schuyler from St. Louis. But any humor fled at the look in the other man's eyes; most likely he was high on something other than liquor.

"Take it easy, pal," he said, watching carefully.

"Can't tell me what to do."

The guy lunged, and Carl grabbed the hand holding the weapon, twisted his attacker around and kicked the legs out from under him. Within seconds he was handcuffed on the floor next to his friend.

His deputy had dealt with the third guy with equal speed.

"Okay, Noah, let's get them loaded in the cruiser."

"Adrenaline must be like Novocain, Carl," Noah gasped. "You're bleeding."

Carl glanced down and saw an expanding red stain on his khaki uniform shirt.

Damn.

Noah got on the radio while the white-faced bartender held out a handful of clean bar towels.

"Thanks." Carl pressed the towels to his rib cage. "Sorry about the mess on the floor. Noah, I'll have this stitched later. We'll get these yahoos into lockup first."

Though Noah looked doubtful, he didn't argue. But while they were loading the trio into the back of the cruiser, another sheriff's vehicle screeched to a stop nearby. Two men jumped out.

"Hey, boss." It was another one of his deputies, George Winston, and he calmly surveyed Carl's injury. "I see you've sprung a leak."

"It's not too bad."

"Good to hear, but we'll book these guys while Noah takes you to the clinic."

"That won't work—it's closing time there," Carl said quickly. "The one in Windy Bluffs is open later."

"Nope, the Schuyler clinic is expecting you."

"But—"

"No buts." George crossed his arms over his chest. "Your rule, remember? You get hurt, you see the doc. Noah will drive you. Take my cruiser."

Carl growled under his breath and swung into the second vehicle. He'd set protocols for this type of situation but hadn't expected to be caught in one. A minute later Noah slid behind the wheel.

"Take me to Windy Bluffs," Carl ordered.

"Sorry. The Schuyler clinic is the best in the area, and you're bleeding like a stuck pig."

That was the problem. Carl had spotted Lauren going to work that morning, and she might still be on duty. He didn't want to take a chance of reminding her how much blood could come from a relatively minor knife wound.

It was revolting that he was still hanging on to hope for a relationship.

"How about the emergency room?" he suggested.

"George called them. The ER said that since you're mobile and conscious and they're swamped right now, you'll see someone faster at the clinic. If needed, the clinic will transfer you for hospitalization."

"Hospitalized for *this*?" Carl rolled his eyes.

Noah pulled up at the medical clinic. The door swung open, and Lauren ran to the vehicle, followed by a nurse.

"I'm all right," Carl insisted. "It's barely a scratch."

"Obviously it's a little more than that," Lauren said calmly.

Groaning, Carl stepped down from the cruiser and followed them into the clinic. The slice across his ribs hurt, but he had enough experience to know it wasn't serious.

Lauren was completely professional in the exam room as she examined the wound.

He hadn't wanted her to see it, but now he wondered if it was just as well. It hadn't felt entirely honest inventing excuses to see her.

"I guess you can see what it's like in law enforcement," he told her as she began to clean the wound.

She gave him several injections around the cut. "This should help with the pain while I stitch you up," she advised, ignoring his comment.

"Thanks. As I was saying, my work has its risks. No wonder so many women don't want to be involved with someone in law enforcement. I'd never ask a woman to try something she didn't think she could handle."

At that she looked up. Her eyes were filled with surprise and something else he didn't recognize.

"That's very straightforward," she finally responded.

He nodded, wishing he could convince her that it was possible to tackle life together. But he didn't have any business doing that—she'd already made her feelings plain.

LAUREN CAREFULLY STITCHED the cut in Carl's side. The blood horrified her, but not because she was squeamish. She saw blood every day...just not spilling out of Carl Stanfield.

She forced her thoughts into a detached, clinical mode. Carl didn't need someone to break down and cry; he needed someone to take care of his injury.

"Ordinarily the emergency room is the best place for something like this," she said as she finished.

"This wasn't serious."

"No, it wasn't serious, so I'm glad we could help out. You'll need to take some time off, however, to let it heal properly. Two weeks at a minimum."

He made a face.

"I mean it," she insisted. "What if you got into another confrontation and someone punched you there? You could go down, and whoever needed your help would be out of luck."

There was startled respect in Carl's eyes when she finished, and he held up his hands in mock surrender. "Okay. By the way, have you heard any more from Tara? She's been gone a long time, and I know how much you were looking forward to her visit."

"She's called a couple of times. Josh McGregor joined the camping trip and brought a satellite phone. She hasn't wanted to stay on and run up his charges, but she's having fun. She's going to stay longer when she gets back, so we'll still have the same amount of time together."

"Glad to hear it. Look, I hoped we—"

"Sorry, I should get the doctor," Lauren interrupted. "He's staying late to check you, as well."

She was glad to escape the exam room and the intense emotions Carl inspired, along with whatever else he'd started to say. He had tried to tell her that he understood how she felt, but it was clear he didn't, at least not completely.

The risks of his job were only part of why she'd resisted getting involved. Loving a man in daily danger *would* be difficult, but it wasn't the only reason.

She didn't know what to think. If she was less concerned about a relationship breaking down, would she be able to deal with Carl's career, especially since it meant so much to him?

Lauren sank into her office chair, depressed, thinking she'd probably never have the opportunity to find out.

As Josh washed another load of gravel, he realized he was enjoying the interlude in the mountains, at least when he wasn't frustrated by his libido.

"A table would be nice for sorting," he told Tara as he sat next to her on a flat rock and balanced the sieve on his knees. His jeans were perpetually damp from water dripping off the gravel, but it was easier than setting the box on the ground and bending over to sort. It was the reason Tara often wore shorts to work...which was much more comfortable for her, and excruciating for him. She had terrific legs.

"That's how they do it at a Montana mine I read about. People buy buckets of raw material, then wash and sort it on trays set out on tables."

"You sure did your research. I'll admit that I know more about agates than gemstones. It never seemed necessary to study them, so I'm glad you did some groundwork"

"I wanted to help Walt," she said simply.

"It's admirable, especially since it isn't easy for you to get close to people."

Tara was quiet for a long moment. "After a few different homes, I wouldn't let myself care about anyone. It was safer, because I knew everything was going to get ripped away, sooner or later."

"Yet you seem to value what my grandfather says about Grandma Evelyn and the cost of love."

Tara shifted her tray. "One part of my brain accepts that love should be worth the risk, but it's hard to overcome a lifetime of conditioning. I don't know if you can imagine what it was like to start loving foster parents, only to have a social worker pick you up from school and say you're being sent somewhere else. There weren't any explanations or goodbyes, only paper bags filled with a few of my belongings."

Josh hated the thought that any child could be treated that way. He knew the foster care system could work out okay for kids, but it had been lousy for Tara.

"You seem to be getting closer to Lauren," he murmured. "I know I mentioned something about it before, but maybe meeting her is helping you open up to other possibilities."

She shrugged. "I suppose, but it would be harder moving from place to place if I got too attached. I have a good life, so don't think I'm whining."

"I'd never think that," he affirmed. "You seem to take everything in stride and deal with it. The ability to do that came at a high cost, but maybe it's one of the few good things that came out of your childhood."

"Maybe."

She hurriedly jumped up and went to wash another load. Rather than return to sorting, Josh watched her work. Physically she was a stunning woman who chronically made his jeans uncomfortably tight. But as much as he hadn't wanted to see it, there was a whole lot more to Tara than beauty.

JOSH STARED AT the full moon through the tree branches. This adventure had reminded him of how beautiful Montana evenings could be.

Grandpa was snoring nearby on the raised air bed, which had turned out to be Tara's idea, along with the odd-looking air chair. He still took pain medication, especially at night, and usually slept deeply. With the hard work, Josh normally did, also, but at the moment he was curiously alert.

A faint noise on the other side of the fire caught his attention. It was Tara, slowly easing from her sleeping bag. Eyes half-shut, he watched as she gathered her bag of bathing supplies.

He gulped, picturing her in the moonlight.

The temptation was extreme.

Carefully, he got up, as well. He hesitated before searching in his pack for the condoms he'd packed on his last trip down to the ranch. *Just in case*, he thought, with a hint of self-disgust—he couldn't assume Tara wanted to make love with him again, but being prepared was an old habit.

He grabbed his towel and made his way up the dark path.

Tara was in the water when he arrived. She turned his direction.

"Mind if I skinny-dip?" he asked.

"Why not? I am."

Heat instantly surged through his groin. Shucking his clothing, Josh stepped into the pool and swam lazily, thoroughly warmed by the water that steamed more than usual in the cool night air.

It felt as if he'd wandered into another world and that Tara was one of the fairy folk from the tales he'd been told as a boy. If he approached too quickly, she might disappear in a flash of silver light.

WHEN TARA HAD SEEN Josh at the pool's edge, naked and already erect, various thoughts had raced through her mind. She'd come to the pool because she'd been unable to sleep. Their discussion that afternoon had left her with an ache in her gut that wouldn't go away.

It also annoyed her. She'd made peace with herself about her life and lack of connections, hadn't she? But Josh was right. Discovering a twin sister and trying to form a relationship with her had changed the game. Now she felt an unaccustomed hunger for affection, a hunger she'd thought was long since under control.

Sex wasn't the same as love, but it was a kind of intimacy. The first time with Josh had been quick and satisfying, but if it was going to happen again, she wanted it to last longer.

So she let him circle, waiting. If he wanted to have sex, he'd let her know. Finally he drifted within a couple feet.

She extended a hand, and almost unerringly, their fingers met and laced. He tugged her closer.

"You were smart to bring the air bed and chair so Grandpa doesn't have to get down and up from ground level as often," he murmured.

"I bought them in Helena when I drove up to exchange my rental. Luckily I got them to extend the second rental period indefinitely by saying I'd go to another company if I had to."

Their legs brushed, and electricity tingled through Tara.

Josh stroked her breasts with his other hand, teasing and coaxing, then tipped her head back to kiss her throat. It was slow and languid, the opposite of the blood pounding through her veins.

Finally he lifted her in the water so she floated, his lips exploring each of her curves, drifting to her belly and below.

Spasms went through Tara's abdomen. In the back of her mind she wondered if Josh had practiced foreplay in the water with another woman or if he was just naturally gifted. Surely not here, though. He'd claimed the hot spring pool had been unknown to him before.

Tara explored his hard frame as he pulled her to him again. She had muscles, but his seemed carved from stone…particularly when she caressed his erection. Almost as if they were dancing, they left the water. The grass was cold against her overheated back, but Josh quickly dropped down to cover her.

When he fumbled with the condom, she took it from him and unrolled it over his hard length. A moment later he was inside her, and she climaxed immediately. He seemed aware of it; she saw his faint smile in the moonlight as he played with her breasts and began moving in slow, pulsing thrusts. Unbelievably, the heat built again and she shattered a second time, just seconds before his own release.

Josh collapsed over her, chest heaving, and she wished they were in a bed, warm and secluded, where she could spend the night in his arms.

Stupid.

Those kinds of fantasies belonged to women who were comfortable with their partner *and* their own sexuality.

When Josh's chest had stopped heaving, she wiggled free, briskly toweled the remaining dampness off her skin, dressed and walked back to camp. After all, she was a master at taking what came along and dealing with it.

Even Josh had said so.

CHAPTER SIXTEEN

JOSH TRIED NOT to look at Tara too much as they worked alone the next afternoon.

A deep frustration had taken hold of him when, for the second time, she'd rushed away from their lovemaking as if nothing had happened. He finally understood why women resented it so much when their partner fell asleep quickly or hurried to get dressed and leave. He'd done it himself, hoping to avoid conversation. Yet he would have enjoyed a little afterglow with Tara.

Still, his frustration didn't make sense. What else had he expected? He ought to be *glad* she wasn't gushing or making assumptions. To his old way of thinking, Tara was actually the perfect lover, never seeming to expect a commitment. But he'd been wrong to think that she was cool and emotionless. As Grandpa had said, her eyes told the whole story, provided someone was willing to look hard enough.

"There's nothing here," he said unnecessarily as he dumped the debris into a bucket.

His grandfather had decided they should pile their discards near the alluvial deposit where they'd been working, so they could smooth it over again later. He'd said it was to keep casual visitors from speculating about why someone had dug there. Despite their lack of success, Walt remained optimistic that sapphires were a possibility and was determined to keep "sapphire rustlers" in the dark.

Josh appreciated his grandfather's unshakable belief that they'd find gems. Yet it also reminded him of something Tara had said...something that had bothered him ever since.

"Tara, a while back you told me I concentrated on rocks instead of gems. What did you mean by that?" he asked.

Her eyes widened. "Nothing bad, and as soon as I said it, I reminded myself that value is in the eyes of the beholder. An agate is as beautiful as a sapphire, just in a different way."

Josh nodded. One of his favorite stones was polished aventurine, yet aventurine was inexpensive and easily obtained. But he was also aware that he'd barely looked at his collection in years. He'd concentrated on ranching, ignoring almost everything else.

It was hard not to make comparisons between that and what his grandfather had been telling him.

Josh had always thought that putting the Boxing N first meant that Grandpa hadn't valued his wife. It wasn't true. Walt and Evelyn had shared a good life together, but in their minds, they'd been saving their best times for retirement. Then all their plans had been taken from them.

It was entirely possible that Grandpa both loved and hated the Boxing N the way Tara seemed to think. The ranch was part of Walt's heritage, passed to him by his forebears. Yet it had also gotten more of his attention than the love of his life. Would he ever be able to make peace with it?

Josh piled more rocks into his sieve and began washing them. He'd read that the questions were more important than the answers. He hoped that was true, because he had a whole bunch of questions that might never get answered. And some of the biggest ones had Tara's name on them.

LAUREN READ THE CHART for the next patient, and her breath caught in her throat.

Carl was in for his first checkup. No doubt he was hoping to get his stitches removed and permission to return to work early. Lauren set her jaw… Not if *she* had anything to do with it. The past few days had been much more comfortable for her, knowing he was safe at home. Or at least that he wasn't in uniform. And she didn't want him going back before he was 100 percent fit.

In the examination room, Carl was sitting easily in a chair, reading a *National Geographic* magazine. He tossed it to one side.

"Good morning," she said brightly. "How are you feeling?"

"Fine. I heal fast. I gashed my arm as a kid when I was stupid enough to ride my bike while carrying a mason jar. The doctor was amazed that I tried it again two days later."

"Did you have another accident?"

"Nope."

Lauren glanced down at his chart, then blinked and looked up again. "Why were you carrying a mason jar?"

"I was collecting fireflies. I was under the mistaken impression they would make a bang-up nightlight for my little sister."

She grinned. That sounded like Carl. "Well, your vitals look good, but I need to check the cut to see if the stitches can be removed yet."

"Okay." He stood, then sat on the exam table. "The nurse wanted me to wear one of those gowns with the little ties. I told her I could pull up my shirt as easily as one of those dignity-sucking outfits."

Lauren held back a laugh. "No problem."

Still, when he lifted his shirt it evoked bedroom images she'd rather not think about. So she locked them firmly into a mental drawer. Shutting out disturbing thoughts was a trick she had employed during training.

She removed the bandages. The slash on Carl's ribs was healing well, but she thought the stitches shouldn't be removed for another few days.

"Are you sure?" he asked.

"It was a long cut," she pointed out. "And it's in an area that gets stretched every time you bend or move. But I think you can start showering again."

"Good."

From the expression on his face she suspected he'd already showered at least once. But the wound showed no sign of infection, so it was likely all right. She applied a new, more compact bandage.

"Be sure to keep an eye on it," she told him. "Come back if it gets red or swollen or you have more than a small amount of clear drainage."

"Sure." He sat up and tucked his shirt into place.

"Uh…" Lauren hesitated, but it wasn't right to let him keep assuming his risky job was the only barrier between them.

Carl raised an eyebrow. "Something else?"

"There's something I need to clarify," she said carefully. "The other night you…well, assumed that my problem with us getting involved is that I can't handle your job. That's just part of it."

"I'm only your patient until this thing heals," he returned sharply. "In fact, the next time I come in, I'm asking for another PA. You're fired, as of right now. So you can forget the doctor–patient thing as a reason for not getting involved."

Lauren gathered her courage. "That isn't what I meant. The thing is…I…I don't deal well with conflict. Maybe that isn't terribly unusual, but it's particularly acute for me."

Fumbling, she tried to describe her childhood and how any kind of conflict between people left her irrationally convinced it meant the end.

"You're strong, and I knew before we ever went out that you needed someone who could be strong with you," she concluded miserably. "My old boyfriend in Los Angeles thought it would be okay, and he was a store manager, not a cop. But ultimately he got tired of it and called me 'the gutless wonder.'"

"That was cruel and uncalled for," Carl said quickly. "Besides, you can't judge me by what he did."

"Maybe not, but I know my weaknesses. I only brought this up because I think you're making a mistake to back off whenever a woman is worried about your job. Surely you *want* to be with someone who cares about your safety. So don't try to make that decision for someone else. That isn't fair, and it will cheat you both."

Lauren rushed from the room, blinking tears from her eyes. The thought of Carl dating someone else hurt, but she'd said what she needed to say.

TARA SHOOK HER head emphatically. "You're wrong, Josh. The designated hitter rule in the American League has a lot of value. There *ought* to be something that distinguishes between the two leagues.

And another benefit is that it can extend the career of a great baseball player."

"It's a ridiculous way to play the game. Everyone who hits should fill a position, and vice versa."

"In that case, maybe the first- and third-base coaches should be position players, too."

"That isn't the same thing."

"It doesn't seem that different to me." They'd debated the subject for the past ten minutes, and it was plain they would never agree. That was all right. Tara had learned to love baseball while living in Japan and had strong opinions.

When Josh had insisted on staying with her and Walt, she'd expected endless arguments whenever they were alone. Instead, while they'd debated and occasionally sniped at each other, they'd also discussed everything under the sun. Naturally the times he'd ridden down to deal with ranch business had been less stressful, but they'd also felt curiously flat.

She still disliked him, right?

Sexual compatibility didn't mean she'd changed her mind about him being pushy and unreasonable, though admittedly, now that she understood some of the reasons for his behavior, it was easier to forgive.

Not that it mattered. In another ten days or so, Tara estimated their combined supplies would be exhausted. She hadn't told Walt; it still worried her how he'd respond if they didn't find any sapphires.

"Is something wrong?" Josh asked. He'd grown more adept at recognizing the tiniest shift in her mood.

"Just thinking about Walt. He's sensible, but I'd hate to see disappointment setting him back."

"Grandpa knows you're concerned. I doubt *he* knows how he'll react, but even if we don't find something this time, it doesn't mean the search is over."

"True. And I'm sure he sees value in simply making the trip. Even a failed attempt can be a valiant quest."

"That sounds like a fairy-tale conclusion."

"Because I called it a quest?"

Some of the things they'd debated were words and their uses or meanings and emotional impacts. Josh was smart, well-read and as opinionated as Tara was herself.

Fortunately, the one thing he hadn't tried to discuss was their lovemaking—or sex, or intercourse, or whatever term was most accurate. Tara had always thought "making love" wasn't the right term unless two people were actually *in* love. Anything else was just about satisfying a physical need.

A quiver of desire ran through her veins as she remembered the pleasure she'd experienced that night at the pool. Sex was more powerful than she'd ever believed, but she wasn't in love with him.

After all, who wanted a handsome rancher who thought raising organic cattle was the most important thing in life?

Once she left Montana, she would surely regain her balance.

JOSH SHARED TARA'S worries about his grandfather, though he agreed that Walt would be able to find value in the attempt. Her insight was impressive, particularly when he considered her bleak childhood.

He had to smile when he recalled her firm command not to think she was whining. Tara didn't feel sorry for herself. And while she didn't brag, he'd figured out enough to know she'd gotten through college mostly on her own dime and was in demand in her field.

Actually, it was almost laughable that she'd been willing to clean out the Boxing N ranch office and sort its records. She could write her own ticket anywhere in the world, yet she'd taken on the Boxing N for a fraction of what she could charge elsewhere.

Then, when an old man desperately needed a new interest in life, she'd cheerfully traveled into the mountains to sleep on the ground and spend twelve hours a day in hard and dirty labor.

Josh wondered where his own brain had been for so many months, butting heads with Walt and grinding his teeth because he wasn't getting exactly what he'd dreamed of. He'd completely missed the reason Walt couldn't let go.

"Is this one of those Montana agates?" Tara asked, holding out a stone for him to examine.

"Yeah," he said, struck again by the fact he'd spent little time on his rock-hound hobby lately.

She tucked it into her pocket. "At first I wondered whether having agates and other stuff all mixed up meant it was ridiculous to think sapphires might also be here. Then I realized that's the point of looking in alluvial deposits. Everything gets washed into streams and rivers and mixed up together."

"Sure. Stones have been carried by water, so you could have various things from all over the place."

Tara glanced toward the mountains west of them. "I've been thinking, though. If there are sapphires in alluvial deposits, they'd have to come from somewhere higher up."

"Probably. Grandpa thinks this area is where the original sapphires were found, and that's why he wanted to search here. But eventually we may need to look elsewhere."

As he spoke, Josh was aware that he was now completely hooked on the search. He'd had more fun the past few weeks than any other time in recent years. Part of it was his growing relationship with his grandfather...and part of it was spending time with Tara. But it wasn't just the possibility of more incredible sex; she was also good company. She had intelligence and humor in spades and wasn't shy about giving him hell when she didn't agree.

Tara stood and stretched. "I'm going to dig for a while," she said. "I like to have a good pile for Walt when he comes back."

"Just a minute," he said, standing and leading her to the shady spot where the tiny waterfall made their work easier.

Pulling her close, he laid his lips over hers. Lord, she smelled good.

"What was that about?" she asked with the same nonchalance about their intimacy that she'd shown before. Except now he thought it meant more to her than she revealed.

"I wanted to find out what it was like to kiss you without having warm water all over us."

"But you kissed me in the office once, remember?"

He definitely remembered.

"True," he agreed. "But that was different."

"I don't see how."

Josh smiled. "I could show you, but Grandpa might come back early, and I'm not an exhibitionist."

The blue in Tara's eyes darkened. "I suppose we could meet at the pool tonight, after he's asleep. Not to go in the water, since you want to satisfy your curiosity about…dry skin."

"We could always swim afterward."

"True."

Determinedly she pulled away and marched toward the shovel.

Josh watched, torn. Sharing his life with Tara might mean more than all the other goals he'd worked toward and he couldn't escape the fact that he'd fallen in love and wanted a lifetime together. The revolution in his ideas about his life stunned him. But Tara didn't *want* to live in Schuyler. Just the day before, she'd talked about which country she might pick next, and whether she ought to take a one-year contract over the usual two—because that way she could see more of the world.

And what if he *did* convince her to marry him? One day she might get tired of ranch life and wasting her abilities. There weren't any businesses around Schuyler that truly needed someone with her qualifications. How would he feel once she took off for London or Tokyo or one of the other places she loved?

Perhaps it would be even worse if she *didn't* leave. She was loyal and gritty and might stay to make the best of things. Josh's stomach rolled at the thought, because it meant he'd be doing the same thing to her that he'd always assumed his grandfather had done to Evelyn.

STUNNED, TARA STARED down at the translucent green lump in her fingers. She'd glanced down as she was digging and the sun had caught it just right in the pile of dusty rocks.

Dirty, rough and irregular, it looked exactly like the photos of raw green sapphires she'd seen while researching Montana gemstones.

Dropping the shovel, she hurried to where Josh was sorting rocks.

"I found one," she practically shouted.

He straightened and looked carefully at the stone, a cautious expression on his face. "Interesting. What makes you think it's a sapphire?"

"I know it isn't blue, but they come in all sorts of colors. This is exactly like one of the green sapphires I saw on the internet."

"They aren't just blue?" All of a sudden Josh groaned. "I'm sure I haven't seen any stones like this up here, but they've been right in front of me my entire life and I never recognized them. None of us did."

"What do you mean?"

"Have you ever seen one of those old canning jars—the ones that used to have zinc lids and eventually turn lavender?"

Tara wasn't familiar with them, but she nodded anyway and waited.

"There's one in the kitchen," he continued. "Grandma kept it in the window because it was full of marbles and rocks and she liked the sun shining through them." Josh held the sapphire up and shook it. "There are several in there that look quite a bit like this one."

Tara tried to choke down a laugh.

"Go ahead," he said. "Laugh your head off. It's the best and worst joke that's ever been played on the Nelson family."

It bubbled out of her, and he reluctantly joined her.

"Sapphires," he said at length, pulling her close. *"Sapphires."*

His kiss was full and deep, and Tara returned it with all her strength, but when his hands slid under her T-shirt, she stepped backward.

"Whoa, we need to go tell Walt."

Josh grinned. "Yeah."

Back at the campsite, Walt was seated in his chair and looked up eagerly when they catapulted into the clearing.

"Look what Tara just found," Josh exclaimed, handing the raw gem to him. "It's a green sapphire."

Walt's eyes gleamed. "Do you know what this means?"

"Sure. It means my great-great-grandfather found sapphires a century ago and the proof has been staring us in the face every time we wash our hands."

"What?" Walt demanded.

"The jar that Grandma kept over the kitchen sink…remember what's in there?"

Comprehension dawned on Walt's face, and he groaned exactly the way Josh had groaned. Then he chuckled. "Ah, well, water under the bridge." He held the gem in the air and admired it. "Let's get to work. Where there's one, there could be more."

"Absolutely," Josh agreed enthusiastically. "We may have finally hit the right layer."

Tara was amazed by his zeal.

"We might not find any of gem quality," she cautioned them both.

"Who gives a rat's ass?" Walt asked.

"That's right. You just found a sapphire, and no one can take the fun of it away from us," Josh declared.

Relaxing, Tara nodded. "Then let's go."

Walt walked with a new bounce in his step as they returned to the dig site.

They carefully pulled out more piles of dirt and stones. Tara discovered a tiny blue sapphire in her sieve an hour later, and Walt got one soon after. It wasn't until nearly dinnertime that Josh exclaimed and held out a translucent brilliant blue stone in his fingers.

They forgot about food and everything else as they worked. It was dusk when they reluctantly returned to the campsite to eat trail mix and crawl into their sleeping bags.

But Tara hadn't forgotten her suggestion to Josh about meeting at the hot spring pool. When she saw him quietly slip away, she sat up and checked to be sure Walt was asleep.

Why not enjoy it while she could? She would never be in these circumstances again, and she wanted Josh with every cell in her body.

CHAPTER SEVENTEEN

JOSH WOKE THE next morning, knowing that if he were a rooster, he'd be crowing at the top of lungs, hardly the attitude of a twenty-first-century man. Tara had joined him at the hot spring pool, turning into a temptress, bewitching him as she pulled off her clothes and lay on the tarp he'd spread in hopes she would come.

They'd made love not once but twice in the brilliant moonlight. Afterward, they'd gone into the warm water, swimming and playing as if they were children instead of adults who'd enjoyed all the pleasures of their sexuality.

Later, Tara had dressed and returned to bed, barely acknowledging him as she departed.

Why did she act that way? He was certain she didn't take sex casually, but he was equally certain he didn't know what was going on in her head.

He kept returning to the thought of what it would be like to share a life with her. But if he couldn't figure out why she was so remote after making love, he certainly couldn't fathom how she'd feel about marriage.

Except he *did* know. She'd made her feelings

perfectly clear when he'd stupidly declared he wasn't interested in a long-term relationship. Who would have guessed he'd come to regret his adamant declaration?

He was finally getting a clue. Love and home and family were important, and it had taken a woman who'd grown up without any of those things to remind him of that.

CARL ABSENTLY SCRATCHED his ribs. The cut was starting to itch like crazy. It was a normal part of healing, and he could try getting something at the drugstore to help. Stopping by the clinic was also a possibility, but he didn't want to risk running into Lauren.

Eileen, the day manager and emergency dispatcher, grinned when she saw him come through the door.

"Welcome back, boss," she said. "Got a release from the doc?"

"None of your business. I'm just here to visit and see if the station is still in one piece."

"We considered moving to Vegas so we could play the slot machines when things got slow, but decided it would lengthen response time too much."

Chuckling, Carl grabbed the mail from his inbox and went through it. There were more get-well cards, dozens of which had already been delivered to his apartment by Noah Mercer.

Noah had been coming by each day, and Carl

shook his head as he thought about the deputy's worried face. Finally Noah had confessed that he felt responsible for the way things had gone down out at the Roadhouse.

"I should have been faster dealing with that guy," he'd said. "Then you wouldn't have been fighting two of them."

"Don't be ridiculous," Carl had assured him. "We had three guys to handle, and you took down the biggest one. You're a great deputy, and I'm glad to have you on the force."

It appeared to be the right thing to say; Noah had calmed down and been less stressed on his next visit.

Over the next few hours, Carl dealt with his mail and talked with his deputies.

At noon he sat back and considered whether to go down to the café for lunch. Before being injured, he'd gone regularly on the days he knew that Lauren was working, in the hopes of running into her. Now he'd lost track of her schedule.

Lauren's revelations troubled him.

Conflict sometimes *did* end relationships. He'd known that since he was a kid. His mother had been anguished by the danger his father faced as a cop and it had finally torn them apart.

But from what Lauren had said, her parents had fought over everything, and sometimes over nothing. As a child who'd finally gotten what any foster kid would want—a family—it must have been terrifying to feel it could all be snatched away again. It sounded as if her new parents hadn't trusted each other enough to argue and still know that they'd both be there when it was done.

Conflict was inevitable in any relationship. But he didn't believe Lauren lacked courage; she just needed to trust him enough to know that he wasn't going anywhere. Ironically, she'd also done the very thing she'd warned him against…deciding for *him* that he wouldn't be able to deal with her issues.

Everything was in a damned tangle. Lauren obviously didn't realize his feelings were serious, but she was right that he'd always pulled back whenever a woman expressed concern about his career. It was a pattern set well before they'd ever met. He'd tried to protect people instead of giving them the right to choose for themselves.

Maybe it was time to try a different approach.

THERE IN THE DARK, it was so quiet that Tara could hear Josh's breathing a few feet away.

For the past week he had been slowly edging his sleeping bag closer to hers, though she wasn't sure what to do about it.

A slash of light shot across the gap between the trees, and she sighed. The wonder of shooting stars never seemed to go away. Despite knowing they were simply little bits of rock burning up in Earth's atmosphere, she still wanted to make a wish and see if it came true.

"Beautiful, isn't it?" Josh whispered.

"Incredible."

"Right now it seems as if the mountain is singing."

Tara knew what he meant but didn't want to say so.

"That sounds fanciful," she said instead.

"I find myself getting more and more imaginative up here, as if anything is possible."

"It's a nice way to think."

"But you don't agree."

Tara turned on her side toward him. "People say anything is possible, but that means that bad things are possible, too."

"Don't tell me you're a pessimist."

"I think I'm more of a realist."

"But some things have gone right for you, haven't they?" he asked.

"I'm not complaining. I've found my sister, traveled and done okay in my career."

"We've also found sapphires. The potential for good things is endless."

"Perhaps."

He shifted to face her, as well. "Is it just your childhood that makes you skeptical, or something else?"

Tara pressed her lips together; there was no reason not to reveal more about her life, except she wasn't used to sharing.

"Obviously it's up to me to break the revelations logjam," Josh murmured, "so I'll admit to sneaking off to Spain and running with the bulls one year. My girlfriend thought it was the perfect way to prove how much I loved her."

"Yikes."

"Afterward I told my folks I busted my shoulder playing football with my friends. I also realized that if Celine had really loved me, she would never have demanded something so reckless."

"Too bad you didn't figure it out before busting your shoulder."

"How about you?" he asked. "What's one of the skeletons in your closet?"

"Pierre Montrose," she said reluctantly.

"Tell me more about him."

She wasn't obligated to say anything, but the night felt surreal, as if it really *was* confession time. "What would you like to hear?" she asked lightly. "He thought he was a great lover who deserved a girlfriend who was both a nun and a call girl."

"He sounds about as mature as Celine."

"I wasn't in love, any more than you were," she acknowledged.

"Have you ever been in love?"

"I went last. It isn't my turn for another confession."

"Yeah, but I went first. Isn't it fair for you to fess up before I go again?"

Part of her wanted to know what Josh might

confess next, but it also seemed dangerous. The more she understood him, the more her heart got involved.

"Who said life is fair?" she countered.

"Come on, truth or dare," he urged.

"That's a fool's game."

"Not the way I play. We could have fun."

Tara could imagine the dare he'd use, and it *would* be fun, but she wasn't prepared to answer any more questions.

"What do you say?" he whispered.

"Go soak your head."

"Soaking *something* sounds like a fine idea."

"Do you ever quit?" she asked in exasperation.

He chuckled. "Rarely."

Suddenly, Walt's voice intruded. "If you kids are going to keep talking, then stop being rude and speak up so I can understand you."

A sputter of laughter burst from Tara's throat.

"Sorry, Grandpa," Josh called. "We thought you were asleep."

"I would be if you let me have some peace and quiet."

Tara snuggled down into her sleeping bag, unable to turn her gaze away from Josh. Firelight gleamed in his blue eyes, still fixed on her. Slowly she grew sleepier, and everything circled into a blur.

When she woke up, dawn was unfolding in glorious colors and she tried to convince herself that everything was as it should be.

LAUREN WAS FIXING DINNER when she heard a knock on her door. She peeked through the curtain and saw Carl, dressed in full uniform.

Her stomach flip-flopped—one of the doctors at the clinic must have given him a medical release.

She didn't want to talk to him, but he didn't look like a man who intended to go away easily.

Blast. She might as well face whatever was necessary rather than wait. Anticipation was usually worse than reality.

She opened the door and fixed a casual smile on her face.

"Hi, Carl. I see you're back at work. How is it going?"

"Everything is fine and I feel great. May I come in?"

"Uh, sure."

He walked into the apartment and pulled off his shoulder holster. Her eyes widened when he removed his service revolver and checked the safety before placing it on the coffee table.

"I want to know if you think you could get used to seeing me come home armed this way every night," he announced calmly. "Because I'll always come home to you, no matter what arguments we might have. And if a bullet ever stops my heart, my spirit will still come home to you, because I love you more than anything else in this world."

He stopped and gazed at her. Trembling, she

opened her mouth but couldn't get any words out.
A declaration of undying devotion was the last
thing she'd expected.

Drawing her close, Carl dropped a gentle kiss
on her lips. "I just need you to trust me," he whispered, "because I have faith that you'll stick with
me through everything, as well. Besides, turnabout
is fair play. You said I shouldn't make decisions
for someone else, so you shouldn't make them for
me. Can we discuss this?"

Carl was staring down at her with a burning
hope that she couldn't disappoint.

She nodded, but still pulled away and dropped
onto the couch. He sat nearby in an easy chair.

"Darling, everyone is affected by what they
learn in childhood," he said urgently. "Some of
it is good, some isn't. Sometimes we let go of
the bad things, while others keep coming back.
You learned conflict can sometimes end love. I
learned that a dangerous job can tear people apart,
so maybe I've been too quick to assume a woman
can't deal with it."

"Well…that's what it sounded like, but it wasn't
any of my business to say something."

"I invited you to make it your business."

With a smile, he lifted her hand from where it
rested on the arm of the couch and kissed her fingers.

"My folks got divorced when I was a kid," he
continued. "They eventually got back together,

but only after Dad retired. They got married right out of high school and thought they knew what they wanted, but then my father decided to become a cop. He didn't talk to Mom about it, just announced that he was going to the police academy. It terrified her."

Lauren knew it must have been awful for his mother to suddenly have her husband change the direction of their lives. Obviously she'd stayed in the marriage for a while, but it must have seemed unfair that he'd made the choice for them both.

"For years Mom would go to the library and read criminology books or find articles about police officers hurt or killed in the line of duty," Carl murmured. "Then she'd warn Dad to be careful about one situation or another. It was ghoulish."

"It sounds like a coping mechanism."

"I suppose." A puzzled expression filled Carl's face. "Strangely, it was my father who left. He insisted that Mom didn't ask him to go, but I never believed him."

"Are you sure?" Lauren asked. "Maybe he couldn't deal with the pain he was putting her through. It's hard doing that to someone you love."

Carl stared at her, and Lauren wondered if this was a possibility he'd never considered.

It had certainly made *her* think. Bitter, stupid, petty arguments were hurtful. Would her adoptive parents have argued that way if they'd loved each other the way she loved Carl? Would they have said such horrid, hateful things?

"I never thought of it that way," he admitted. But you may be right. Dad *could* have been the one who decided he couldn't take it any longer."

"Did they ever seriously discuss the danger or get counseling?" Lauren asked.

Carl frowned. "Not that I know of, but that might have been part of the problem. I talked to Dad this week. He told me he'd chosen a different life for them as a couple and always felt guilty because he didn't even ask how she felt about it. He didn't want to hear how hard it was for her, so when she tried to warn him about something, he just felt worse."

Lauren nodded, trying to decide whether *she* could face the dangers of Carl's work. Being a sheriff in Schuyler wasn't nearly as dangerous as being a big-city police officer, but obviously there were hazards. A knife wound, a gunshot, an accident from a high-speed chase… Any number of possibilities could become realities. She could lose her husband without warning, and her children could lose their father.

On the other hand, if she turned him away now, she'd lose him anyway.

"What are you thinking?" Carl asked.

"Just that there may be worse things than knowing the person you love is doing a dangerous job. Not that it's something I'd enjoy. No one would."

"No, but as you've said, I wouldn't want to be with someone who didn't care enough to be concerned."

"Right," she agreed slowly. "And I couldn't promise I wouldn't freak out about it sometimes."

He chuckled and began to look more hopeful. Still, his career wasn't their only problem, as Lauren knew too well.

"Wh-what about the rest of it?" she asked. "Wouldn't you rather be with someone who isn't so afraid of everything?"

"Only idiots don't get scared. It's what you do with it that counts. But I *would* want you to trust me enough to argue with me. Do you think you could ever do that?"

Lauren caught her breath. Trust. That was the thing she needed, to trust that he'd never push her away or leave. To trust that he'd never get petty and pull the tricks her parents had pulled on each other…to trust that he'd keep on loving her, no matter what. To know there was a line that neither of them would ever cross, because you didn't do that to someone you loved.

"I believe in you," he added. "More than I can say."

"And I believe in you," she choked out through the emotions clogging her throat. "I love you so much."

He leaned over and pulled her into his arms. It would take time and patience, but surely they could make a life together.

JOSH WAS THOROUGHLY enjoying himself. Never in his life could he have imagined getting along with Grandpa so well. Jokes and laughter filled the air as they dug deeper into the alluvial deposit. The creek they were working on had once been a larger river, so the possibilities were intriguing. Still, it didn't mean they'd find any more sapphires than they already had.

But it really didn't matter. The gems that counted were the renewed life in his grandfather's smile and the mysterious secrets in Tara's vibrant eyes.

Nevertheless, two days after they'd found the first sapphires, more began appearing. While none of them were experts, some of the stones appeared to be good quality, and many were a brilliant cornflower blue. Josh held a large one up to the light, comparing it to the wide Montana sky. It was almost as if a piece of that sky had crystallized and fallen to earth.

The following days were equally fruitful, especially now that they'd figured out what to look for and how to best use the sieves for washing the rocks.

And every night, he went to the pool. Tara sometimes joined him there, sometimes not. But she never discussed it, or acted as if anything had happened between them.

"The food is getting low," Tara announced, eleven days after she'd found the first sapphire.

Jake knew the only reason it had held up so long was because he'd brought some back with him after his last trip down to handle the ranch payroll. He'd considered bringing more, but it was easier to do the return trip in a day without leading a pack horse.

"Dang it," Walt grumbled.

"I could fetch more supplies, Grandpa, but we can't stay up here the entire summer," Josh told him. "There are a few things that have to be done on the ranch."

"You made Clyde Hawes the foreman, didn't you?" Walt demanded.

"Sure," Josh agreed, hiding a smile at how agreeable Grandpa now found the decision to put someone else in charge. "But it's still a new arrangement, and other things weren't planned for ahead of time."

"You have your phone."

"That isn't the same as being there. Tell you what, we can come back in the autumn."

"Yeah, well…" Walt glanced at Tara, who was bending over the fire. Josh suddenly understood. *They* could return later…but Tara wouldn't be with them. Her absence would leave a gaping hole.

"How much longer can we stay?" Josh asked.

Tara assessed the remaining food. "Two days, with breakfast on the third, but just a handful of trail mix on the way down."

"I don't mind," Walt said quickly.

"Me, either," Tara agreed, and Josh nodded, though he knew it wasn't smart to push things.

Like his grandfather, he wished they had weeks left, but he had a feeling time wouldn't make a difference to something that mattered more than sapphires. They needed to return to their lives...and make some decisions.

So after their final breakfast, they packed up camp before going to cover the area they'd been digging through.

Then they mounted their horses and made their way off the mountain.

A SINKING SENSATION hit Tara as they rode into the Boxing N's large barn. It was back to real life. Of course, it was always a downer when returning from a holiday. She enjoyed her real life, but adventures were hard to beat.

Andrew Whitlan met them.

"Hey, boss," he called. "Hi, Tara, Mr. Nelson. How was the camping trip?"

"Terrific," Josh answered. Unable to tell the ranch hands the real reason for their absence, he'd told them his grandfather had wanted time away to think about things, and that he'd decided to do the same. With Clyde in charge, it had apparently sounded reasonable to them.

"Is everything in good shape here?" he asked.

"You bet."

While Josh chatted with Andrew and some of the hands who'd ridden in when they spotted them coming, Tara unsaddled her horse, groomed the gelding and put him into a stall. "Good, Ringo," she murmured, giving him a last rub on the nose.

She expected to help with the pack horses, but one of the cowhands stopped her, saying, "We're taking care of them, miss."

"Thanks."

Josh had gone to talk with Clyde, so she turned to Walt. "I'd better get back to my apartment and check in with Lauren."

"It's been a good trip, kid."

Smiling determinedly, she nodded. "The best. I'll see you in a day or two. I still need to finish organizing those historical records."

Holding back unexpected emotion, Tara hurried to her car. She'd expected to find a thick coat of dust on the paint, but someone must have washed it. After loading everything into the trunk, she got in and drove toward Schuyler.

Already the weeks she'd spent on the mountain seemed like a glowing dream.

On the passenger seat was a pouch of raw sapphires. She hadn't wanted to accept the gift, but Josh and Walt had insisted. The two men seemed to be getting along well. The entire ride to the ranch, they'd amicably debated the merits of using the sapphires for commercial purposes or saving them as a private family treasure trove.

Hopefully, they'd keep making progress on their relationship now that they were home. It concerned her because the Boxing N was an emotional trigger for them both.

Dropping by the grocery store first, Tara bought vegetables, something she'd been craving; freeze-dried stew had some nutrients and they'd supplemented with dried fruits, but that was no replacement for fresh, crisp veggies.

At the apartment she started a load of laundry before dialing her sister's number. She got voice mail.

"Hi, Lauren," she said. "It's Tara. I'm back from the mountains and everything is fine. I'll talk with you tomorrow. Right now I'm looking forward to crawling into a real bed."

She prepared a large salad, but it didn't taste as good as she'd expected—maybe it lacked the savor of mountain air. Her shower was equally disappointing, though she'd expected to revel in having modern plumbing again. Of course, a fiberglass shower stall couldn't compare to a hot spring pool out in the wild, but at least it was easier to wash her hair.

Trying to push away the memories, Tara finally sat down with a biography of Mary, Queen of Scots, that she'd picked up at a library sale. While it wasn't the most uplifting reading material, she hoped it would help her stop wishing for the impossible.

JOSH WENT INTO Schuyler to shop and get a pizza to share with his grandfather.

They ate in the kitchen, and memories of Grandma Evelyn crowded in. It was obviously worse for Walt, but the tension eased when they opened the old mason jar from the window over the sink. Sure enough, sapphires had been in plain view all the time.

Yet knocking around in the back of Josh's head was the memory of seeing Tara's car driving away. Why hadn't she waited to say goodbye? He'd only been gone a few minutes.

It shouldn't surprise him. She was great at leaving; he didn't know if she'd ever be good at staying.

Later he and his grandfather sat on the porch, watching the sun drop low on the western horizon.

Josh hated to spoil the companionable moment, but he finally leaned forward. "Grandpa, I've been thinking. Let's split responsibilities on the Boxing N. Your first love has always been horses. Why don't you take over the horse-breeding program and leave the cattle ranching to me? That way we won't step on each other's toes."

Walt scratched his jaw. "I suppose you still want to buy bull semen from Texas."

"I want to get into producing organic beef. It takes a while to be certified, but I can build the herd until then. Upgrading our other cattle is a good idea, too, and the best way is through artificial insemination."

"That isn't how we've always done things."

"I know, but the business is changing, Grandpa. Property owned by a family for generations is being sold or turned into dude ranches. I don't want that happening to the Boxing N, which is one reason I want to tap into the organic market. A lot of our acreage won't support as many cattle, but organic beef commands high prices, which should make up for that."

Josh could tell he'd scored a point. The Boxing N hadn't turned a profit for several years—mostly because the way Grandpa did things was stubbornly out-of-date. They both knew it, but it wasn't necessary to be hurtful. Walter Nelson had worked hard and done his best.

"My pop used to say, 'The view is nice, but it isn't real sustaining,'" Walt said slowly. "I still don't understand this organic thing, though."

"Does it matter, if we get more money?"

Walt chuckled. "Nope. You know…there's room in the foaling barn for more mares."

"That's right."

As they continued discussing how to work things out, Josh saw relief on his grandfather's face.

"How does Tara fit into all of this?" Walt asked abruptly.

A humorless laugh escaped Josh. He shouldn't be surprised. Grandpa was too smart not to have realized something was going on. He'd probably even guessed before leaving on his sapphire quest.

"I'm not sure," Josh admitted. "Tara enjoys cities and travel and living in new places. She doesn't put down roots, so I doubt she'd consider staying in Schuyler, even if her sister is here."

Walt's eyes narrowed. "Does that have to end things between you?"

Josh stared, confused for an instant. Then understanding crept in…why *should* Tara be the one to give up her lifestyle? What about compromise? He'd been thinking about whether she'd be willing to settle down in Schuyler, but that wasn't the only choice.

TARA WOKE LATE the next morning, a surprise because she'd been rising at sunrise for weeks. Unfortunately she hadn't gotten to sleep for hours last night; the bed had been too soft, the sounds of the town too loud and a feeling akin to claustrophobia had kept her restless.

It was just a case of getting used to civilization again, she decided. After all, her first weeks in Schuyler had been a shock after living in Paris, and adjusting to Melbourne after her trip to the outback had taken time, as well.

She dressed and walked over to her sister's apartment. Lauren must have seen her coming from the window, because she threw open the door and rushed out for a hug before Tara could knock.

"I've missed you so much," Lauren exclaimed. "And I have incredible news. Carl Stanfield and I are engaged!" Her nose wrinkled. "Go ahead and say, 'I told you so.'"

"Okay, I told you so. But it's also wonderful. Congratulations," Tara said, despite the hollow sensation in her midriff. "I want to take you both out to dinner to celebrate."

"Carl is attending a law enforcement seminar in Rapid City right now, but we can go when he gets back."

FOUR EVENINGS LATER Tara watched her sister and her fiancé together, determined not to envy their happiness. They practically glowed, and there was a subtle, unspoken communication between them that said more than anything they could have told her aloud.

Lauren falling in love and getting married would change things. They'd likely have a family soon, so there probably wouldn't be any trips abroad to visit her twin.

That's okay, Tara thought determinedly. Her sister deserved to be happy.

She returned to her small apartment after saying good-night and sank onto the couch. Honestly, there wasn't any reason to feel lonely. She'd found a sister and soon she'd have a very nice brother-in-law. Everything was the way it should be... Lauren was the kind of woman who got married and had children, same as her friend Emily.

It turned out that Walt had gotten back barely in time for the big event; Emily had gone into labor two days after their return from Smaug's Mountain. Tara had hoped to spend an extra day at the Boxing N office with Walt practicing email and Skype, but instead he'd been at the hospital to greet his new great-grandson.

She sighed and glanced around her living room. It was rather dull—decent furniture, but with no distinctive character. Other than buying flowers, she rarely personalized the places she lived. The exception was a digital-photo frame that rotated through photos of her travels, sitting on the divider by the kitchen. She'd plugged it back in that morning, and the photographs on the memory card were from Great Britain.

The British Isles were beautiful, green and rich with ancient history. Yet as Tara watched one scene dissolve into another, she felt even more alone. There weren't any people she knew in the photographs, just strangers who'd seemed interesting—a fish seller in Liverpool, a child staring up in awe at a Buckingham Palace guard, that sort of thing. The slide show could have been scanned from a magazine or culled from the internet.

Tara raised her chin. The photos meant something to her because she'd seen those places and taken them. Ultimately, pictures were the only belongings she cared very much about.

Determinedly she took her camera out of her duffel bag. She copied the memory card to her computer and began going through the recent images. There were lovely shots of Montana countryside, a number of Lauren, and a great many of Walt and Josh. This would be a very different set of pictures to put in the digital frame.

Yet she hesitated. She wasn't ready to have photos of Josh in her apartment, so she carefully backed them up on a portable hard drive. It was something she usually did, but there was no denying she was taking special care this time.

In the living room was a small knickknack shelf. On it she arranged the sapphires from her pouch. She wasn't sure what to do with them. Perhaps they could be a wedding gift for Lauren and Carl. She could sell them, but she didn't need the money. And keeping the gems would be a painful reminder of Walt...and Josh.

No, she wasn't going to think about it that way.

Walt would continue to be a friend, and his grandson would be a pleasant memory. After all, few women had the opportunity to swim by moonlight in a mountain hot spring pool and enjoy the company of a very proficient lover.

But now it was time to go back to her normal life and think about what came next.

CHAPTER EIGHTEEN

A WEEK AFTER returning home, Josh and his grandfather met with Clyde Hawes to discuss their plan for operating the ranch. The birth of Emily and Trent's son had taken precedence over everything else, but with the excitement settling down, they needed the Boxing N foreman to know how things were going to operate in the future.

Questions or problems with the horses would be referred to Walt. Anything to do with the cattle would come to Josh.

Clyde was too diplomatic to comment on the arrangement, but he was clearly pleased. "One of the new guys seems to have some extra horse sense, Mr. Nelson," he said. "If you want, I can assign him to muck out the foaling barn for a few days so you can get a feel for his work. His name is Hector Morales. He's young, but very keen. He grew up on ranch near Tulsa."

Walt nodded. "I'll check him out."

As Clyde left, Josh glanced toward the ranch office. "Is Tara finished sorting out the files?"

"Yes." His grandfather's expression became dour. "She left notes on everything, including a set for you. I'll miss seeing her every day, but she's shown me how to do email."

Josh nodded, amused. "Email is a great way to keep in touch."

"I like Skype better," Walt returned seriously. "That way we can see each other when we talk."

Hearing his technology-hating grandfather casually mention Skype was almost more than Josh could handle. "I used to Skype with the family when I lived down south."

"Yes, well, Tara has promised to keep me up to date on all her travels, one way or another."

Pain went through Josh at the idea of Tara so far away. Never in his life could he have imagined caring for a woman the way he cared for her.

Walt cleared his throat. "I, uh, was thinking I'd like to go to the cemetery and bring flowers to Evelyn."

Josh tried to keep his expression neutral. Grandpa had been too badly injured to attend the funeral and had refused to visit the cemetery since being released from the hospital. Josh had taken that as confirmation of how distant his grandparents' marriage had been, but no longer. Now he knew how hard it must have been for Walt to consider going to his wife's graveside. Wanting to go now might mean Walt's soul was healing as well as his body.

"Are you sure you're ready?" Josh asked.

"I think so. But if you don't mind, I'd like Tara to come with us."

"I'll ask her."

After Walt left, Josh considered phoning Tara, but thought it would be better to tell her the latest development in person. At her apartment he knocked, wondering if he should have called first. Then he heard her light, quick footsteps and the door opened.

"Hi."

Instead of jeans and a T-shirt, she wore a graceful black skirt and gray blouse, with sparkling blue sapphire solitaires in her ears. Lord, she was beautiful.

"I came to ask a favor," he said. "It's for Grandpa. He wants to bring flowers to the cemetery, and he wants you to come with us."

"I don't know," Tara murmured. "Visiting a grave... Isn't that a family thing?"

"Not really, and even if it was, Grandpa's wishes are what matter."

"Yes, of course. In that case, I'll be happy to go."

"Great. I'll call later and we can work out a good time."

LATE THE NEXT AFTERNOON Josh drove his grandfather to Schuyler's community cemetery. Tara had wanted to meet them and was waiting at the gate, looking distinctly uncomfortable.

They walked toward the Nelson family plot.

"The McGregors are over there," Walt told Tara,

gesturing across the cemetery. "So I guess in the end, we're all going to rest in peace together."

It was a curious thought that after all the rivalries and tensions between the two families, they'd lie together in common ground.

There were fresh flowers on Grandma Evelyn's grave, and Josh knew someone else had been there recently. A pang went through him; there was no sign now of where the turf had been removed and replaced. How could that much time have passed? It still seemed like yesterday.

"I need to get a proper stone," Walt said, looking at the small metal plate with his wife's name. "Your mother wants me to choose one, but I haven't been able to do it. Makes the whole thing too real, I suppose."

Walt bent and set down the bouquet of flowers he'd picked in the garden and along the road. "Evelyn loved the flowers she'd planted," he said. "And she loved the flowers of Montana."

Josh's eyes burned, remembering his grandmother working in the garden, or sitting and painting pictures of wildflowers.

"I couldn't come when you were laid here," Walt said softly, talking to his wife. "But I hope you know how much I love you."

As Josh glanced down and saw Tara's fingers laced with his, the memory of holding Grandma Evelyn's hand in the hospital rushed back.

"She knows, Grandpa," Josh said, Tara's firm

grasp helping him to get the words out. "I'd forgotten, but she reacted at the hospital when I told
her I was going to see you."

Walt's eyes sharpened. "Did she say anything?"

"Not with words," Josh answered, wishing with
all his heart he could say something different. "I
was holding her hand, and she brushed my palm
with her thumb. Three times. It was very distinct."

Grandpa pulled in a sharp breath, and Josh saw
tears gathering in his hazel eyes.

"She always did that when we held hands," Walt
said, his voice choked. "In the beginning Evelyn
could never get our anniversary right. She remembered the date she'd proposed to me, but not the
wedding. So I started tapping her hand four times
for April, and she'd tap back three times. It was for
the third of the month, to remind herself." Walt let
out a watery chuckle. "It became our special code.
I used to tease that it was a good thing we hadn't
gotten married on the twenty-ninth."

Josh grinned back. "She would have lost count
before getting that far."

"Uh, why don't you two go for a walk," Walt
suggested. "I'd like to be alone with her."

TARA WALKED BESIDE JOSH, wondering how to pull
her fingers free without being obvious. She'd been
trying to support him, but now it seemed too intimate.

"It's really something," he said after a few minutes. "All this time I knew something that Grandpa needed to hear, and I never realized."

"Maybe she did it with the others, too, hoping someone would get the message through," Tara suggested.

"Possibly." He glanced over at her. "Has this tempted you to become a sentimentalist?"

"This isn't sentimentality," she insisted. "It's sentiment—that's different."

"I'm not so sure the dictionary would agree."

The debate felt like a continuation of their discussions in the mountains. But the familiarity wasn't comforting; she needed distance, not friendship with Josh.

"By the way," he murmured, "thanks for coming today."

"I haven't done anything."

"You didn't need to. Being here was enough."

"I'm surprised Walt didn't ask his daughter."

"After the weeks we all just spent together, I think it seemed right."

It did feel right, and that was part of the problem. Tara wasn't sure how to handle the sense of connection. Her life had been so much simpler when Walt had been her only friend and Josh was an annoyance.

Caring about Josh was far more dangerous.

LAUREN STUDIED THE ENTRIES on the internet, made her decision and picked up the phone to make an appointment with a counselor in Helena. There might be someone closer, but she wanted a person unlikely to ever become otherwise acquainted with her or Carl.

Briefly she explained to the receptionist what she wanted to discuss. The first appointment was set, and she put the receiver down, knowing it was the right decision. Still, it was daunting to think about telling a stranger the story of her childhood.

She hurried to the stove and took out the pot roast she'd prepared. Carl would be at the apartment at five for his dinner break—he was working an evening shift this week.

Half an hour later, she opened the door at his knock. "Hi," she said as cheerfully as possible.

Carl gave her a heart-stopping kiss but afterward gazed down at her in concern.

"Something up?"

"Nothing, it's just that I…" She hadn't intended to tell him about the counseling appointments. On the other hand, she'd have to be gone for the better part of a day whenever she went, and he'd be curious. Besides, it seemed dishonest, even if she wasn't directly lying.

"Darling?" he prompted.

"I…um, just made an appointment with a counselor in Helena."

He frowned worriedly. "Are you having second thoughts?"

"*No*. But it might help with my…issues."

"I thought we were working on them together."

"We are," Lauren assured quickly.

When her old boyfriend had suggested counseling, she'd known their relationship was ending. But she also hadn't loved him the way she loved Carl.

"I love you," he said intently. "You can trust me. I'm not going anywhere."

She knew in a way he was trying to convince her she didn't need a counselor; deep down he might even be hurt because it might sound as if she *didn't* trust him. But trust wasn't the question—it was because she cared so much that she wanted to deal with her fears.

It was ironic; this was their first disagreement. He'd said he wanted her to speak up when it happened. She had to have faith that he'd meant it.

"I know you love me." Her throat was so tight it hurt. "Everyone thinks love is enough, and maybe it should be. But I have enough experience now to be aware that sometimes love *and* counseling is best."

Carl gazed into her eyes for a long time.

"Okay," he murmured finally.

"What if…" Lauren's heart pounded. "What if the counselor wants you to come to some of the appointments?"

He pulled her close. "I'll go," he promised. "If that's what you need, I'll go."

Relief washed over her. She probably should

have talked to a counselor years ago. She'd just never had enough incentive until now.

As they ate dinner and discussed it further, Lauren saw that Carl was getting used to the idea. She was serving their dessert when his cell phone rang.

At the end of the call, he jumped to his feet. "Sorry, honey. This isn't an emergency, but I have to deal with it."

Lauren kissed him, knowing she'd always worry, even when it wasn't an emergency. "Are you coming over after you get off duty?" she asked.

"You'll be in bed by then, but I'll call to let you know I'm home safe."

A smile curved her lips. "You can tell me that in person just as well. And there are other benefits to delivering a message...personally."

A chuckle rumbled through him. "You are *so* right. I'll see you later."

IN THE DAYS following the trip to the cemetery, Tara tried to forget the mixed emotions it had evoked.

During the daytime it wasn't too difficult. Several businesses in town still wanted her services, so she dived in, working longer hours than usual.

At night it got harder.

When looking for possible family, she'd done other research and learned that her parents were buried in the Los Angeles area. Though she didn't remember them, it seemed wrong that their graves were marked with just a number, so she'd ordered a stone to be placed. But the idea of their grave had been rather abstract, not unlike the tombs she'd visited of famous people. Those places were solemn and meaningful, of course, but not as emotional as seeing a family plot and the name of Josh's grandmother on a temporary grave marker.

The grief on his face had hurt more than she'd thought possible.

Then on Friday evening, Tara came home at seven to find Josh sitting on the front doorstep, leaning against her apartment door.

"Hi," he said. "I'd love company for dinner and was hoping you'd take pity on me."

She eyed him. "You have a huge family and plenty of friends, I'm sure. Can't one of them keep you company?"

"I don't know anybody else who can turn freeze-dried stew into a delicious meal. It's only right I feed you."

Knowing it would be wiser to refuse, Tara nodded. "All right. Give me a few minutes to change my clothes."

She almost balked at letting him into the apartment, but after their intimacy in the mountains, making him wait outside would be ridiculous.

"Wear something casual," he called as she started into the bedroom.

Pizza, she thought. They were probably going to a pizza parlor.

But apparently she'd guessed wrong. Josh drove through town to the county park where she and Lauren often walked. The two of them had begun meeting again in the early mornings, but it was different now. Lauren was looking forward to being married and all that it meant.

"I brought a picnic," he explained.

Tara hiked an eyebrow. "Haven't you had enough alfresco meals for a while?"

"Not a chance. After so much time outside, the house is oppressive. It's like living in a box."

"I know what you mean." Tara would have mentioned plumbing as one of the minor compensations, but she didn't want to evoke images of the hot spring pool where they'd bathed and done *other* things... She still didn't want to call it making love.

"I picked up stuff at the deli," he said, pulling out containers of fruit compote, potato salad, grilled chicken and a tray of raw vegetables. "After so much reconstituted food, the fresh fruits and veggies have tasted really good."

"I haven't been able to get enough myself." Tara crunched down a piece of cauliflower. "How are things going at the Boxing N?"

"Grandpa and I have worked out a compromise for how to run the ranch without getting in each other's way."

"Oh?"

"Yeah. Horses are his first love, so he'll handle

all the horse breeding and training while I focus on cattle."

The sensible arrangement impressed her. "That's terrific."

"And much more peaceful. Word is getting around, and the cowhands who quit are already looking to get their jobs back. It would be great if you came out to see how it's working."

"Oh. I'll try, but I've taken on some new clients, so I'm pretty busy right now."

"Grandpa really misses you."

"I miss him, too, but he's coming to lunch on Sunday."

"That's nice."

Josh's expression seemed hopeful, but Tara determinedly kept from saying anything stupid... such as inviting him, as well.

Coming here today had been a stupid move. What she needed was *more* distance, not less.

As THEY ATE, Josh could see Tara was putting up her defenses.

He could hardly blame her. Especially in the beginning, he'd treated her as a globetrotting princess who had no business in Montana. On top of that, he'd tried to pry her out of the ranch office and had suggested she was being careless about Grandpa Walt's welfare.

It was little comfort to know he'd probably behaved that way to protect himself; he must have realized Tara had the potential to turn his world upside down. True or not, it was no excuse for being a jerk.

Yet Tara *had* changed everything. She was the reason he'd started really talking to his grandfather and seeing him more clearly. She'd also gotten him to see how narrow his life had become.

Josh took a long drink from his bottle of water, embarrassed to remember how often he'd complained that Grandpa was closed off when *he* hadn't been any better. At least Walt and Evelyn had loved each other without reservation. The only things Josh had were brief relationships and meaningless sex.

Now he could see a whole array of intriguing possibilities and wanted to explore each and every one of them with Tara.

But how could he convince her that he was worth the risk?

After they ate, Josh suggested taking a walk. "The sunset is beautiful by the river."

Tara shook her head. "I should get back and have an early night. My schedule is intense right now."

"Come on," he coaxed. "It's a beautiful evening, too nice to spend inside."

"All right, just for a while."

Around a bend of the path, out of sight from potential observers, Josh stopped and drew her close. He kissed her gently and felt the briefest response before Tara pulled back.

"No hot spring here," she said, "and casual sex was out of character for me, anyhow. Find one of your other women to snuggle with in Schuyler."

"I might be able to find somebody, but there's only one woman for me now."

"Don't be ridiculous." Tara turned and gazed at the river. "That isn't funny."

"I agree, one hundred percent. I've been an idiot, which is hardly any fun to realize."

"Josh, I don't want to discuss this *or* what happened up in the mountains. I thought you understood that."

"I'm not talking about sex. I'm talking about love."

She jerked and wheeled around to stare at him. "That's even more ridiculous."

"Tara, I want a future with you. I don't want to keep prioritizing the wrong things. We can work on that together so we won't miss out on anything in the years ahead. I love you, and that's all I care about."

Tara shook her head. "You've got the wrong woman. I don't know *how* to love. Remember, I'm the difficult foster kid who pushed everyone away."

"You're wrong," he refuted steadily. "You know how to love, and you do it so well that you've been protecting yourself against the pain of it ever since you were little."

"This is an insane discussion," she insisted. "I'm

tired and I want to go back to my apartment. I'll walk if necessary."

Josh sighed. After all, he hadn't expected this to be easy. Life with Tara would never be easy, but it would be worth every challenging minute.

"Okay, I'll take you home. But I'm not giving up on the best thing I could ever have. Don't forget, I'm both a Nelson and a McGregor. We're a stubborn lot and sometimes thickheaded, but once we see the truth, we're tenacious. Please think about it."

Neither of them said anything else. At the apartment Tara slid silently from the truck and let herself inside.

Josh sat, watching the front room lights go on briefly before turning off again. Obviously she'd meant it about wanting to go to bed. He would give anything to be under the sheets with her... anything *except* the future he was trying to convince her to share with him.

So what was going to be his next move?

TARA LEANED AGAINST her bedroom door, trying to regain her composure. She'd expected Josh to suggest spending the night together, not to declare he loved her.

She blinked.

Had he actually suggested that he wanted to get married?

A normal woman would be over the moon instead of being vaguely depressed with a side order of panic.

Feeling as if she was slogging through thick mud, Tara stepped into the shower, letting the water stream over her. When the tank finally ran cold, she crawled into bed and lay staring into the darkness. Josh had asked her to think about it, and she'd told herself not to do anything of the kind.

But his words came back to her, over and over. He'd claimed that despite what she thought, she *did* know how to love. What had he said...that she knew how to love so well, she'd had to protect herself against it?

The thought was flattering. Tara just wasn't sure it was true. Memories of childhood and the parade of foster parents she'd known flooded back. In the beginning, she'd quickly become fond of each new family, hoping they would love her in return. Some of them might have cared a little, but she'd also learned that foster parents weren't *supposed* to get too attached.

By the end, she'd refused to feel anything. She'd been polite, done the chores assigned to her, obeyed the rules and studied hard. If nothing else, she'd wanted her records to stop saying she was difficult. But it had been a relief to leave for college and no longer live with people who weren't her family and never would be.

Then she'd met Pierre...handsome, ardent and

determined to marry her. She'd thought her luck was turning.

But time had passed, and she never seemed to be what Pierre had expected. After a while he'd begun saying she was cold and unresponsive... that he would have to teach her how to make love the way he liked.

Tara rolled over and punched her pillow. Josh had never complained that she was cold; he'd seemed quite pleased with the way she responded to him. Heat suffused her body as she remembered a few aquatic explorations they'd both found exciting.

So why did Pierre get the deciding vote on her ability to love? Now that she thought about it, while Pierre had been passionate, he hadn't actually been *warm*. So what did he know about the subject?

Exasperated, Tara sat up and grabbed the biography on Mary, Queen of Scots. Unfortunately she'd reached the section where poor Mary was discovering her second husband wasn't quite the man she'd thought.

Tara tossed the book down with disgust.

All right, she loved Josh. Despite her best efforts and fervent wish not to get hurt, she'd still fallen in love with him. That didn't mean they could have a relationship. He was a Montana rancher, and she'd never lived in one place for longer than two years.

He'd always wanted someone who knew and loved ranching the way he did.

That wasn't her.

He'd expected to wait until he'd achieved his ambitions before considering marriage and family.

That wasn't now.

How could anyone build a future on such a shaky foundation?

CHAPTER NINETEEN

JOSH SAT ON HIS PORCH. He'd called Tara's cell phone at least two dozen times, without success. How could he tear down her defenses?

There had to be a way.

At night he pictured her in his bed. In the morning he imagined sunlight dancing across her cheeks as she woke next to him.

He hadn't said anything to her about *how* they'd work out a life together. It had been a mistake. Weeks ago, he'd expressed his feelings too clearly to her; she had every reason to think he expected her to turn into a rancher's wife, the only travel being trips to Helena to shop for the items not available in Schuyler.

If Tara couldn't stay in Schuyler...well, he was a smart guy. He could find ways to make it work. Jackson and Kayla were managing. They spent a fair amount of their time in Seattle. Josh had thought his brother a fool to consider anything except an all-or-nothing proposition. But now he realized Jackson was a genius.

At 5:00 a.m. Josh drove to the grocery store; they had a decent flower selection and he chose a dozen yellow roses. At Tara's apartment building, he quietly laid them against her door.

The next day he got orchids.

The day after that, he found some beautiful Dutch irises.

She wouldn't talk to him, but one way or the other, he'd convince her that he wasn't going away. And if she left, he'd follow.

TARA OPENED HER DOOR three weeks after her dinner with Josh, hoping she wouldn't find another bouquet. But she also knew if there *weren't* any flowers, she'd be disappointed.

She found a sheaf of roses on the step—white, with the faintest blush of pink.

Her apartment was filled with flowers, various odds and ends serving as vases. Lauren thought it was great, though she'd refrained from pushing her sister too hard to make a decision.

Tara just wished she knew what she wanted.

She was a city woman, with a career and travel plans. But she couldn't deny the appeal of a home and family. That was what she could have in Schuyler, along with a husband she loved. Josh said he didn't want to keep repeating the same mistakes, but what did that mean in real life?

While she could work as a consultant via the internet, most of what she did couldn't be accomplished long distance. If Josh was serious and she married him, it would mean giving up everything except part-time jobs around Schuyler. It was a romantic ideal to sacrifice everything for love, but it was also terrifying. What if she did that and a relationship with Josh still fell apart?

Carefully she arranged the white roses in an empty pickle jar and put them on the coffee table. Curling up on the couch, she gazed at the blooms. They were beautiful, the bare blush of color reminding her of innocence. She couldn't remember ever feeling innocent, full of hope and expectation for the future.

The world had serious problems that needed to be fixed, but surely children should have as much carefree joy as possible. She'd want that for her own kids, if she ever had them.

Josh would want a family, and Tara had a feeling he'd be a good dad. And Walt would be around, too, making sure his great-grandchildren were raised right, along with grandparents and aunts and uncles and cousins. They'd have everything she'd lacked growing up—an extended family that would shower them with love and attention.

Tara smiled. With so many McGregors and Nelsons around, a mother would have to fight for her children's independence, to keep their lives from being planned out the way Josh's had been. Though on reflection, there were worse things that could happen.

Before meeting Josh she'd figured children weren't part of her future. After all, what sort of mother could she be? She couldn't bear for her children to think they weren't loved the way they deserved.

Her cell phone rang. It was Josh, but she didn't answer, just as she hadn't answered the last two or three dozen times. After a while she listened to the message.

"Hey, it's me," said Josh's strong voice. "I'll be around the ranch center all day. As I've mentioned before, I didn't say a lot of the things that need to be said. I'm not going away, Tara. I love you."

Tara's finger hovered on the screen, but she didn't delete the message the way she'd deleted all the others, saving it instead. Hearing Josh say "I love you" made her knees go weak.

He was right. She *did* have the ability to love; it was her courage to do it that was in question.

She sat up and swung her feet to the floor. The scent of flowers was really getting to be too much, and the place looked like a flower shop.

It was time to sort things out with Josh, if only to keep from drowning in irises, roses and orchids. Besides, she wanted to see Walt.

A half hour later she experienced an odd sense of déjà vu as she turned off the main road and drove under the Boxing N sign. Or perhaps it was a sensation of homecoming, which was absurd. Pulling into the spot where she'd always parked gave her the same sense, and she almost left immediately. She wasn't going to be seduced by either sentiment *or* sentimentality.

She went to Josh's house and rapped firmly.

No answer.

Then she went to the large house and knocked.

Still no answer.

Wishing Josh had been at home so they could have met privately, she picked her way slowly to the foaling barn, then to the large barn where the dance had been held. From the outside she could hear voices, and one of them was definitely Walt's.

Inside, Josh and Walt were standing with their backs to the door, chatting, clearly on good terms. It was an amazing contrast to the days when she'd first come to the Boxing N.

Walt said something and Josh threw back his head, laughing.

Tara swallowed, unsure why a man laughing should get her by the throat.

JOSH HAD NEVER realized how well his grandfather could tell a joke. Actually, two months ago he would have sworn Grandpa didn't *know* any jokes.

All was going smoothly, except for the thing that mattered most of all—settling things with Tara. He'd delivered flowers to her door every day for three weeks and was prepared to keep it up as long as it took. If she left the country again, he'd follow her.

He was almost ready. He'd applied for a passport and hoped to get it soon. Once it came, he'd keep it in his pocket as a reminder that his horizons had expanded beyond the borders of the Boxing N.

He had something else in his pocket, as well.

Suddenly, his grandfather turned, and his face lit up.

Josh swiveled to see Tara standing just inside the barn door. She wore casual clothing, a sign she wasn't working that day. But he could tell nothing from her face.

Walt hurried forward. "Hey, Tara. I've missed seeing you every day."

"Me, too, Walt."

Josh just stood, drinking in the sight of her.

"Right now, I've got some phone calls to make," Walt said, casting a knowing glance at his grandson. "You'll come up to the house later, won't you, Tara?"

"Sure. I still haven't seen the famous sapphires on the kitchen windowsill."

Walt chuckled. "We're leaving them there as a reminder not to get too cocky." He left the barn with just the bare suggestion of a limp.

"Let's take a walk," Josh suggested when they were alone, aware that one of the ranch hands could appear at any moment.

"I… Sure."

As they strolled toward a grove of trees, Josh

decided to take Tara's hand in his. She didn't pull it away, and a small flicker of hope went through him.

Once they were out of sight among the trees, he whisked her close and did what he'd been dreaming of for weeks.

THE SENSATION OF Josh's lips moving against hers threatened to dissolve any resistance Tara had left. She could hardly breathe and didn't want to; having his arms around her was the only thing that mattered.

After an endlessly pleasurable moment, Josh pulled back a fraction of an inch.

"Have you been thinking about it?" he asked hoarsely.

"Yes," she managed to answer. "But I don't have an answer."

Tara stepped away and began walking again. Josh fell in beside her.

"There's something I want to show you," he said.

She knew that from the cryptic notes he'd left with each bouquet of flowers—"We can work it out," "I have something important to show you," "Our future is more than Montana" and the last saying simply, "Anywhere."

Josh dug in his pocket, and Tara decided she'd slug him if he showed her a condom. Instead he handed her a photocopy of a passport application.

The air whooshed from her lungs.

"I've changed my ways," Josh said. "I don't want a life bound by Boxing N property lines, no matter how many sapphires might be here. I know you don't want to stay in Schuyler full time, so I'll find a way to come with you part of the year. In fact, I'm not sure you should *try* staying. It's a big world out there, and I want to see it, too. Not learning from Grandpa's regrets would be a terrible waste, so no waiting for us. No putting off hopes and dreams and adventures."

She stared. It was the last thing she'd expected him to say. An argument to convince her to remain in Schuyler, that she could find work here, that nothing was as important as love…*that's* what she'd expected. But she'd never thought he would leave Schuyler if she wouldn't stay.

"I was thinking, maybe it's possible for you to work here part of the time," Josh continued. "When you need to be gone, I'll get a ranch manager to consult with the foreman. But even if you want to live on the ranch for extended periods, we'd still plan long trips every year, whether we have kids or not."

"You want to have children?" Tara managed to ask.

"If you want them, too. I think we could make beautiful kids together. Besides, they'd be so lucky to have such a wonderful mother, they might not mind having a dolt for a dad."

Tara choked back a laugh. She couldn't picture how the plan would work, and she didn't care. He was saying he would put her first, ahead of everything. It was an extraordinary promise and more than she'd ever expected. He meant it, too. Josh wanted to embrace a life that went beyond his ranch, and he wanted to live it with her.

She turned and surveyed the Boxing N land. As much as she had loved the many countries in which she had lived, she had also always wanted to have a place she could call home.

Josh slipped his arms around her, tugging her against his chest.

"This is the only home I care about," he whispered, and her heart sank a moment. "For me, home is where you are."

She looked up at him. She'd never thought of it before…that home didn't have to be a place. It could be a person. At the same time, she'd fallen in love with Montana, along with Josh. She loved him so much that the thought of going anywhere without him was unbearable.

JOSH RECOGNIZED THE conflict in Tara's face and knew what a huge leap of faith he was asking her to make.

"I believe we can do it," he said. "And together, maybe we can get Grandpa to Italy after all."

A small smile danced on her lips. "Surely you aren't talking about taking him along on a honeymoon…"

Hope beginning to bubble inside, Josh grinned. "Much as I love my grandfather, that isn't happening."

He groped in his pocket and took out the small box he'd been carrying. "This was Grandma Evelyn's engagement ring. Grandpa said he had a feeling it would fit."

Her quick intake of breath and the ragged way she let it out was a sign of the emotion she was always so reluctant to show. He didn't know how he could have thought she was cool and unemotional; she was the most caring person he'd ever known, even if she didn't show it well.

"I love you," Josh whispered, slipping the ring onto her finger, "forever and forever."

The ring fit perfectly, and the gold glittered in the sunlight, but the joy growing in Tara's eyes shone even brighter.

"Forever," she agreed and kissed him.

* * * * *

LARGER-PRINT BOOKS!
GET 2 FREE LARGER-PRINT NOVELS PLUS
2 FREE GIFTS!

H HARLEQUIN®

Romance

From the Heart, For the Heart

YES! Please send me 2 FREE LARGER-PRINT Harlequin® Romance novels and my 2 FREE gifts (gifts are worth about $10). After receiving them, if I don't wish to receive any more books, I can return the shipping statement marked "cancel." If I don't cancel, I will receive 4 brand-new novels every month and be billed just $5.09 per book in the U.S. or $5.49 per book in Canada. That's a savings of at least 15% off the cover price! It's quite a bargain! Shipping and handling is just 50¢ per book in the U.S. and 75¢ per book in Canada.* I understand that accepting the 2 free books and gifts places me under no obligation to buy anything. I can always return a shipment and cancel at any time. Even if I never buy another book, the two free books and gifts are mine to keep forever.

119/319 HDN GHWC

Name	(PLEASE PRINT)

Address	Apt. #

City	State/Prov.	Zip/Postal Code

Signature (if under 18, a parent or guardian must sign)

Mail to the **Reader Service:**
IN U.S.A.: P.O. Box 1867, Buffalo, NY 14240-1867
IN CANADA: P.O. Box 609, Fort Erie, Ontario L2A 5X3

Want to try two free books from another line?
Call 1-800-873-8635 or visit www.ReaderService.com.

* Terms and prices subject to change without notice. Prices do not include applicable taxes. Sales tax applicable in N.Y. Canadian residents will be charged applicable taxes. Offer not valid in Quebec. This offer is limited to one order per household. Not valid for current subscribers to Harlequin Romance Larger-Print books. All orders subject to credit approval. Credit or debit balances in a customer's account(s) may be offset by any other outstanding balance owed by or to the customer. Please allow 4 to 6 weeks for delivery. Offer available while quantities last.

Your Privacy—The Reader Service is committed to protecting your privacy. Our Privacy Policy is available online at www.ReaderService.com or upon request from the Reader Service.

We make a portion of our mailing list available to reputable third parties that offer products we believe may interest you. If you prefer that we not exchange your name with third parties, or if you wish to clarify or modify your communication preferences, please visit us at www.ReaderService.com/consumerschoice or write to us at Reader Service Preference Service, P.O. Box 9062, Buffalo, NY 14240-9062. Include your complete name and address.

HRLP15

LARGER-PRINT BOOKS!

HARLEQUIN

Presents®

GET 2 FREE LARGER-PRINT NOVELS PLUS 2 FREE GIFTS!

PASSION
GUARANTEED
SEDUCTION

HPLP15

REQUEST YOUR FREE BOOKS!
2 FREE WHOLESOME ROMANCE NOVELS IN LARGER PRINT
PLUS 2
FREE
MYSTERY GIFTS

✵✵✵✵✵✵✵✵✵✵✵✵✵✵✵✵✵✵

HEARTWARMING™

✵✵✵✵✵✵✵✵✵✵✵✵✵✵✵✵✵✵

Wholesome, tender romances

YES! Please send me 2 FREE Harlequin® Heartwarming Larger-Print novels and my 2 FREE mystery gifts (gifts worth about $10). After receiving them, if I don't wish to receive any more books, I can return the shipping statement marked "cancel." If I don't cancel, I will receive 4 brand-new larger-print novels every month and be billed just $5.24 per book in the U.S. or $5.99 per book in Canada. That's a savings of at least 19% off the cover price. It's quite a bargain! Shipping and handling is just 50¢ per book in the U.S. and 75¢ per book in Canada.* I understand that accepting the 2 free books and gifts places me under no obligation to buy anything. I can always return a shipment and cancel at any time. Even if I never buy another book, the two free books and gifts are mine to keep forever.

161/361 IDN GHX2

Name	(PLEASE PRINT)

Address	Apt. #

City	State/Prov.	Zip/Postal Code

Signature (if under 18, a parent or guardian must sign)

Mail to the **Reader Service**:
IN U.S.A.: P.O. Box 1867, Buffalo, NY 14240-1867
IN CANADA: P.O. Box 609, Fort Erie, Ontario L2A 5X3

* Terms and prices subject to change without notice. Prices do not include applicable taxes. Sales tax applicable in N.Y. Canadian residents will be charged applicable taxes. Offer not valid in Quebec. This offer is limited to one order per household. Not valid for current subscribers to Harlequin Heartwarming larger-print books. All orders subject to credit approval. Credit or debit balances in a customer's account(s) may be offset by any other outstanding balance owed by or to the customer. Please allow 4 to 6 weeks for delivery. Offer available while quantities last.

Your Privacy—The Reader Service is committed to protecting your privacy. Our Privacy Policy is available online at www.ReaderService.com or upon request from the Reader Service.

We make a portion of our mailing list available to reputable third parties that offer products we believe may interest you. If you prefer that we not exchange your name with third parties, or if you wish to clarify or modify your communication preferences, please visit us at www.ReaderService.com/consumerschoice or write to us at Reader Service Preference Service, P.O. Box 9062, Buffalo, NY 14240-9062. Include your complete name and address.

HW15

LARGER-PRINT BOOKS!
GET 2 FREE LARGER-PRINT NOVELS PLUS 2 FREE GIFTS!

H HARLEQUIN®

INTRIGUE
BREATHTAKING ROMANTIC SUSPENSE

YES! Please send me 2 FREE LARGER-PRINT Harlequin® Intrigue novels and my 2 FREE gifts (gifts are worth about $10). After receiving them, if I don't wish to receive any more books, I can return the shipping statement marked "cancel." If I don't cancel, I will receive 6 brand-new novels every month and be billed just $5.49 per book in the U.S. or $6.24 per book in Canada. That's a saving of at least 11% off the cover price! It's quite a bargain! Shipping and handling is just 50¢ per book in the U.S. and 75¢ per book in Canada.* I understand that accepting the 2 free books and gifts places me under no obligation to buy anything. I can always return a shipment and cancel at any time. Even if I never buy another book, the two free books and gifts are mine to keep forever.

199/399 HDN GHWN

Name	(PLEASE PRINT)	
Address		Apt. #
City	State/Prov.	Zip/Postal Code

Signature (if under 18, a parent or guardian must sign)

Mail to the **Reader Service:**
IN U.S.A.: P.O. Box 1867, Buffalo, NY 14240-1867
IN CANADA: P.O. Box 609, Fort Erie, Ontario L2A 5X3

Are you a subscriber to Harlequin® Intrigue books
and want to receive the larger-print edition?
Call 1-800-873-8635 today or visit www.ReaderService.com.

* Terms and prices subject to change without notice. Prices do not include applicable taxes. Sales tax applicable in N.Y. Canadian residents will be charged applicable taxes. Offer not valid in Quebec. This offer is limited to one order per household. Not valid for current subscribers to Harlequin Intrigue Larger-Print books. All orders subject to credit approval. Credit or debit balances in a customer's account(s) may be offset by any other outstanding balance owed by or to the customer. Please allow 4 to 6 weeks for delivery. Offer available while quantities last.

Your Privacy—The Reader Service is committed to protecting your privacy. Our Privacy Policy is available online at www.ReaderService.com or upon request from the Reader Service.

We make a portion of our mailing list available to reputable third parties that offer products we believe may interest you. If you prefer that we not exchange your name with third parties, or if you wish to clarify or modify your communication preferences, please visit us at www.ReaderService.com/consumerchoice or write to us at Reader Service Preference Service, P.O. Box 9062, Buffalo, NY 14240-9062. Include your complete name and address.

HILP15